EXOPOD
by Joe Gillespie

EXOPOD
By Joe Gillespie

ISBN: 9781912092703

First published in 2017 by Arkbound Ltd (Publishers).

Arkbound is a social enterprise that aims to promote social inclusion, community development and artistic talent. It sponsors publications by disadvantaged authors and covers issues that engage wider social concerns. Arkbound fully embraces sustainability and environmental protection. It endeavours to use material that is renewable, recyclable or sourced from sustainable forest.

Arkbound
Backfields House
Upper York Street
Bristol BS2 8QJ
England

www.arkbound.com

For Maevis, Oscar and Edgar

EXOPOD

Exobiology:
a branch of biology concerned with life outside
the Earth.

Cephalopod:
any of class Cephalopoda including squids, cuttlefish and
octopuses.

Table of Contents

Chapter 1 - Hunter

There was a damp coldness in the air. Grey water lapped between the marsh reeds. In the distance, a halo of mist blended the small lake and sky to become one. A lifeless tree trunk, twisted round to meet itself again, like a great arched serpent frozen in eternity.

Not far from the muddy shore, a procession of water fowl left an undulating pattern of vees on the surface as they sped by on a deliberate path to nowhere.

An occasional bird's cry or beating of wings was all that disturbed the calm.

Somewhere in the long reeds, a shadow moved. Slowly and silently, two rugged arms parted the thick vegetation. A rough, bearded face rose briefly from the rushes only to disappear again.

The air was heavy with moisture and the dank smell of waterlogged earth. A trio of birds glided towards the shore, occasionally pecking just under the surface of the water and casting silver pearls of water across their backs.

The world stopped.

And while it waited, a long, dark outstretched shape curved through the air without a sound. With a mighty splash, a flurry of brown feathers lifted from the water.

One shape slapped the surface with its wings before disappearing back into the grey mist with a loud quack. Two others hung struggling, their necks gripped by powerful hands.

A broken-toothed smile spread across the hunter's face as the birds' last twitches subsided. Clad only in mud, he waded back to firmer ground and proudly laid his prey beside a dry bundle and flint-tipped weapon.

The man shivered. He wiped the cold wet mud from his body and unwrapped the bundle of furs on the ground.

In turn, he took the pelts and attached them to his body with thick twine. Feeling a lot more comfortable, he lifted the two limp birds with one hand, his spear with the other, and set out across the lonely fenland towards higher ground.

As grass gave way to bracken, and bracken to bramble, he trundled along a barely discernible path. Thoughts of little smiling faces and a warm fire gave every step purpose.

The path was clearer now. Small trees formed a canopy on each side and the carpet of soft moss and pine needles added a spring to his step.

A faint rustle in the thicket brought him to a sudden halt. He crouched and drew a long, slow breath. Laying the two birds at his feet, he slowly moved his hand along the spear, finding its balance point and gripping it tightly.

Another movement in the undergrowth betrayed the presence of a small horned creature grazing on some sweet roots. The hunter held his breath and waited for it to come closer.

It nibbled at the ground, lifting its head and chewing from side to side.

The hunter could not see why it was suddenly startled. It didn't seem like his fault, yet he could hear nothing else. The goat rushed towards him. As he stood up sharply and raised his spear, it skidded to an acute turn. He charged after it. Branches brushed hard against his face and thorns tore his skin. This prize was his.

Finding its path blocked by denser undergrowth, the animal paused for a second and turned to face him again. Its eyes held terror like he had never seen in an animal. He launched his spear. The smooth shaft cut through the dry forest air and buried itself deep into the soft earth. He straightened up. Not only had he missed his target, the goat was nowhere to be seen. He crouched down and listened.

Nothing.

He raised himself slowly and stepped forward. Feeble rays of yellow sunlight illuminated the small clearing. Pulling his spear from the ground, he looked around. There was something strange, something unfamiliar.

He wiped the cold sweat off his forehead and blinked twice. A vertical wall of air in front of him rippled like a pool.

From the centre of two concentric rings of ripples, two twig-like objects were suspended in mid-air, wavering slightly. Had they been bull-rushes poking from the surface of a lake, the vision would have made more sense, yet this pool was upright.

He edged closer to the apparition. As he stared, his mind wrestled with the incredulity of the situation. For the first time, in his dry mouth, he tasted fear.

Raising his spear, he prodded and poked at the bulbous protrusions.

They moved. They multiplied.

Five, six, seven ... reached straight out from the ripples towards him, a blue light danced on their surfaces.

He gulped.

Suddenly, the illusion before him exploded in a thrashing mass. Twisting and coiling around his body, he coughed blood as the agglomeration tightened around his body and lifted him from the ground. He ripped at the whipping black thongs feebly as they wrapped around his arms and legs. As they touched his bare skin, they stung like fire and his flesh swelled and suppurated. The grip tightened. His body spasmed.

Limp and still, he was lifted back into the vortex and was swallowed by nothingness.

The ripples in the air closed around him, diminished and disappeared.

The forest slept.

Chapter 2 - Lagoon

Fernando and Miguel were the worse for a gutful of grog. They had been left aboard to watch the sailing ship as the landing party went ashore in search of fresh food and water. Supplies were very low. The small island to starboard was a gift from God.

Fernando looked out across the forecastle in the moonlight and drew a deep breath of sweet air. He could smell the island's vegetation through the saltiness and longed for Lisbon.

Miguel was leaning on the side of the ship, gazing across the lagoon and whittling a piece of wood. He wasn't carving anything, it was merely a distraction whilst he gathered his thoughts.

Smoke rose from the onshore camp. Even at this distance, they could smell it. Fernando's mouth salivated at the thought of roast boar when the shore party returned. They had been eating dried beef and maggot-infested sea biscuits for the last month or more. Soon, he would be having proper food. He licked his lips in anticipation.

"Miguel," he called. "Is all quiet?"

There was no answer. Fernando walked across to the other side of the foremast.

"Miguel?"

Miguel was staring up at the sky, mouth agape. The look of astonishment spread across his weather-beaten face. Above him, the moonlight played strange tricks. The rigging seemed to sway and ripple in the breeze. What looked like a pile of rope fell onto Miguel from out of the sky. It was not unknown for rope to fall from the rigging, but it was heavy and could seriously hurt someone standing it its way.

Fernando started towards him. Something was wrong. What should have been at rest was twisting and squirming violently. Miguel was screaming in pain. There was a blue flash. He went stiff.

As he got closer, Fernando froze in his tracks. Coils of … something … were engulfing his shipmate's body. As he struggled in sheer terror, Fernando could only watch helplessly. The writhing mass, and his friend, rose from the deck and disappeared into the St Elmo's Fire in the sky.

He looked at the sky and then back down at the decking. All he could see were wood shavings and a horn-handled knife glinting in the blue moonlight.

How was he going to explain this to his captain?

Chapter 3 - New York

Gus Lubinski put his knuckles on his hips and strolled along the steel girder, as if he were jaywalking on East 42nd Street. The fact that this particular steel girder was hanging several hundred feet above East 42nd Street, suspended on four stout steel ropes, didn't matter to him. He was showing-off to his workmates. They all did it. In Manhattan in the early 1930s, they were lucky to have jobs. Skyscrapers were being built and somebody had to do the steelwork.

Gus hopped from the swinging girder onto a much more stable support beam, which was being riveted in place by his friends Sean and Salvatore. Sean was inserting the yellow-hot rivets into holes with a pair of grippers and Salvatore was whacking them with a heavy hammer and a hollow-headed chisel. Sparks flew. The hot metal cooled rapidly so the hammering had to be quick.

"Hey Sean, my brother in law told me a good one last night. He works at a Buick dealership over on Long Island. He was telling me that when customers brought their cars in for a service, they expect the head to be taken off and cleaned and a new gasket to be fitted. That takes time and trouble so…" he winked over at Salvatore, "what do they do? They get some yellow paint and a fine paintbrush and paint a nice new line around the cylinder head. Looks just like a new gasket has been fitted. I tell you, I wouldn't take my car into that place – if I had one."

"Ah, baloney," Sean grumbled, as the others laughed.

"Maybe I should bring up some silver paint and paint on a few rivets here and there?" he joked. He sent the empty bucket back down for another load of hot rivets. Salvatore stood up and stretched, his back ached from being bent over for so long.

"Soon be time to knock off," said Gus, looking at his watch. "Anybody fancy a cold beer down at the speakeasy?"

"Naw, can't afford it," Sean sighed. "Bernadette would kill me."

Gus looked over at Salvatore with raised eyebrows. Salvatore just shook his head. Being a foreman, Gus had a little more money in his pocket, the other two were having the same hard time as everybody else. He shrugged. He put out a hand and grabbed hold of a passing rope, stepped onto a girder and went sailing skywards.

"I don't think that Gus knows what it's like to have six kids," frowned Sean. "I used to like a drink myself when I could get one, but these 1932 prices for black-market hooch have made a teetotaller out of me. An Irish teetotaller. Can you believe that?"

"Back home in Sicily, we were given wine from the age of ten," said Salvatore. "Come to the great United States of America and the strongest thing they drink is coffee, and it's not even good coffee."

A bucket of hot rivets arrived at Sean's feet.

"Better get on with it," he said, pointing at Salvatore's hammer.

Salvatore was just knocking in the third rivet when he stopped suddenly. He pointed across to a suspended steel girder where Gus stood.

"What the hell is Gus doing now?" he asked.

Gus appeared to be walking backwards along the beam.

"Madre di Cristo, is Gus trying to kill himself?"

As the beam swung closer, Sean and Salvatore could see Gus holding up his hands as if to ward off some unseen assailant, though they couldn't see what was bothering him. There was a slight ripple in the air, like a mirage, but that wasn't unusual on a late summer afternoon in New York. The smoky air often played tricks in the city, and they were near the East River, which often sent odd reflections dancing off the steelwork.

"Gus, watch out you bloody eejit!" yelled Sean.

Gus was paying no attention. He continued stumbling backwards along the long girder seemingly oblivious that he was getting closer to the edge. The girder was too heavy for the weight of one man to unbalance it – unless they were close to the end. Gus was getting that close, and the steel beam was beginning to tip.

For a fraction of a second a long black object streaked out towards Gus. It never reached him, as Gus was already hurtling towards the ground with a piercing scream.

"My God," cried Sean. Salvatore put his hands

across his mouth and closed his eyes.

"Gus, Gus my friend, what have you done?" Sean whimpered, shaking his head slowly. There was no sound from below. No heart-rending crash. No gasps from onlookers. They were too far up and the constant din from the building site masked all but the loudest of noises.

"What did we just see, Sal?" asked Sean. "I can't believe my eyes. Did you see it?"

Salvatore mumbled something in Sicilian that Sean didn't understand.

"What did you say, Sal? Please speak English."

"When I was told ghost stories as a bambino, they frightened the hell out of me," he began. "As I got older, I realised that they were all assurdità. I didn't believe in ghosts anymore. Now, I have just seen one with my own eyes…"

The rivets had gone cold.

Chapter 4 - Steve

A clenched fist fell hard, and completely missed the snooze button. The alarm radio stayed on. The arm pulled back under the duvet.

Steve Markham groaned and rolled over, wrapping the bed covers tightly around himself.

"...further flooding in Bangladesh yesterday has left thousands more homeless..."

"Aren't you getting up?"

Steve peered over to where the voice had come from. A semi clad figure leaned over a vanity mirror.

"Uh?"

"...postal workers in the South East voted to return to work today. The backlog of mail..."

"Oh, get up Steve, you know I have an interview at half past nine, and I need a lift to the station."

The heap in the bed rolled over again.

Julie walked over and gave him a shove. She did not see the hand slip from beneath the duvet and grab her just above the knee. A sharp tug pulled her off balance and she fell on to the bed. Another arm threw back the quilt and pulled her beneath.

"Steve, I'm in a hurry. Stop it!"

Steve and Julie had an arrangement of convenience. She lived with him, she even shared his bed, but it was a loose relationship. On the odd occasion when Julie didn't come home in the evening, he didn't ask any questions. He didn't care much whether she came back or not, but she always did –

eventually. Steve wasn't into long-term relationships, even with the beautiful Julie.

"...local people are helping police comb woodland in Buckinghamshire for a youth who has gone missing..."

Julie pulled free and rolled off the low bed taking the duvet with her as she stood up.

"...this is the second person reported missing in the last twenty-four hours. Earlier..."

"It's alright for you, you can go in whenever you like."

The young man tumbled out of the other side of the bed and stretched. He ran both hands through tousled fair hair and neatly trimmed beard.

"As it so happens, I have to start early today anyway. I have to go out of town. "

"Where?"

"Oh, just down past Cobham, I won't be too late."

"Are you taking the car?"

"Uh? Oh, yes. It's not near a station."

"Steve. Do you really have to put all that butter on your toast? It's all fat you know. Why can't you use the low-fat spread?"

Steve didn't have an ounce of fat on his whole body.

He went on spreading the toast and dolloped a liberal blob of jam on top. Julie sighed.

Deliberately, he lifted the toast to his mouth and took a huge chomp. His greedy eyes rolled from side to side in defiance. An empty yogurt carton caught him squarely on the forehead.

"Hey!"

"Come on! Its five to eight." She tugged at his arm.

"Where's my camera case?"

"Wherever you left it."

Steve reached over the back of the sofa and pulled out a green canvas bag. He ripped open the Velcro fastener and did a quick check of the contents.

"So, what's on at Cobham then?" Julie asked, pulling on her short leather jacket.

"You won't believe it, but I'm taking photographs at a village fête."

Julie pulled a cheeky face.

"Oh, Steve Markham, ace freelance photojournalist is covering Women's Institute cake competitions now, is he?" she taunted.

"No, actually, it's a very enterprising church vicar who has booked Donna Fry as the star attraction..."

"Donna Fry, the page three girl?" Julie laughed, holding her hands out from her chest about six inches.

"Yes, it's a bit like the actress and the bishop. I don't know how the twin-set-and-pearls brigade are going to react," grinned Steve. "Still, I've got to hand it to him. He's got a visit from a national daily out of it. "

"So naturally you were the first to volunteer when you heard about Miss Cheesecake!"

"Very funny, but she's not my type. All bust and no brains. Have you ever heard her speak?" Steve shrugged.

"I bet you wouldn't push her away if she came smooching up to you," Julie mocked.

"Well ... it was Malcolm's idea, not mine. He reckons it will sell newspapers. He runs a newspaper, who am I to argue?"

Steve's devilish grin was met with a contemptuous look and a good hard shove.

The rusty old Fiat pulled up sharply at the station steps.

"Oh, no. Look at the ticket queue," moaned Julie. "I'm going to miss the train."

She fumbled in her bag to find the dog-eared interview appointment card and looked at the time on it. 9.30.

"Do you know where this is, Steve?"

Steve took the piece of paper and glanced at it.

"It's a film production company that wants somebody to act as PA and general runabout, but the pay's pretty good," she explained.

"Sure. It's in Soho. Just off Wardour Street. Oxford Circus tube is probably your best bet."

He paused and looked at her with a peculiar expression.

"Julie, my love. What day is it today?"

"It's Wednesday ... the 5th ... isn't it?" She stared at him for confirmation.

"Yes, it's Wednesday – but it's not the 5th!"

Julie shook her head. "What do you mean? "

"It's Wednesday the 4th," said Steve with a pitiful

smile. "Your interview is tomorrow!"

Julie flicked through her diary, and back.

She snatched the card back off him, slapped her head and groaned, "I've been looking at the wrong month. "

She turned away and stared out of the window in silence.

"Well I suppose I'd better get a bus back," she half asked.

Steve knew her well enough to interpret the comment as, "aren't you going to give me a lift home?" and answered accordingly.

"Sorry love, I haven't got time. I've got a long drive..."

Julie gave one of those looks that said, "Huh, sorry I asked!"

She opened the door and started to get out.

"Hey! If you're not doing anything, why don't you come with me. A nice day in the country ... eh?" He nudged her with his elbow.

Julie let go of the door handle and paused. "Yes. I think I will. Just to keep an eye on you!"

Steve grimaced and slipped the car into gear. The 8.20 to Waterloo pulled in as they left.

Chapter 5 - Poor cow

"Ho! Get this."

Duty Officer Jeffries grinned at the desk sergeant.

"An absolute nutter of a farmer has just rung in with some cock and bull story about one of his calves disappearing into thin air – right in front of his eyes!"

Sergeant Paul Rorke raised his eyebrows and tapped the desk with his pencil.

"Who was it?"

"Edwards, Mulberry Farm."

"Frank Edwards?"

"Yes."

Rorke frowned and twisted in his swivel chair.

"Frank's okay, he's a good friend of mine. He's a sidesman in the church. I can't see him telling tall tales if there wasn't something to it."

Jeffries wiped the desk with his hand and didn't look up.

"Sounded like a loony to me."

"Well, be a good lad and try and get a unit out to see him."

"Might be difficult, we're getting a lot of bacon and eggs on the radio."

Rorke stared at Jeffries with a strange look.

"You're what?"

"Oh, it's a kind of crackling noise like bacon and eggs frying."

The Sergeant went over to the set and picked up the mic.

"Mobile Two, Mobile Two, come in please. Over."

There was a light hiss.

"Mobile Two to Base."

Rorke looked around at Jeffries and continued.

"Mobile Two, would you get over to Mulberry Farm on the Hillsbury Road? There has been a report of a missing animal. Over."

"Mobile Two. Is this really police work? Over."

"Just do as I say Twilly. Over and out."

The panda car bumped down a narrow lane sending streaks of mud over its blue and white paintwork. It pulled into the farmyard and stopped beside an ageing Land Rover.

Officer Twilly stepped out. A scruffy mongrel came scampering over and yapped at his feet. He waved it away with little effect.

"Buster ... here boy."

A woman, wiping her hands on a towel, was standing at the door. The dog barked again and ran towards her.

"Sorry about that," she called.

Twilly walked over to the door.

"Good watchdog," he smiled.

"No, just a bit crazy. Barks at anything."

"So, I hear that you've been having a little trouble?"

The farmer's wife scowled.

"I think you had better come inside officer," she said, opening the door wide." Frank's in the kitchen."

The policeman put his hat down on the kitchen

table and looked back at Mrs Edwards. The farmer had his elbows on the table and his head buried in his hands.

"I suppose they're saying I'm mad?" he moaned, without looking up.

Twilly looked at Mrs Edwards again.

"Well, if you'd just like to tell me what it's all about, Mr Edwards, perhaps we can sort something out."

He took out his notebook and found a clean page.

At last, Edwards looked up.

"What's the point?" he muttered." Things like that just can't happen."

"Things like what?" asked the policeman, puzzled.

"Look, son. I've been through the war in the army and I've seen things that I wish I could forget. But what I saw this morning…" He trailed off, shaking his head and shuddering.

"What did you see?"

There was no reply.

"Go on Frank, tell him what you told me," prompted Mrs Edwards.

She leaned over to Twilly.

"Mightn't get a lot of sense now, I think he's in a state of shock."

The farmer waved his hand in disagreement, but stared down at the table as he spoke.

"I was down in the back meadow this morning. It was about seven o'clock, I think. Well, I saw that something was disturbing the cattle."

The officer scribbled in his book.

"I thought it might have been a dog or a fox that had put the wind up them, so I went down to the trough in the corner. One of the young calves was kicking up a din, and at first I couldn't see what was troubling it. Then I noticed that it had ... like, a rope tied around its neck. The thing was..."

He paused for a moment and looked up.

"The rope was sticking straight up into the air."

"Tied to a tree?" offered Twilly.

The farmer looked back at the table.

"No, there are no trees down there, just a few hedges."

"Well, what was it tied to then?" quizzed Twilly.

Edwards shook his head to and fro.

"Nothing. That's it. Nothing at all. Like one of those Indian rope tricks."

The policeman looked at Mrs Edwards. She stared back blankly. He wrote something in his notebook.

"Then ... there were more ropes," continued the farmer, still shaking his head." Except..." he hesitated," they weren't actually ropes…" He trailed off again, trying to find the right words to describe them." Have you ever seen 'Twenty Thousand Leagues Under the Sea'? The giant squid? Well they were just like tentacles, and they were coming out of nowhere."

Mrs Edwards walked around to her husband and put a hand on his shoulder.

"As quick as a wink, it had pulled the calf right off the ground and into the air. I don't know where it went. It was just like there was a hole in the sky..."

The policeman's expression changed and he bit at the end of his pencil.

"No. I didn't believe it either," said the farmer quickly." Look, maybe it's best that we forget the whole thing."

Mrs Edwards stroked the back of his neck.

He looked up and winked.

"Maybe we should just forget it officer. Sorry to have wasted your time. I'm sure you have better things to do..."

Twilly made a few more notes and tucked the book back into his chest pocket.

"I'm going to have to file a report back at the station."

The farmer nodded.

"Come on Frank," said Mrs Edwards." I think you should have a lie down. You go up to bed and I'll bring you a nice cup of tea."

She looked around at Twilly.

"Will you excuse me officer, I think..." She nodded in the direction of the door and helped her husband from the chair.

"Oh yes. Well, I think I'd better be off now. I hope that you feel better when you've had a rest. If you want to tell me anything more, you know where I am."

Edwards nodded and took his wife by the arm.

"I'll see myself out. Bye now."

Twilly climbed into the car and picked up his

radio handset.

"Mobile Two to Central, come in please. Over."

A tinny voice replied.

"Central, there's something fishy here. I'm going down the meadow to have a look around. I'll get back to you in five or ten minutes. Over."

He walked down past the barn and opened the gate at the back of the house. He couldn't see the bottom of the field from where he stood, as it was hidden by the curvature of the land. He closed the gate and headed towards the dip.

Looking back at the house, he saw the curtains close in an upstairs window. He stepped over the soft ground carefully, avoiding the wettest patches and cow pats. Now he could see the water trough at the bottom of the meadow and headed straight for it.

The trough was an old rusty cast iron bath, green with moss and dripped with wet slime. It was surrounded by a liberal carpeting of cow dung.

No. There weren't any trees close by, just a ragged hedge dividing the field from the pasture beyond. At the end of it, he could just make out a dip that could only be a ditch, or small stream. His eyes followed it along and sure enough, there was a stone bridge over the road in the distance.

He stood for a minute and looked about. Everything was exactly as it should have been. He shrugged and walked back up the hill.

"Mobile Two to Central."

He held the radio mike in his left hand as he steered up the cratered lane.

"I'm on my way back. Over."

Driving with one hand was difficult on the rough terrain but he managed to hold the mic and steady the steering wheel with the ball of his hand.

"Central to Mobile Two, have you sorted it out? Over."

Twilly braked at the main road junction.

"Don't know Central. I just don't know!"

Chapter 6 - Marion

"Oh, what an absolutely adorable room."

Rachael Hartmann paused in the doorway of the study, her eyes darting from one curio to the next.

"Come in Miss Hartmann, it's so very nice to see you."

The neatly dressed young woman with tied-back hair and small oval glasses stepped in and revelled in the atmosphere of a real Oxford academic's study.

"I'm sure you would like some tea after your journey," said the mousey-haired older woman, indicating a large floral armchair by the bay window.

"Yes, that would be wonderful," came the reply in a soft Californian accent.

"Or would you rather have coffee? I have some fresh Arabica beans."

"Oh no, tea please Professor."

The middle-aged lady smiled and adjusted her black, thick-rimmed glasses. She went off into the next room.

"By the way, it's Doctor, not Professor," she said casually on the way out.

The study was a strange marriage of a library, museum, office and living room. It was large and airy, but held so many objects of fascination. It definitely had a woman's touch. The soft pink wallpaper and floral drapes somehow contradicted the oak panelling around the open fireplace and the heavy leather-topped mahogany desk with its brass desk lamp didn't quite belong with the delicate porcelain figures on the mantelpiece.

A rattle of teacups heralded the return of the doctor. She pushed the heavy door open with her foot and squeezed in with a wooden tray holding a flowery china tea pot and matching cups and saucers. Her visitor had her head tilted sideways as she scanned the titles of the tomes on the floor to ceiling bookshelves.

"Oh, do you take sugar Miss Hartmann? I think I am rather low, I don't use it myself."

"No thank you Professor, I mean Doctor, I don't take sugar either. Oh, and please, call me Rachael," she added, looking up momentarily before returning her gaze to the bookshelf.

She took down a leather-bound volume from the top shelf and opened it carefully. She smiled.

"This is an odd thing to find on the shelf of Doctor Marion Calvin, one of the world's most eminent research anthropologists."

"What is that, my dear?" she asked, pulling down her spectacles.

"'The Time Machine' by H G Wells. It's a very old copy if I'm not mistaken."

"It's a first edition," answered the doctor, in a matter of fact tone. She arranged the cups and spoons on the saucers with precision.

"You mean it's an original?"

Rachael paused as she turned the next page.

"It's autographed!"

"Yes, I do believe it is."

Marion lifted the teapot lid and stirred the tea.

"It must be worth a fortune," gasped the American woman.

"Probably. My Father gave it to me as a present shortly before he died. That was more than thirty years ago," reminisced the doctor, pouring the tea out. She held up the cream jug.

"Just a splash," said Rachael, carefully turning the precious yellow pages. She closed the book and returned it to the shelf.

"I've read some of your papers on co-existent states," Rachael continued, as she sank back into the opulent arm chair." Surely you weren't influenced by H G Wells?" she smiled.

The professor tapped her nose." Maybe more than you think!" she said, holding out the cup and saucer to her guest.

"Anyway, how are things at Stanford?"

"Oh, fine," answered Rachael, stirring her tea slowly.

"I haven't been to The Farm since nineteen-seventy-nine. I hate flying, goes for my ears." The doctor rubbed her left ear as she spoke." So, tell me, how is old Brad?"

She reached out with a plate of biscuits. Rachael took one and set it on the edge of her plate.

"Well, he's up and about again, but he's had to take it very easy since his stroke. Anyway, he sends his best wishes and said to tell you to watch your driving."

Rachael frowned as she passed on the message, as

if searching for an explanation.

"He's not talking about golf by any chance?" she asked with a puzzled look.

The doctor put down her cup and saucer and tried to hide her amusement.

"The last time Brad was here, we had a teeny mishap in my car. Nothing serious, but he has teased me about it ever since."

Rachael sensed that there was more to it, but politely changed the subject.

"Where did you get this?"

She lifted a small, black, carved figurine and examined it.

"It's from your country."

"It's American?"

She looked even more closely. "It's not Native American."

"Hawaiian," corrected the doctor. "At least, that's where I picked it up, but I suppose it could have come from any island in the South Pacific."

"And what were you doing in Hawaii?" asked Rachael, setting the object back in exactly the same place that it had come from.

"Just some research for one of my papers," Marion replied. "Are you fond of old things then?"

"Oh yes. Very. I'm just dying to have a look around some of your antique shops while I'm here."

Dr Calvin leaned forward and put down her cup.

"More tea?" she asked, lifting the pot.

"Please." Rachael passed her cup over and nibbled at her biscuit.

"Actually, I have a very good friend in Thame who has a little antique shop," said the doctor causally. "Nothing too fancy, mind. Perhaps we could pop over there this afternoon. I'm sure he would be delighted to meet you."

The idea obviously found favour, as Rachael's eyes lit up.

"Are you sure you can spare the time Doctor?"

Marion waved her hand in the air.

"My time is yours Miss Hartmann, sorry, Rachael. Any friend of Bradley Johnston is an honoured guest as far as I'm concerned."

Chapter 7 - Margaret

Margaret Blair was a fusser, but in a good way. She liked to get things right, and usually did. Her husband, Reverend Hubert Blair, was the vicar of St Augusta's Parish church. He was what could only be described as a boring old stick-in-the-mud. It was fortunate that his lady wife was there to organise things for him.

It was the time of year for the church fête. The steeple was desperately in need of repair, so they needed to raise several thousand pounds to get the most urgent work done. The rest would have to wait.

When Margaret suggested having a celebrity along to bring in the crowds, Hubert wasn't sure. The idea of a cheap publicity stunt seemed somehow, ungodly. Margaret went ahead anyway.

Celebrities don't come cheap. She tried a few local dignitaries first. They all had their excuses. It was Eddie, the gravedigger, who came up with the idea – a page three girl. Margaret was broad-minded enough to know what a page three girl was.

"What an excellent idea, Eddie," said Margaret." I don't know what Hubert will say. Maybe I will describe her as an actress. He won't know the difference."

So, Margaret started making phone calls. She called the tabloid newspapers, but they fobbed her off. Then she started ringing modelling agencies. They weren't quite so unhelpful, but quoted silly prices. Margaret had nearly given up on the idea when some guy at a modelling agency suggested a name and a price of two hundred and fifty pounds. It was a lot less that other people were asking. Margaret had never heard of the girl, Amanda Fry, but when she told Eddie, he nodded and grinned.

"Those will bring 'em in!"

Margaret did a double-take, then realised that he was talking bosoms.

"Err, yes, Eddie. We all have to look to our God-given talents. The agency is sending me some publicity photos. I do hope that they are decent."

When the large brown envelope fell on her doormat the next morning, Margaret opened it with a degree of trepidation. She needn't have worried; somebody had used their good sense and had sent fully-clothed photos of a pretty girl. She just wasn't a *young* pretty girl. It dawned on Margaret that there was a reason behind the low appearance fee. No matter, nobody was going to get that close to Ms Fry. She was still quite a stunner from a few feet back. Margaret was quite mercenary when she had to be. She rang the agency and confirmed the booking. Now all she had to do was break the news to Hubert.

"Are you mad?" yelled Hubert.

"This is the house of God. We can't employ showgirls to parade around in the altogether at our church fête."

Margaret wasn't sure how the words 'showgirl'

and 'altogether' had come to Hubert. She had only described her as an actress – a perfectly respectable occupation. Hubert knew more than he was giving away. When Margaret told him that Amanda Fry was only going to charge two hundred and fifty pounds, he put his head in his hands. She thought he was praying.

"No, no, no!" he stamped.

"I have already confirmed the booking Hubert, we will have to pay whether she comes or not."

Hubert didn't speak to his wife for the rest of the day. Apart from a few prudes, everybody else she told thought the idea was sheer brilliance. She used the publicity photos to make some posters.

'St Augusta's Grand Celebrity Fête, featuring Miss Amanda Fry. Come along and have your photo taken with her. Support our steeple fund. Raffles, Tombola, and prizes to be won. A great day for all the family.'

Chapter 8 - Amanda

"St Augusta's Grand Celebrity Fête."

The white banner stretched right across the country road and fluttered in the gentle breeze. A youth in blue denim with a very official looking armband was directing cars into an already packed field.

Steve wound down the window of his elderly Fiat and leaned out.

"Some turnout!" he called.

The young man grinned back and waved another car through.

"The Reverend really knows how to pull them in."

Steve saw that he was blocking the way and sunk his foot on the accelerator. The car bucked over the uneven ground and pulled into the next empty space. Two other cars immediately took their places to his left.

"Where are they all coming from?" asked Steve, looking all around.

"Probably all randy, young newspaper photographers," sighed Julie, looking the other way.

Steve twisted his face and turned the engine off. Leaning over to the back seat, he grabbed his camera case and slid out of the car.

"Well, you've picked the right day for it," called Steve to the young marshal, who was desperately trying to squeeze in just one more car.

"Couldn't be better," he shouted back.

Julie closed the door with a slam.

"When does it all start?" she asked the youth.

"It's been going on for over an hour now, but the official opening ceremony is at two o'clock."

Julie took a long, deep breath of fresh country air. It was a long time since she had smelled green grass. She liked it.

The walled garden beside the church was ablaze with colour. Red and white striped awnings were bedecked with flags and bunting and the smell of frying onions mingled with the charcoal smoke. Two prim ladies by the gate were busy taking money and handing out tickets. Steve patted his "Press" badge as he walked past. Julie stopped and set a two pound coin on the slatted table.

"That's for him too," she excused, as Steve disappeared into the throng. Julie pushed after him.

"Try your luck at the hoop-la, Miss?" a white-haired old gentleman called. "Only twenty-five pence!"

Julie smiled and shook her head. She could just see Steve in the distance, jostling towards the central stage.

A tent guy-rope almost sent her sprawling. A helping hand steadied her as she caught her balance.

"Thanks," she sniggered, and immediately tripped again.

An almighty squeal cut through the air and made her jump.

"Testing one, two, three. Testing. Testing."

The PA system settled down to a quiet hiss.

"Ladies and gentlemen, boys and girls, I would like to welcome you to St Augusta's Grand Celebrity Fête on this beautiful summer's day."

Julie could see a black clothed figure at the microphone on the stage.

"I think you will find that there is something here for everybody today, all the fun of the fair. As you probably know, the proceeds of today's fête are going to the Steeple Fund, so please give what you can to help restore our magnificent sixteenth century building."

The fresh-faced young curate swaggered with the microphone in his hand. Julie could only think of Butlin's. The exuberance of the crowd spurred him on as he joked and bantered through his inaugural speech. Julie pushed on, until she finally managed to catch hold of Steve's jacket. He was too busy to notice. Trying to line up a clear shot of the stage, he was oblivious of Julie's presence, or the speech.

"We have some celebrities here today who have graciously accepted our invitation, and who I know you can't wait to see. We will be introducing them shortly, but first, I would like to offer my thanks to you all for coming today. I would also like to say thank you to the many members of the congregation, and their friends, who have put so much hard work into the organisation of this great day..."

Steve manoeuvred into a position that gave him a good view of the stage. As yet, there was no sign of Amanda Fry, or anyone else he recognised.

Julie tugged at his arm.

"You know, I think the minister has a little problem," Steve mouthed sideways at Julie, who was standing on her tiptoes to try and see what was happening.

"What do you mean?" she asked.

"I think that he has either been stood up, or it's all been a con. There's no Amanda Fry!"

"No, they wouldn't pull a con like that," protested Julie. "Not a vicar surely..."

"So, first this afternoon, let me introduce you to our good lady mayoress, Her Worship Mrs Julia Netherwood. Give her a big hand everybody!"

The vicar helped the stoutish blonde woman in a pale blue frock up onto the platform and clapped wildly. A section of the crowd cheered.

The overweight dignitary nodded and waved, with a totally detached look on her face.

"Kermit the Frog!" said Steve. "That's who he reminds me of, the vicar." He pointed over at Hubert, who was slipping a folding chair under the lady mayoress's ample derrière.

Julie sneered and then giggled.

"...And just back from the Ecumenical Conference at Brighton, the Right Reverend Arthur Copeland..."

A sour-faced clergyman mounted the wooden steps and did his best to smile to the cheering crowd. The elderly man took the microphone from the young curate, clipped it back on to the stand and launched into a speech that was too quiet and boring to listen to.

"So, these are the celebrities," he smirked.

Steve twisted the barrel of his zoom lens and took a few spot meter readings from different parts of the scene in front of him. As he fiddled with the controls on his camera, he was just aware of a momentary drop in the light level. He looked up at the sky. There were no birds, no aeroplanes, just light fluffy clouds hanging motionless in the blue nothingness.

He paused, shook his head, and continued adjusting his camera.

Behind the old clergyman, the younger curate was now in deep conversation with someone out of sight behind the platform. He gesticulated excitedly. In front, the old one gave a pathetic wave that indicated that his speech had reached its conclusion, and bowed to the two applauding people at the front of the stage. The young one stepped up to the microphone and took it in his hand.

"Thank you, Reverend Copeland. Most enlightening. And now Ladies and gentlemen, I think you will all join me in giving a great big St. Augusta's welcome to a young lady who has very kindly taken time from her packed schedule to come here today..."

Steve's ears pricked up.

"He's not..."

"Ladies and gentlemen ... Miss Amanda Fry!"

The flaps of the marquee tent pulled aside and a farm tractor chugged out into a small roped off area in front of the stage. In the driver's seat, a smiling young man in jeans and a chequered shirt swung it around in a tight turn. On a small wooden trailer behind and almost obscured by bunting, a figure in a white tutu stood up and waved a magic wand. The crowd roared.

Aided by many helping hands, she jumped down to the ground and bounced up the steps on to the rostrum.

Cheers and wolf whistles filled the air.

The Fairy Queen smiled sweetly, curtsied and blew a kiss out to the crowd.

Steve's camera clicked and whirred. He laughed.

"That vicar has sure got style," he shouted, as Julie craned her neck for a better view.

"I would just like to say how lovely it is to be 'ere. Have a nice day..."

Amanda handed the microphone back to the curate as if it were red hot. He took her hand and held it high in the air. When the cheering subsided, the curate spoke again.

"For the autograph collectors amongst you, Miss Fry will be around for an hour or so and will, for a price..."

A moan went up from the crowd.

"...For a price, will be happy to give you her autograph."

"If you would like a selfie, there is a price for that too. Remember, it's all for a very good cause – the church steeple fund. Please give generously."

"She's a bit of alright," grinned Steve, trying to get a better angle of the unlikely group on the platform.

"Was, a bit of alright," said Julie, sarcastically.

Steve twisted and screwed at his zoom lens. An elderly parson was getting in the way and filling the viewfinder with his scowling face. Steve could not get a clear shot.

Suddenly, a shriek pierced the air, followed by gasps and more screams. A chill ran through the crowd. Something was wrong!

"What's happening?" called Julie." What's that?"

Steve dropped the camera from his eye.

An impossible whirlpool had materialised in the air just a few feet above the platform. What seemed like sparks, or miniature lightning bolts, leapt down from the anomaly towards the blue-clad mayoress.

She convulsed.

Steve brought his camera to his eye, zoomed back and held his finger on the shutter release.

"Clack, clack, clack."

His camera was making exposures at eight frames a second.

"Christ, what kind of stunt is this?" he asked.

The PA system screeched and squealed.

"Clack, clack, clack, clack."

As he zoomed in, Steve could see her plump, pink face frozen in a grotesque mask.

"Clack, clack, clack."

Steve lowered the camera just in time to see the limp figure disappear into a blur in the sky. A split-second hush was followed by pandemonium.

The ripples in the air smoothed out and were

gone.

"I don't believe this," screamed Julie." Will someone tell me what just happened?"

Six hundred voices asked the same question, but there was no answer.

Chapter 9 - Andi

Julie was still in a state of shock. The church fête had ended in panic and the crowd evaporated within half a minute. Only a few stunned onlookers still stared at the sky waiting for an explanation that would never come.

"You don't suppose that it was something religious, an act of God or something?" asked Julie. She had had a Christian upbringing as a child and had only half rejected the ideas in later life.

"Don't be silly," said Steve.

"What was it then? How do you explain it?" asked Julie.

"I don't know," said Steve." All I know is that those shots are going to make me a fortune."

The journey back to London was fast. Steve had the scoop of a lifetime on the SD card in his camera and was determined to milk it for every pound. He was excited. He didn't know what he had photographed, hadn't a clue, but he did know that it was something very special.

Steve fumbled with his phone.

"Steve, you can't make phone calls when you are driving!" yelled Julie.

Steve put on his left indicator and pulled onto the hard shoulder.

"You drive then," he barked, getting out of the driver's seat. Julie got out and swapped seats with him. As they headed back out into the traffic, Steve was tapping numbers into his phone.

"Hi Nick, Steve Markham here. You've no doubt heard about the incident at the Cobham church fête?"

"Yes, Steve. We've already had some shots sent in."

"Damn, damn, damn," said Steve under his breath. He was hoping to have the scoop.

"…But they were mostly mobile phone shots. I can't tell what is happening. Too far away or there's people standing in the way. Were you there?"

"Yes, I was there and I've got some good close-ups," said Steve.

"What is it all about then, Steve? I am very confused," said the news agency guy.

"Something grabbed a woman at the fête and hauled her off into oblivion, that's what," said Steve.

"And you have shots?" asked Nick.

"Yes. Good, clear shots," replied Steve.

"How quickly can you get them to me?" asked Nick.

Steve thought for a moment.

"In a few minutes," he said.

"Good," said Nick." You could be onto a winner here."

Steve rang off and gave Julie some directions. He was headed towards the residence of his old boss, Paul, a still-life photographer.

"Just down there to the left," ordered Steve. His

old car pulled into the driveway of a big house.

"Just wait here for a minute," he told Julie, and rang the doorbell.

"Oh, hi Steve," said the short-haired blonde girl who answered the door.

"Hello Andi," replied Steve." My, you've changed since the last time I saw you."

She smiled sweetly.

"Is your Dad in?"

"No," said Andi. I think that he is out searching for props."

"Andi, can I use the studio computer?" asked Steve.

"Oh, there are a couple of computers there now. It's a bit different from when you worked here," smiled Andi." I have your job now as studio assistant. Don't touch the big iMac, there is a smaller one with a guest account that he lets clients use."

"That's fine," said Steve pushing past her." I need to get some shots to the news agency chop-chop."

Andi stepped aside. Steve knew the way to the studio at the back of the house. The last time he had seen her, she was waif-like with long blonde hair in plaits and a school uniform. She was still skinny, but had a short, fashionable bob-cut, eye makeup and turned up dungarees. She liked to hang around her dad's studio when he was working and had obviously learned a lot. Now, she was an alluring young woman.

Steve connected his camera to the computer and copied some shots over. He viewed them on the large screen.

"Whatcha got?" asked Andi inquisitively. She didn't quite know what she was looking at over his shoulder.

"This, my dear, is a small fortune," said Steve with a grin.

"What is it?" asked the girl, "a garden party?"

"Yeah, something like that," replied Steve, as he emailed the folder of shots to Nick at the agency.

Andi looked bemused. "Yeah?" she said. "Nice."

"Tell Paul 'thanks'," said Steve, patting the girl on the shoulder. He deleted the folder of photos from the desktop and unplugged his camera.

"Tell him I'll give him a ring sometime," said Steve as he rushed out the door.

"Thanks, Andi."

He gave her a quick peck on the cheek.

Steve's shots made the evening news on television, and the front page of just about every newspaper around the globe the next day. So preoccupied was he about the thoughts of huge royalty payments, he didn't stop for a minute to think about the scene he had witnessed and the ramifications of that event.

But someone else did!

Chapter 10 - Rachael

Steve's phone rang before he had even finished his first coffee. He hadn't slept well at all. He had tossed and turned all night as visions of his experience haunted him.

"Steve Markham?" asked the American voice at the other end of the phone.

"Yes, can I help you?"

"My name is Rachael Hartmann; I wonder if I could ask you something?"

"Sorry, I have no time for American journalists," said Steve.

"Oh, it's not like that," said Rachael. "I have someone here who would really like to talk to you."

Rachael handed the phone over to Doctor Marion Calvin. The mild Edinburgh accent reassured him.

"Mister Markham, I got your phone number from the news agency – after a lot of arm twisting, I might add. I really do think that we should meet up."

"Why?" asked Steve. "Who the hell are you anyway?"

"Ah, Mister Markham. You won't have heard of me. I am Doctor Marion Calvin and I am a research anthropologist at Oxford University."

"And…" said Steve, with more than a hint of annoyance in his voice.

"Mister Markham, you have taken some remarkable photographs in the past few days. I would very much like to see them. I must point out, I don't want to buy anything, I just want to look. I am an academic, not a newspaper. Can we meet?"

"I'm very busy," said Steve. "I can't spare the time to drive down to Oxford."

"You mean up to Oxford?" came the reply.

"Whatever," said Steve. "Up, down, I don't give a…"

"Then, Mister Markham," interrupted the doctor," it seems that we will have to come and see you."

Steve, finding it hard to refuse, gave her his home address in Chiswick, and suggested a time the following day.

"Myself and my colleague will be with you at eleven sharp. See you Mister Markham."

Steve's doorbell rang at exactly eleven o'clock the next morning. He ushered the two women into his small living room.

"Doctor … Calvin, is it?" he asked.

"Yes, that's right, and this is Rachael Hartmann. She is visiting me from California."

Steve gestured them towards a sofa.

"How can I help you Doctor?" he asked.

"Let me explain, Mister Markham…"

"Please Doctor, call me Steve. Mister Markham was my Father."

Marion Calvin smiled.

"Alright, Steve. Apparently, you took some photographs yesterday at a church fête. Photographs that showed something very unusual."

"You can say that again," he replied.

"Steve, my main area of expertise is anthropology, but I do have another interest on the side. Something more … unusual, you might say."

"Yes," said Steve in expectation.

"What you witnessed yesterday," said the doctor." That is not as unusual as you might think."

Steve's eyebrows raised.

"There have been cave drawings, hieroglyphs in Egyptian tombs and etchings in old manuscripts. They all show what your photographs do. An entity that can reach through time and space, snatching living creatures from our side and whisking them through to … what I can only refer to as 'the other side'."

Steve sat in stunned silence.

"Steve, have you ever heard of a trapdoor spider?"

Steve nodded, "I think so."

"Well, this is a trapdoor spider, of sorts. It lurks on the other side of a rift in space and time and pounces out on its prey in our world."

"No," said Steve, shaking his head. "That's just not possible."

"Steve, could I ask you to show us your photos?" asked the doctor." I would like to see them in chronological sequence."

Steve fetched his laptop and inserted the camera's SD card.

"There," he said." A ripple in the sky appears and the lady mayoress is yanked off the stage and taken away by … something that sparked."

Marion peered at the photos closely. She pointed out features to her companion, Rachael.

"Mister Markham, Steve, you have been extremely helpful. I won't take any more of your time. I have seen exactly what I wanted to see. We shall be off now. Thank you most sincerely."

"Wouldn't you like some prints?" he asked.

"No, no thank you. That won't be necessary – for the moment anyway," said the lady. "Your photos have been seen across the World, I don't have to knock myself out to convince anyone ever again."

Steve passed off the visit from the Doctor as that of a harmless crank and thought no more about it. Online, he watched the payments roll in from the news agency. He was feeling very pleased with himself.

Chapter 11 - Paul

Next morning, Steve was checking his emails. Among the payment notifications from the news agency, he spotted a message from Dr Marion Calvin. She thanked him profusely for his time on the previous day and asked if he would mind forwarding some of his photographs by email. She was most interested in the sequence of events and, in particular, how the incident started and ended. She took great pains to point out that the photographs were for academic research purposes only, and that she would gladly pay any reasonable fee if they were to be published.

Steve assembled a collection of photos that he figured would interest her most, attached them to an email and hit 'send'.

With the pictures still on his screen, Steve scrolled through them. He had only taken a casual look previously. He had been much more interested in the scoop than the content. The photos showed the distortion in the air. It looked like ripples spreading out across a pond, and that something was extending from the ripples. First, two blobs on the end of bendy sticks, then a lot more. Only the first two had the blobs, the rest tapered to blunt points. They flickered with electricity.

He zoomed-in on his computer screen to look at the blobs. He couldn't see any detail. As he zoomed-in further, the image pixelated. That wasn't going to work. Then an idea struck him. Grabbing the phone, he quickly dialled the number for Paul Atwood, his old boss. Andi answered.

"Yes, he's around somewhere Steve, I'll just go and find him."

After a few pleasantries, Steve got down to the point.

"Paul, I remember that you used to have an app that could enlarge images way past their native resolution. Do you still have it?"

"I think so," said Paul. I haven't used it for a while. I think it is still on the old Mac Pro."

"Could I pop around and run a few shots through it?" asked Steve.

"Sure, any time. If I'm not around, Andi will let you in. Remember, you're going to be producing enormous file sizes so bring plenty of USB sticks."

"Ah," said Steve." I'll pick some up in Kingston on the way over. It will be mid-afternoon."

Steve thanked Paul and loaded the shots he wanted to process onto the USB sticks he had.

"Hi, Andi", said Steve as she opened the door.

Andi smiled and held out her hand in the direction of the studio.

"You want to enlarge those weird shots you took at the fête?"

"Yes, I used to do it with a program on the Mac Pro. I can't remember what it was called."

"Can't help you there, I'm afraid. I haven't used that machine. It's been gathering dust since he got his new iMac."

It didn't take Steve long to find the app. He set it to magnify a shot ten times. The result was big, but soft. The detail wasn't there. Andi was watching over his shoulder.

"Can I try?" she asked, taking the mouse from him. She set the magnification to four times and introduced a degree of unsharp mask.

"There, is that what you are after?" she asked, smirking.

"Exactly," said Steve, with a modicum of 'I knew that,' in his voice.

He took back the mouse and processed six more pictures, saving each onto a USB stick as he worked.

"Looks like two big creepy eyes on the ends of stalks," commented Andi, pointing at the image on the screen.

"I think you're right," said Steve, looking closely at the screen." I know somebody that will be very interested in this!"

Back home, Steve made a composite image which included the original shot cropped to exclude the extraneous stuff around the periphery. Then, he superimposed the magnified detail of the 'creepy eyes', as Andi had called them. He emailed two different shots to Dr Calvin. Ten minutes later, he had a phone call from the doctor.

"Steve, these are fantastic. I understand now that these two initial stalks are eyes of some sort, as you suggested. They appear to be spying out the situation on this side of the rift, before it grabs its victim. It does remind me of Idiopidae, the armoured trapdoor spider found across the Southern hemisphere. It has eyes on stalks too, but it's mainly the vibrations of its prey that it picks-up before it pounces and drags it back into its burrow."

"Fascinating," said Steve.

"Do you mind if I share these photos with some colleagues, Steve?"

"No, that's okay, go ahead. Glad to be of help. If you need anything else, just let me know."

"These are great. I can finally understand what some of the old engravings were getting at. Now that I see them as eyes, it makes things a lot clearer. The other protrusions are not tentacles as we know them either, they seem to be quite smooth. Most cephalopods have suction cups, or other mechanisms, to help hold on to what they catch. This thing seems to only use friction and sheer brute strength."

"I would love to see some of these old illustrations, said Steve. "Are they online anywhere?"

"Oh, no," said Marion," to publish those pictures would be jumping the gun at this stage. Your photos will, hopefully, make my colleagues sit up and take notice. Steve, would you be prepared to come down to Oxford for a day and speak to some of these people?"

"Well, I could do. I haven't got anything in my diary for Friday."

"Friday it is then," said the doctor, "I will email you a map and directions. It's a bit tricky to find."

Chapter 12 - Oxford

All that Steve knew about Oxford was that it was very difficult to park. Luckily, the doctor's directions took him to a very small private courtyard with a vacant space.

Steve was led by Marion Calvin into a wood-panelled meeting room. There were four other people waiting – three were seated at a big mahogany table, the fourth was examining the bookshelves.

Doctor Calvin turned to the group. "Everyone, can I introduce Steve Markham? He took all those wonderful photographs you have been seeing on television and on the front pages."

"You have already met Rachael Hartmann, who is visiting me from Stanford. This is Professor Colin Marshall, who works with me here at The University."

Steve shook the outstretched hands.

"Here, we have Leana Butler. I don't quite know how to describe her." Marion screwed up her face.

"An interested party," said Leana, who looked exactly like a librarian might look in Steve's eyes.

"And this is Michael Doherty, who just happens to be over from Trinity College in Dublin. There are several other people who would have loved to be here, but couldn't make it at such short notice."

"Yes, Hans Müller couldn't get over from Germany," said Leana. "He's unreachable at the minute."

"And my good friend Bradley Johnston from Stanford. He has made this phenomenon his lifetime's work, but he's too ill to travel. He was prepared to jump on a plane to be here, but I told him we would pass on the details of the meeting," said the doctor. "So there. Now, as an eye-witness to the event in Cobham, can you please describe exactly what you saw, Steve?"

Steve recounted the story about the page-three girl and seeing the lady mayoress being whisked-up into a hole in the sky. The people around the table listened attentively. Leana Butler was hastily scribbling notes. Rachael Hartmann was recording the discussion on her phone.

"Can I ask a question?" interrupted Michael Doherty.

"Of course," said Steve. "I'll help you if I can."

"It is more of a general question, I'm asking everybody. Why Cobham? Why a church fête?"

Marion tapped the table with her pen.

"As far as we can tell, these events happen at random. What we do know, is that they seem to be happening more frequently now than ever before. The problem we have is that a lot of sightings go un-reported. People think they will be laughed at – you can't blame them, but in the last month I have received reports of two other incidents. One was from a farmer in Devon, who described in great detail, how he saw one of his cows being taken from a drinking trough in a field. Another report is about a young man hiking in the Lake District with friends. He vanished before their very eyes into a mirage in mid-air. That is three reports in one month! Steve here is the only reliable witness, and he has the photographs to prove it. Let me show you something…"

Marion pulled a projection screen down from the ceiling behind her and pointed a remote control at a projector mounted at the top of the wall opposite.

"This is a photograph I took in a cave in France. Look at the circle with lines coming through it. See the small animal entwined in it and the hunter with the spear standing well back."

She changed the slide.

"Here we have a drawing of the deck of a sailing ship – Portuguese, I believe, Fifteenth Century. It shows a hapless sailor hanging from what look like ropes, but note the wavy circles just above him."

The next slide was a clipping from a New York newspaper dated 1932. It described the experience of two men who were erecting steelwork for the Chrysler Building and saw their foreman being assailed by a thing with tentacles before falling, horribly, to his death.

The final slide was the composite that Steve had emailed to her.

"Now, we see that the thing has two eyes, necessary for stereoscopic vision, and it obviously picks its target. In this case, it is the biggest, plumpest one."

"Could it be that there is more than one of these things?" asked the visitor from Dublin.

"There's no way of telling," said the doctor. "We

don't know if it's the same creature inhabiting an expanded space and time domain, or a multiplicity of them breeding and matching our own time span."

Steve shook his head. This talk was all beyond him.

"Of course, this is all speculation," said Leana," we can only whisper about it all between ourselves. Releasing it to the greater scientific community would only bring scorn and ridicule."

"Ah, so what you want is for me to go and catch one," said Steve. "Tie a cow to a winch on a crane and go fishing?"

The joke fell flat; these people were too serious.

"Wish that it was as simple as that," said Leana. "When you go fishing, you have a pretty good idea where the fish will be. When something like this pops up at a random time and place, it makes things a lot more difficult."

Marion switched off the projector and pulled on the spring-loaded screen to retract it.

"The best we can do," said Marion, "is to collect as many reports, sightings and even rumours, as we can. Then maybe, just maybe, we might see a pattern to it all."

Chapter 13 - Maderia

As a freelance press photographer, Steve found it nigh impossible to take a holiday. He could not afford the time nor the money. Julie was so delighted when he produced two airline tickets to Madeira.

"I've always wanted to go to Madeira," cried Julie, jumping for joy.

"Yes, you did mention it a few times," smirked Steve, "along with a lot of other places that we couldn't afford. Now that I'm having a bonanza with my fête shots and you have a new job, we can afford a short holiday."

"I don't know how they will take to me going off on holiday after only being in the job for a few days," said Julie, worriedly.

"Mmm, hadn't thought about that," remarked Steve.

"Damn it, we're going," said Julie. "If they object, I'll tell them where to stuff their job. Don't like it much anyway. 'PA', is how they described it, but I'm nothing but a glorified gofer. Sod them, we are going to Madeira!"

Steve had been warned about Funchal Airport. It is one of the trickiest runways to land on in the world, being built out over the sea at the bottom of a mountain. He needn't have worried. It was as smooth as any landing he had ever had before. That wasn't many. He and Julie took a taxi to the hotel. It was right on the seafront, just a short way out of town. The taxi driver gave them a card and told them to ring him if they wanted to take a scenic drive at any time. Steve put the card in his shirt pocket and paid the man.

The hotel was huge. It seemed to be interconnected with two others, probably all the same company, so they had a choice of six different restaurants and three swimming pools. Their room was spacious and airy, with a marvellous view out over the swimming pool and the sea beyond, but Steve had another agenda in mind. In reception, he had noticed a sign showing what was on the big-screen television in the bar – a Chelsea match!

"Oh, you go ahead, Steve," said Julie, waving him away. "I'd rather read my book on the veranda."

Steve didn't have to be told twice, and headed off to the bar. It was still early afternoon, but the bar was quite full and it became immediately obvious that there were more than a few Chelsea supporters staying at the hotel.

"Come on the Blues," came the shouts.

At half time, there was no score. Steve felt guilty about leaving Julie alone so he dived into the mini-market in the hotel lobby, bought a bottle of chilled wine and took it up to their room. Luckily, it had a screw cap and not a cork. Steve retrieved a glass from the bathroom and half-poured a glass of wine for her.

"Here, got to get back for the second half," he said, rushing out again.

Julie blew a kiss as he left.

The second half was just as boring, ending in a nil-nil draw. Steve had drunk a few beers by this time and was getting quite pally with a couple of the other guests. John and Freda had already been in Funchal for a week and knew the lay of the land. They suggested a visit to the floral gardens high above the town via the cable car, a trip on the tethered balloon at the harbour and a ride on the town's sledges, which ran down the hillside over the cobbled streets, guided by men with straw hats. Also, there was the town market with fruit and vegetables that were totally unknown in England and the spectacular Nun's Valley high above the town. Steve arranged to meet them after breakfast to see some sights.

One thing missing in Funchal was a beach. The mountains just swept down into deep blue water. There was a very large open-air seawater pool where a beach would have been with some hardy swimmers in it. Steve preferred to stick to the hotel pool, it was cleaner and warmer.

In the bar that evening, Steve introduced Julie to John and Freda. They seemed to hit it off. John worked in engineering somewhere in Essex and Freda was a hairdresser. When Julie told them that she worked at a film company, they were very impressed. She omitted to tell them that she had thrown in the job to come on holiday.

Freda told Julie about all the places they could go. Steve had already done that but Julie listened with interest to the woman's perspective. Talk finally got around to Steve's job and Julie was only too ready to brag about his scoop photographs. John and Freda didn't seem too interested in 'current affairs'. It transpired, later, that 'affairs' without the 'current' was more their kind of thing. Later on, they all had dinner together in one of the hotel restaurants. Steve noticed that John was taking just a little too much interest in Julie. He couldn't keep his hands off her. He put her napkin on her lap and brushed a loose hair of her shoulder. It wasn't until Freda started coming on to him that he realised that they had hooked up with a pair of swingers. He wasn't really in to that kind of thing. Freda just wasn't his type. Julie was soaking-up all the attention from John, oblivious of what was going on.

"I'm sorry folks," he said across the table. "It's just that we are not too wild about the wife-swapping thing."

Julie stared at him in utter surprise.

John waved his hand.

"It's okay, really. Some are, some aren't."

"I think we had better head off," said Steve, taking Julie's arm.

"Okay, good night then," said John. "See you tomorrow."

On the way up to their room, Julie quizzed Steve about what had just happened.

"They were a couple of swingers," explained Steve. They wanted to swap partners for the night."

Julie looked shocked.

"Yes, I know," said Steve. "I didn't fancy Freda,

too much war paint."

"Do you mean that if she had been a little less dolled-up, you might have considered it?"

Steve shrugged, "We'll never know."

"Oh," said Julie in exasperation. "We are not going anywhere with those two tomorrow!"

"Quite," said Steve.

Chapter 14 - Roberto

John and Freda were not in the breakfast lounge next morning. Steve called the taxi driver whose card was in his pocket. Ten minutes later, he was holding the back door of his cab open outside the hotel.

The taxi wove up the winding roads surrounded by lush vegetation, cacti and banana trees. The driver was very chatty and told how he had his own allotment and grew vegetables. As they climbed higher into the mountains, valleys of terraced vegetable gardens could be seen over the roadside wall. It was a steep drop, but the view was spectacular.

The taxi stopped at a little cafe in the middle of Nun's Valley. There was a small car park leading to a pathway up to a viewing platform. The taxi driver, Roberto, told Steve and Julie that it was the best view in Madeira. After they made the long climb to the top, the reward was both stunning and unforgettable. The valley below was shrouded in mist and clouds wafted past beneath them.

Steve had left his professional camera at home. For the holiday, he was travelling light. He had a small compact camera and took some pictures of Julie with the magnificent backdrop behind her.

When they had had enough, they made the long trip back down to the car park. Their driver was having a snooze in the car, so they decided to go into the cafe for some refreshments.

Roberto was sitting upright in his seat when they came out. He jumped out and opened the back doors of the cab. On the way back down the mountainside, he was even more talkative. He gave a running commentary on the scenery around them and its history. Eventually, as they got back into the upper heights of Funchal, he asked Steve about his occupation.

Steve was only too happy to tell him about his exciting job as a newspaper photographer – all the events, all the celebrities. Then, he mentioned the incident at the fête. Roberto slammed on the brakes.

"You took those pictures?" he asked, astonished. "They were all over the papers here, and on the mainland. A relation of my wife's saw the same thing some years ago. He still tells of how he saw, with his own eyes, a sheep being pulled into a cloud."

"Really," said Steve, somewhat taken aback. "Would it be possible to meet this man?"

"Tomorrow," said Roberto. "I will take you to see him tomorrow. He doesn't live in Funchal, he lives in Calvinna on the other side of the island."

"He would," thought Steve to himself. "How much will it cost?"

"For the taxi, eighty-five Euros. Paulo won't charge, he loves to tell the story to anyone who will listen. He doesn't speak any English though; I will have to translate."

"And how much will that cost?" asked Steve.

Roberto laughed.

"I am a taxi driver, that's all I charge for. Talk is free."

* * * * *

The route to Calvinna was not quite so spectacular as the one through Nun's Valley. It was mountainous and pretty, but not 'edge-of-a-cliff' stuff. The mountain forest finally gave way to green pastures as they neared the coast. When they arrived at Calvinna, they were delighted to see the little triangular thatched cottages that Roberto had told them about. With their neat and tidy gardens, it was almost like a deliberately-built tourist attraction. Indeed, it was an attraction, but the houses had been lived-in for centuries. This was real!

They found Paulo's house and were shown in by a toothless old lady who politely nodded at every comment from Julie, even though she didn't understand a word.

Old Paulo was sitting by the window on, what appeared to be, an uncomfortable wooden seat with a few cushions on it.

Steve greeted the man warmly, whilst Roberto started to explain the purpose of their visit. Paulo's eyes widened. Someone had come all this way to hear his story, a story that is normally laughed at and ridiculed. Paulo waved his arms around in the air. Steve didn't really need Roberto's translation, Paulo mimed the entire story faultlessly. When Paulo had finished gesticulating, Steve asked a few questions –

"Where did it happen and when did it happen?"

At that point, the old lady arrived with a tray of drinks and biscuits. It must have been Paulo's wife, sister, or mother, it was hard to tell. Steve and Julie accepted the drinks graciously and politely took one biscuit each.

Roberto continued with the translation.

"The sheep was taken from a pasture just up the hillside outside town. It happened in nineteen-ninety-nine. Paulo was very shocked. He hasn't been well ever since."

Roberto explained something else to Paulo. He gasped and put out his hand towards Steve. He pulled Steve towards him and gave him a warm hug. Steve didn't quite understand what Paulo was saying, but it sounded religious. A blessing perhaps?

They all shook hands and departed.

Roberto took a different route back to the hotel; it was closer to the coast and gave them a completely new and different aspect of the beautiful island.

Back at the hotel, Steve squeezed a hundred Euro note into Roberto's hand and patted his shoulder. The taxi driver gave him a big toothy smile.

Travel arrangements for the rest of the holiday consisted of bus rides. The bus service on Madeira was excellent and very cheap. They went up to the floral gardens and church at Monte, high above the town on the cable car – a treat in itself. They came back down in a wicker sled. It was a nail-biting ride, noisy and a couple of times Steve thought that they were going head-on into a stone wall. Of course, the sled guiders were doing it deliberately, just for the thrills. The entire run was about two kilometres and when they reached the bottom, Steve was amazed to find a guy holding up a framed photo of the two of them half way down with their mouths agape. Steve waved it away, they were asking too much. Julie took out her purse and handed the man the money. Steve bit his lip and said nothing.

Chapter 15 - TV Show

When he got back home, the first thing Steve did was ring Marion and tell her the story about the old man in Madeira.

"Thanks, Steve. Another small piece of the puzzle. How many other people are there out there, like this old man, too afraid to tell anyone about their experience?"

"Would you be prepared to be interviewed for a story in the newspapers?" asked Steve. "I know plenty of journalists who would jump at the chance."

Marion thought for a minute.

"That just might work, Steve. Now that the idea is fresh in peoples' minds, it might encourage some others to come forward. I need to talk to somebody else before going ahead. I will call you back shortly."

Steve thought that Marion had forgotten to ring him back. It was that evening before the phone rang.

"Steve. Sorry, I'm afraid that we can't do it."

"What," gasped Steve, "why on Earth not?"

"I have been in touch with someone, a personal friend that is pretty high up in the government. I won't mention his name, but you will surely know it. He has taken advice from appropriate people and they say that it must stay hushed-up. They say to let people think what they like, but any mention of our … monsters … would lead to wide scale panic that would be uncontrollable, and could bring this country – and maybe others – to their knees."

"I understand," said Steve. "It was worth a try, although there was no wide-scale panic when my photos were published."

"Yes, I know, but I have my funding to think about," said Marion. "It is tight enough as it is. Can't go rocking boats."

"What if the story was not attributed to you, but to some anonymous person? It could start a buzz on the internet."

"Absolutely not," said the Doctor firmly. "I don't want my cause associated with the cranks and loonies that put stuff on the internet. This is serious academic work. We will just have to bide our time, get the right people on board. It will come out eventually, but it will have to be from a greater power than me."

After a couple of thinly disguised threats, Marion hung up.

"I was only trying to help," Steve muttered to himself.

Julie was out job-hunting again. She followed-up on some that she had seen on an online job agency, but she had no luck. It was either a case of not enough money or being too far away. She was beginning to wish that she hadn't gone to Madeira now. Maybe that film company job hadn't been so bad after all.

* * * * *

Steve found three messages on his answering machine when he came back in. One was from Marion, one from Paul Atwood and one from somebody he didn't know, a 'Tony Bishop'. He dealt with them in order.

"Hello Doctor Calvin, Steve Markham. You rang?"

"Yes Steve, I rang to apologise for my conduct yesterday. I shouldn't have spoken to you like that. I was under a lot of pressure; I hope that you understand?"

"Yes, of course I do. Think no more of it."

Steve didn't really feel the need for apologies. It just didn't happen in the newspaper industry.

They said goodbye.

"Steve, thanks for ringing back," said Paul Atwood. "Look, I have a favour to ask. I have a location shoot next week and I could really do with some help?"

"Can't Andi help you?" asked Steve, "She seems to know the business."

"That's the thing, Steve. Andi is applying for art college. She has an entrance exam and interview that day."

"What are you going to do when she's away at college?"

"I'll have to get a replacement then, but I'm really stuck for next week. Can you spare a day?"

"Well, yes. I think I can squeeze that in."

"Excellent," said Paul. "Always knew I could depend on you. Now, here are the details…"

Steve scribbled the address and time down and hung up. It was very short notice, but he owed Paul.

"My name's Tony Bishop and I'm a researcher for a production company in Soho," said a voice at the other end of the phone.

"What can I do for you?" asked Steve.

"We are putting together a series about unexplained phenomena. I was rather hoping to have a chat with you. Are you ever up in the West End? Meet for a pint maybe?"

Steve was in Soho regularly, so he agreed to meet Tony Bishop at a pub in Dean Street the following day.

Tony was already waiting in the pub when Steve arrived. He didn't know how Tony recognised him but he picked him out and waved him over.

"What are you having?" asked Tony.

"Oh, a pint of lager," said Steve, sitting down on a cushioned chair.

"Can I ask how you got my number and knew what I look like?" asked Steve as Tony set the pint before him. Tony tapped his nose and grinned.

"I'm a researcher. There is no information that I can't get within minutes. I am the best, even if I say so myself."

Steve puckered his lips.

"So, unexplained phenomena is it?" asked Steve. "What's your angle?"

Tony sat down and pulled his chair closer.

He looked around to check that nobody else was listening.

"It's a six-episode series with an option on six more if it goes well. It's going to be a bit…" he shook his wrist … "tongue in cheek, if you know what I mean. We are not making any rash claims that we can't substantiate. We will invite the viewers to make their own minds up based upon the material we present."

"What kind of thing?" said Steve, curiously.

"Oh, fairies at the bottom of the garden, alien abductions, haunted houses and…" He made a gesture towards Steve.

"If you are talking about the Cobham fête incident," scowled Steve, "I don't see how you can bundle it in with those other things. I was there and saw it for myself."

Tony took a sip from his drink.

"Steve, old boy. The material we have is just as sound as your experience. Okay, it might not have made the front pages, but we have reliable witnesses and good photographs."

"They are all hoaxes," said Steve in a raised voice.

Tony drummed on the table.

"Are they? You haven't seen the evidence and you are calling them hoaxes already."

Steve cooled down a little.

"What do you expect of me?"

"What I would like you to do, is sit down with a couple of our guys and give your version of the incident. It won't be filmed. The conversation will be recorded and transcribed. No-one will hear your voice or see your face. We are quite happy to buy a couple of your shots at agency rates for broadcast television. There will be repeat fees too if the show is syndicated."

Even though the pound signs were lighting up in his eyes, Steve was having misgivings.

"Are you going to be quoting me in this programme?"

"Not if you don't want us to, you can remain totally anonymous if you like."

"And nobody will know that I gave you this information?"

Tony smiled. "There were hundreds of people at that fête. Any one of them could have given us the information. As for the photos, they are syndicated from a news agency. They can't be traced back to you directly."

"Well, okay then," said Steve. "If it is all anonymous, you can count me in. Oh, do I get a fee to compensate me for my time?"

"Yes, you can invoice us when we put the programme to bed. Just don't try to be too greedy. Remember, you are getting the photo royalties too."

Steve agreed to come to the company's offices the following week. He just had to work around his location shoot with Paul.

Chapter 16 - Dean Street

The production company's offices were on the very top floor of a mews off Dean Street. They had swish, modern furniture that looked rather incongruous on the old, planked, wooden floor. Steve was ushered into a room where two people were waiting.

"Hello, Steve. Pleased to meet you," said the bearded man in his mid-forties. "I'm Ben Taylor and this is Cissey Townsend. Can you get us some coffees Sally?"

The young girl nodded and pulled the door shut behind her.

"Okay, Steve. I'm going to switch-on this voice recorder because we don't want to be writing notes and miss something. You were at the fête following-up on a story about a vicar and a showgirl, right?"

Steve nodded. Tony Bishop had certainly done his job.

"What was the crowd's reaction when this … apparition appeared over their heads?"

"I don't think anyone noticed. They were all too busy ogling Amanda Fry's cleavage. I didn't notice anything myself until the screaming started."

"And what started the screaming?"

"The tentacle things dropped down from a mirage in the sky just above the stage. I have established subsequently, that the first two … tentacles were actually eyes, looking for a victim. He trailed off, unable to find the word and just made a wiggling shape with his hands.

"Well, it grabbed her and pulled her up into the air. The last thing I saw of her was the mayoress disappearing into ripples in the air."

"And the thing was gone after that?"

"Yes," said Steve. "There was nothing to be seen after the ripples smoothed out."

Ben Taylor rubbed his chin.

"Do you know of any other such happenings?"

"Yes, there have been incidents like this spanning thousands of years right across the globe."

Taylor wrote something on his notepad.

"How do you know about these?"

"I have an … acquaintance who studies such things."

"It wouldn't be a certain lady doctor who works at Oxford University?"

"I'm sorry," said Steve. "I can't discuss that."

Ben rubbed his chin some more.

"We'll take that as a 'yes' then."

Steve jumped to his feet.

"Look, this 'lady doctor' you are talking about is a serious academic and has to answer to people in the government. Don't bring her into this. She has a reputation to maintain."

"Don't worry yourself, Steve. Calm down. The said person will not be referenced in any way in our programme. I was merely trying to ascertain how involved you are in all this. We already know about other sightings and incidents. Tony Bishop is the best, but then I'm sure that he has already told you that?"

Steve smiled affirmatively.

"Now, let's cut to the chase…"

The girl arrived with a tray of cups and a coffee dispenser, set them on the table and left.

"Cissey, would you?" said Ben indicating the cups on the tray.

Steve was beginning to see why Julie wasn't so keen to work in film and television. It was tough at the bottom, especially if you were female. Some girls couldn't see past the glamour.

"As I was saying, Steve, we know all the facts about this 'incident', as you call it. It is my job to suggest some explanations to the viewers and let them draw their own conclusions. In some of our other episodes, we expound the concept of a 'parallel state'. Some people refer to it as 'the other side.' Now, it could be supernatural, it could be pseudoscience, it doesn't matter. All we know is that there is another state of being sharing our existence on this planet. This 'Giant Squid' or whatever you call it…" he paused.

"Cissey, can you come up with a more suitable name for this thing? We can't keep referring to it as a 'Giant Squid', and, while you are at it, we can't call its limbs 'tentacles' either. Find better terms."

Cissey nodded and continued to tap on her laptop. So far, she hadn't spoken a word.

"So, I propose the theory that this creature lives in an alternate reality here on Earth. It can manipulate the wall between the two realities and reach through this wall, as it pleases, taking its pick of tasty morsels on our side – goats, cows, fat mayoresses. Unless you have any other ideas, Cissey, I think we will run with that. Okay?"

Cissey nodded again.

"Right, Steve, I think we are done for now. We might ask you to come in again; we'll see how it goes."

He stood up and shook Steve's hand and led him towards the door.

"Oh, Cissey will send you a purchase order so that you can send us an invoice. Bye, Steve, thanks for your help."

Chapter 17 - Location shoot

"Dr Calvin, Steve Markham."

"Oh, Steve, you don't need to be so formal. My friends call me Marion. What can I do for you?"

"Dr C – Marion, we need to talk. There is something that you need to know. I think you will find it very interesting."

"Really? Then talk we shall. Your place or mine?"

"I'm really busy this week," said Steve." You wouldn't be coming up to London in the near future, would you?"

"As a matter of fact, I am. I have an appointment in Harley Street. It's nothing serious, just a troublesome skin complaint. The appointment is on Thursday morning, how is that for you?"

"Thursday's perfect," said Steve. "I can come and meet you for lunch afterwards. Do you like Greek food?"

"Oh yes, I love Greek food. I haven't had it much recently. Yes, that would be a treat, indeed."

* * * * *

The location photo shoot took Steve to a farm outside Dorking. Paul was already there with his estate car, unloading cameras, tripods and cool boxes.

"Hi Steve, can you give me a hand with these?" asked Paul, indicating the pile of equipment on the ground.

"What are we shooting?" asked Steve.

"It's a shot for some new dairy spread. They want the pack perched on a traditional wooden gate with cows in the background."

Steve had heard it all before and made a 'ho-hum' noise.

"Well, there's the gate and yonder, the cows," said Paul. "Can you set up the big tripod and a couple of smaller ones to put the reflectors on? I would also like the folding table beside the main tripod for my laptop. I just have to tell the farmer we are here. He is expecting us."

"What are you shooting on?" asked Steve.

"The Hasselblad with the digital back," said Paul, as he walked off towards the farmhouse. The grass wasn't too long, having been chewed by countless rows of bovine teeth. He set up the tripods as directed and mounted the two silver reflectors on the two smaller tripods. Angling them to reflect the sunlight onto the top of the gate was the best he could do for now. He opened Paul's silver flight case and took out the expensive camera. He clipped it into the quick release shoe on the tripod and clicked in the short telephoto lens. The digital back was clipped onto the rear of the camera and he focussed on the gatepost. It looked about right.

"Well, we have a good day for it," said Paul, as he came back to the shooting location.

"You've done this before, haven't you?" he smiled at Steve. "Now, let me see what they've sent us."

Paul opened up his laptop and put an image on

the screen. It was a rough mock-up of the shot they had to take; a knife lying across a tub of dairy spread, with a perfect curl of spread resting on the knife.

Paul looked at his own tub of spread. "I don't think ours is going to be able to do that. It's far too soft! I'm going to have to go and ask the farmer's wife if she will stick a few tubs in her freezer for half an hour … and even then, we are going to have to be quick to capture it before it starts running all over the place."

Then Paul placed an open-topped tub on top of the gate and peered down onto the focusing screen. He moved the tripod back and forth to get the right composition.

"Here, Steve. Run off a few shots of that with different apertures. I need to get the cows in shot, not too sharp and not too blurred." He walked off towards the farmhouse again and returned a few minutes later.

"We've been invited in for tea and scones," said Paul. "Bring the camera and flight case. Leave the rest as it is. Nobody will touch it there."

Mrs White was not the round-faced, rosy-cheeked farmer's wife that Steve had envisaged. She was much younger, in her mid to late thirties, and she was slim and quite attractive.

"I've just made a fresh pot of tea; how do you like yours?" she asked with a charming smile.

"Just a splash of milk," said Paul.

"Same for me," said Steve.

"It's a lovely day for it," said Mrs White.

"Yes, I was just saying," agreed Paul.

"Have you been here long?" asked Steve.

"I haven't, myself," answered the woman, "but Bob took the farm over from his father. He's been here all his life."

She held out a plate of currant scones.

"Cream tea, anyone?"

Steve took one and thanked her, Paul waved his hand.

"This might sound a strange question," began Steve, "but have there been any stories about livestock disappearing around these parts?"

Paul gave him a funny look.

"Are you talking about rustlers, Steve? Have you been watching too many cowboy films?"

"No, we don't get many rustlers around this way," said the farmer's wife, laughing. "We have had some diesel and fuel oil taken though."

"Buggers," said Paul.

"Wait a minute," she paused, "I did hear of someone who had a cow disappear in mysterious circumstances on a farm down the road. The farmer only had a small herd of Ayrshires. When he counted them one morning, one was missing. They were in a locked field and there was no way for it to get out. Strangest thing I've heard in a long time. They never did get to the bottom of it."

Paul retrieved the dairy spread from the freezer and checked it. "I'll just take two and leave the others for now. If we don't need them, you can have them," he said, sticking his tongue out and making an ugly face.

It only took a few moments for Steve to put the camera back in position while Paul formed the curl of spread on the knife blade.

"How is the bokeh looking?" asked Paul.

"F8 looks about right to me," said Steve, "but I think that you had better bracket a couple of stops either way to be safe."

Paul turned on the laptop, which was connected to the camera. The screen showed him exactly what could be seen through the camera lens.

"Damn, the cows have all moved down the field out of shot," said Paul." Steve, go down there and chase them up closer."

"What?"

"Shoo the cows up toward the camera."

Steve climbed over the gate and did his best Border Collie impression. The cattle weren't too impressed. Just then, Farmer White came in from the opposite end of the field.

"We need to get the cows in shot," called Steve.

Bob White took a broken branch from the ground and smacked it across the cows' rumps. Reluctantly, they inched up the pasture. Paul was gesticulating with his arm.

"More, more."

As soon as the cows were there or thereabouts, Paul checked the curl of dairy spread. It was holding shape, but only just. He rattled off a couple of dozen shots using a key on the laptop.

"Let me just check that we've got what we need," he said.

He brought up a strip of thumbnails on his screen and played a slideshow. It wasn't ideal viewing conditions in the bright sunlight so he used a reflector to make some shade over the screen.

"Yes, I think they will be happy with those," he said, waving at the farmer. Farmer White waved back.

They packed up the gear and left.

Chapter 18 - Houmous

"Hello, Dr Calvin," said Steve." Was everything alright?"

"Oh, I don't know. You pay a lot of money and get a lot of platitudes. I don't know if the ointment he gave me will be any better than the last lot. It's my skin; it's ageing faster than me! I have wrinkles on my wrinkles."

"Why do you use an expensive Harley Street doctor? I'm sure that your local GP would give you the same thing."

"Oh, didn't I say? He's my brother," smiled Marion.

"He's your brother and he charges you?" gasped Steve.

"Oh, I insist on giving him something. He's still my baby brother at fifty-four."

Steve and Marion strolled down to Greek Street and into an empty restaurant.

"We are a bit early," said Steve. "At least, we will be able to talk in private."

They sat down at a table. There was no sign of a waiter.

"Have you been to Greece, Steve?"

"Err, no. Never been there."

"When I was 'married'," said Marion, forming quote marks with her hands, "we used to go to Greece almost every year, the islands mostly, but we did go to Athens once. Loved it there. I wouldn't mind moving out there after I retire. You can still get reasonably-priced property if you get something off the beaten track."

A waiter emerged from the kitchen.

"Something to drink?" he asked, handing them menus.

Steve remembered this waiter from earlier visits. He made no pretence of charm, and he was even quite rude at times.

"Retsina?" Steve suggested to Marion, with raised eyebrows.

"Oh, yes please," she replied, "and a bottle of fizzy water."

The waiter walked off without any sign of acknowledgement.

"Now, Steve, I am dying to know what you have to tell me."

Steve paused to gather the right words.

"I have been approached by a certain television production company who are in the process of making a series of programs about unexplained phenomena. They offered to buy a few of my photos at television rates, plus repeats, if I would agree to an interview. Well, I did talk to them. I didn't tell them anything that I haven't said publicly before. During the interview, they hinted that they knew about you and your research."

"How could they possibly know about that?" asked Marion, with a surprised expression.

"They have this researcher guy, Tony Bishop. I've

met him, and he is good. Very good. Whatever means he uses, or contacts he has, he has been able to dig up a lot of details about your research. I saw the photos of the cave drawings and the etching of the sailing ship sticking out of a folder he had. I think that I was supposed to see them, they were so deliberately posed."

Marion sat back in her chair and wiped her forehead. Just then, the waiter arrived with the wine, a bottle of water and four glasses. He showed the label to Steve. He nodded. The cork was half out of the bottle with a corkscrew sticking in it. Steve thought that the bottle had been refilled from a bulk wine container in the kitchen. No matter, it was only Retsina. At least there was condensation on the bottle, so he knew it was cold. The waiter poured the wine and opened the twist cap of the water bottle.

"Would you like some starters?" he asked.

"I'll just have the houmous," said Steve and looked at Marion, who was still making up her mind.

"I think I'll have Dolmáthakia Mé Rísi," said Marion, in a perfect Greek accent.

The waiter nodded and wandered off.

Marion leaned forward.

"So, what else did you find out from these people?"

"Oh, they have a theory about these 'things', whatever they are called, that live in a parallel state, manipulating the barrier between our world and theirs. They know that the eyes appear first to identify their prey, before their tentacles…" he said, wiggling his fingers, "…grab the victim."

That is what they are going to suggest to the viewers. He said that they are leaving it to the viewer to decide if it is true or not."

"Oh," whispered Marion. "That is so close to our theory, except I believe that there is only one of these things. Also, it isn't restricted by our chronology, it can move around in time and space at will."

"Why do you think that there is only one?" asked Steve.

"Call it a hunch, if you like. I have no proof to offer whatsoever. I also don't think that its appearances are quite as random as you might think I think they must follow some sort of pattern. I just don't know what it is yet."

The waiter arrived with the starters and pitta bread.

##"Can I take your orders for the main course?"

Steve gestured towards Marion to go first.

"Oh, Kalamarákia for me, please."

"I'll have the Kleftiko," said Steve, pointing at the item on the menu. The waiter disappeared into the kitchen.

"I think we need someone to create a computer model," said Marion, "that plots time of appearance against location. I myself can't think in four dimensions at once. Or even five, maybe?"

Another three men came into the restaurant and looked around. They chose a table on the opposite wall. The waiter eventually arrived to attend to them.

"Do you know anyone with the skills to program

such a model?" asked Steve.

"We are spoiled for choice at the University," she laughed." It's not the coding that concerns me; it's getting someone who can keep their mouth shut. That's not so easy in a computer lab because there's always somebody looking over your shoulder. Whoever does it will have to work in isolation. They could work at home perhaps, although I expect that the number-crunching might be beyond the capabilities of the average PC."

"Don't know much about computers myself," said Steve." Email and Photoshop are about as far as I go."

The conversation slowed as they ate their lunch. Marion obviously had something going on in her mind. She didn't say what it was.

"Marion," said Steve." Can I make a suggestion? Don't jump down my throat."

Marion stopped eating and looked attentively.

"This researcher guy, Tony Bishop, is very clever. He works freelance so he might be happy to dig around for more incidents on your behalf. I don't know what he charges. He might charge less if he was allowed to share his findings with the production company. Between them they would only generate the raw data. You would still be the one organising the information into a meaningful theory."

"I don't know," said Marion." What if they figure out the pattern for themselves?"

"They don't have the resources that you have at your command. It would be way beyond their budget to hire a programmer to write something like that."

"Oh, but they have some very talented programmers in the film and television industry. Just look at all those special effects they do!" said Marion.

"That is something quite different. Yes, they are making three-dimensional models, but aren't they just tweaking existing programs? They don't need Oxford University software engineers for that."

"Well, there wouldn't be any harm in having a word with him. I will hold my cards close to my chest. Can you arrange a meeting?"

"Leave it to me."

Marion thanked Steve for lunch and insisted that it was her turn next time. He promised to get in touch to confirm a meeting with Tony Bishop. They shook hands and went their separate ways at the tube station.

Chapter 19 - Break-up

"Steve, is that lipstick on your cheek?"

Steve put his hand up to feel, even though he couldn't possibly have felt it.

"It might be; I was having lunch with a lady from Oxford University today. She did kiss my cheek as we parted."

That wouldn't be the first time, would it?" raged Julie.

"Huh, you should talk. Who was it that didn't come home last Tuesday night?"

"I was staying over with a girlfriend. I was too drunk to make it back home at that time of night."

"And where was all this drinking happening?" asked Steve.

"We went to a club. The shots were free during the happy hour. Okay, I might have had a few too many. It's no big deal."

"Why do you feel the need to go to a club with a girlfriend? You never go to a club with me."

"I'm a grown-up, you know, Steve Markham. I can do whatever I like. You don't own me."

"No, I don't own you, but remember that you are living here at my expense. You don't have a job. You pay practically nothing to the running of the household. Julie…" He shook his head slowly.

"Well, if you only think of me as your kept woman, then no thanks; I'm out of here!"

Julie stormed off into the bedroom and stuffed

some clothes into a bag. She walked out without another word, slamming the door on the way.

Steve sat with his head in his hands. What had just happened? He had to admit to himself that he had seen it coming. Had he said things that he shouldn't have? No, on reflection. She hadn't taken all her stuff, so she would be back. She still had a key to Steve's flat. She would probably come back when he was out. He didn't really care.

Tony Bishop had given Steve a card when they first met. It was still in his wallet.

"Tony?" said Steve down the phone. "Steve Markham here, remember we …? Yes. Good. What I wanted to know is if you would be interested in doing a bit of research for a friend of mine?"

"Yeah, what kind of research is it?"

"It's very confidential research," said Steve.

"Are you sure that you wouldn't be better off with a private detective?" asked Tony pointedly.

"No, it's not that kind of thing, it's more… academic, if you get my meaning."

"Ah, would it involve a certain lady who resides in Oxford by any chance?" said Tony, in realisation.

"It might," said Steve. "Would you be interested in discussing terms?"

"Well, yes, of course. A man has to earn his bread and butter," said Tony.

Remember the pub where we met last time?" asked Steve.

"Yes."

"This evening?" suggested Steve.

"I can make it about seven," said Tony.

"Great, see you then."

Steve had only just hung up when his phone rang. He expected it to be Tony with a change of plan, but it was Paul Atwood.

"Steve. Guess what? The client doesn't like the shots we took for the bloody margarine ad! I have to reshoot."

"What was wrong?" asked Steve.

"It was my fault," said Paul." My cack-handedness. I had the knife going from left to right instead of right to left. It looks like it was put there by somebody left-handed."

"But wasn't that how it was on the mock-up?" asked Steve.

"Yes, the agency visualizer was obviously left-handed too. I should have double checked with the client. They did originally okay the mock-up with the knife that way around. At least they are going to pay for the reshoot, so it's not all that bad. I think we can do it in an hour, we already know the set-up. I'll just have to give Farmer Bob White the bad news."

"Can't you just flip the image with Photoshop?" asked Steve.

"No. Andi had a go. She's pretty good at that sort of thing, but it just didn't look right. It's quicker to reshoot than mess around for hours on the computer. It's going on a poster so it has to look perfect.

You know me, I'm a bit of a perfectionist. I don't mind retouching a few minor blemishes, but major reconstructions … no way."

"When do you want to do it?" asked Steve.

"They need it urgently. We'll have to do it tomorrow, weather permitting," said Paul.

"Okay, Paul. I'll meet you there."

* * * * *

That night, the pub was packed. Steve couldn't see Tony so he bought himself a pint and found a place to stand near the door. By twenty-five past seven, there was still no sign of Tony. Then, Steve saw his head appear around the door. Tony was beckoning to him. When he got outside, Tony was climbing into a silver car, the engine still running.

"Get in, Steve," he called. "That pub is too full for a quiet conversation."

"Nice car," said Steve.

"Yes, I treated myself a few months ago. What do you drive?"

Steve laughed." A beat-up old Fiat. I need to change it but I just don't have the time."

"I know the feeling," said Tony.

"Where are we going?" asked Steve.

"A pub down in Streatham that I know. It's easy to park and it will be empty on a mid-week night. Hell, it's empty every night. They used to have a band, bloody good they were, but then the landlord decided that he couldn't afford them, he's lucky if he gets two customers a night – two old guys, and they sit over the same pint until closing time."

Steve knew the situation.

"Anyway, Steve, tell me more about Doctor Calvin's proposition."

Steve explained as much as he could without giving the whole game away.

"She is very keen to pin point as many incidents as possible across the country, and elsewhere if at all possible."

"Oh, it's possible, if she has the means," said Tony, looking across at Steve with a wink.

"That's what I wanted to talk to you about," said Steve. "She does have some research funds, but they are little, and for something else. Her research into these 'phenomena' is all under the table, so to speak. I was thinking that you might consider charging her less if you were able to share the results with the television company. I'm sure that they would pay something for the additional detail?"

"I don't know," said Tony. "Television companies don't have bottomless purses these days. The show is only guaranteed for six episodes. They will be making a loss on those in the hope of getting another season out of it."

"Yes, I'm with you. What are your normal rates?"

Tony told him that he had an hourly rate, a daily rate and a weekly rate. If Steve ignored the hourly rate, which was way above what he himself charged, the daily and weekly rates didn't seem so bad.

They got to the empty pub and continued to talk for an hour and a half. After a few pints, Steve was spilling out all his life problems; his lack of work, his girlfriend running off that day and his general lack of prospects for the future. Tony offered Steve commiserations.

"Look, Steve, apart from the production company job, I'm not overly busy. I'll make you a deal. I don't know if I can swing anything with Ben Taylor, but for academic research," he paused, "I'll do half my weekly rate. Okay? That's the best I can do."

"Thanks, Tony. I'll run that past the good doctor and get back to you."

"Steve, normally I would run you to a tube station, but not after three pints. It's not far to Streatham station. I hope you don't mind?"

"No, of course not," grinned Steve. "Nice to see you. Speak soon."

Chapter 20 - Re-shoot

It was just like déjà vu. Same field, same cows. All that was missing was Paul. Steve looked at the time on his phone. He was a little early. It wasn't long before he saw the glint of Paul's estate car bumping along the lane. Steve walked over to the car and was surprised to see Andi in the passenger seat.

"Hello Andi, I wasn't expecting to see you here. Paul doesn't need two assistants."

Paul climbed out of the driver's side.

"We need to do this quickly; rain is forecast for late morning. Andi can do the running back and forth to the freezer in the farmhouse, and maybe chase the cows up the field if need be." He winked at Steve.

"I'm not going near any cows," scowled Andi indignantly. "You won't get me within half a kilometre of those things!"

Paul and Steve laughed.

"How did your art school interview go?" asked Steve.

"Oh, okay, I think. I should hear back next week," answered Andi.

"Right, Steve, if you could just set up the gear as before, Andi and I will go down and see Mrs White. If she hasn't thrown out last week's product, we might be able to start right away."

Paul and Andi headed down to the farmhouse with a freezer box. Steve looked up at the sky. Rain was certainly on the way.

When they returned, they explained that Mrs White had thrown the old spread away so they had to put a fresh one in the freezer to harden it.

"I'll give it twenty minutes. It's not as warm today as last time. That should be long enough."

"Is Farmer White around?" asked Steve.

"No, he's in town at a market, apparently. I think that you are going to have to go down to the field and persuade Daisy, Buttercup and friends to move up this end. My daughter is chicken."

"I don't like chickens either," Andi snapped. "Don't mind little lambs though."

Steve hauled himself over the gate.

"You don't need to be so gentle with them. You saw how Bob got them to shift."

"Yes, but they know him," protested Steve.

"Just be ready to run, and try to avoid the bull!" shouted Paul.

"Bull?" said Steve, wide-eyed. "You didn't mention a bull."

Paul flapped his hand at him and doubled up.

"There's no bull, Steve, just bullshit."

Paul was always pulling his leg. Steve should have known better by now.

Paul sent Andi down to get the dairy spread. She came back with Mrs White, who was wearing jeans and an open-necked shirt.

"Hello," she said. "I'm just curious to see what you are doing."

Paul gave a very quick explanation for the sake of politeness, but he was keen to get the job done before the clouds completely covered the blue sky. He curled some spread with the knife blade, double-checked that it was coming in from the correct angle, refocused and started taking shots.

"Mrs White," said Steve. "Last time I was here, you told me an odd story about a missing cow."

"That's right, she replied. "Fred Marshall, who lives about two miles down the main road, was telling the story at a local farmers' meeting about a month ago. I got the impression that his case was not unique."

Steve was concerned. "Farmer Marshall. Hmm …"

Chapter 21 - New car

"It may be half price," gasped Marion, "but it's still very expensive."

"Yes, Marion, but he is the best," said Steve.

"I will see if I can get a whip-round from my colleagues. My research grant is almost exhausted but if I explain what we're doing, some of them might chip in."

"How long will it take you to find out?" asked Steve. "Tony could get a commission any time and not be available for ages."

"I should be able to let you know this evening," said Marion. "I might have to make a few long-distance calls."

"Can't you use email?" asked Steve.

"Not if we need a quick answer," replied Marion.

Marion rang back about ten o'clock.

"I'm not too late for you, am I?" she asked.

"No, it's alright," said Steve.

"Well, the good news is that I've got the funding. My old friend, Bradley Johnston at Stanford, was more than generous. It was he that got me hooked on this venture some twenty years ago.

"This has been going on for twenty years?" asked Steve.

"Steve, it's been going on for thousands of years!"

"Yes, of course."

"So, Steve, get in touch with this Mr Bishop and

set the ball rolling. I'd rather that he didn't contact me here at the University. If he has any questions, you can act as the go-between."

"Understood," said Steve.

Steve couldn't get hold of Tony. It was late anyway. He would leave it until the morning.

"Okay, Tony. I have funding for a week of your time. You know what we are after; locations and dates. Do you need anything more from this end?"

"No, Steve, I will take it from here, but you are not expecting results in seven days from today, are you? When I quoted you for a week's work, I didn't mean five consecutive days from nine to five. It doesn't work like that. I have other jobs on and it will have to fit around those. I have to put out feelers and wait for replies. You know how it is?"

"Ah," said Steve, nodding. "Oh well, after all these centuries, I don't suppose a few more weeks will make any difference. By the way, I discovered another cow-snatching incident happened at the farm of a Fred Marshall about seven miles west of Dorking. There was also a suggestion that it wasn't the only one."

"Great, I will add that to my list. Cheers, Steve. I'll get back to you when I have something."

* * * * *

Steve was correct about Julie sneaking back in to collect her things. When he came home that afternoon, the drawers were lying open and there were spaces on the CD rack. She wasn't very tidy about it. It was almost as if he had been burgled. He had already bought a new lock for the front door but before he could find his screwdriver to fit it, the phone rang.

"Hi, Steve. It's Paul. We are having a little dinner party on Saturday night and wondered if you and your good lady would like to come around?"

"I don't have a 'good lady' anymore," said Steve, "but if you don't mind singles, I'd love to."

"Oh," said Paul. "Good, well about half past seven then?"

Steve was at a loose end for a couple of days. He didn't have any work lined up, although the phone could ring any minute sending him off to some boring political hustings. His bank balance was looking healthier than it ever had before so he decided that it was time to look for a new car. Well, not a brand new car, but at least something less decrepit than his ancient Fiat. There was a large second-hand car dealership just down the road which he had often passed but had never visited. They had something for every taste and budget. He decided that now was as good a time as any.

As Steve wandered up and down the rows of shiny cars, he was very aware of a young man trailing him. He knew that it was a salesman and wanted to keep out of his way. He didn't like to be pressured.

Eventually, the salesman made his move.

"Can I help you, sir? What exactly are you looking for?"

"Don't know," said Steve, "just seeing what's on offer."

"How much were you thinking of spending?" asked the salesman.

"I don't know," said Steve again. "I'm just looking at what they cost."

"You must have some idea of what you can afford," insisted the salesman – slick suit, wide tie, black shoes, shifty eyes.

"Aw man, leave me alone. If I see something that takes my fancy, I'll let you know."

The salesman shuffled off.

How much did he want to spend? Five grand? That was a lot more than he had ever paid for a car before but he could go to that.

Then he saw it. Sometimes, a man and a car just know that they are meant for each other. But was a two-seater sports car going to be practical? He opened the boot. There was room in there for his camera bag and a small suitcase. He looked through the window. It all looked very spic and span. Would the shiny metallic red paintwork attract parking wardens and miscreants with six-inch nails? Perhaps. He was certainly drawn to it.

"Very nice car," said a voice from behind him.

Steve looked around at the salesman.

"It's quite a bargain too."

Steve had been so taken by the car that he

had totally neglected to look at the price on the windshield. £7499! That was half as much again as he had in mind.

"Would you take a trade-in?" asked Steve. The salesman knew he had him on the line and was slowly reeling him in.

"Perhaps, what have you got?" asked the young man.

"Over here," replied Steve, leading the salesman over to where his Fiat was sitting in the customer parking zone.

"Oh," said the salesman. "It's seen better days." He looked at the car from all angles.

"Can I take a quick drive in it?" he asked.

Steve handed him the keys.

"It runs very well," said Steve. "The paint's a bit faded but I haven't had any trouble with it," he lied.

The salesman was away for about ten minutes. In the meantime, Steve climbed into the car and noticed how the seats fitted his body like a tailor-made suit. He looked in the glove compartment and behind the two seats. He opened the bonnet and looked in at the engine. It seemed clean. He checked the tyres. They looked reasonable too. The number plates told him that the car was about six years old. It was in pretty good nick for a six-year-old.

The salesman clattered back into the parking bay.

"How much were you expecting to get for the Fiat?" asked the salesman.

"Seven fifty, something like that?" asked Steve.

The salesman gave him one of those 'are you

totally out of your mind' looks, and then shook his head.

"I couldn't sell it for that!"

"What can you give me for it then?" asked Steve.

"The best I could do would be four hundred."

"Can't you make it four-nine-nine? I can give you seven grand, cash."

The salesman pondered for a minute and then held out his hand.

"Aren't you going to take a test drive?" asked the salesman.

"Oh, I suppose I should, but we've already shaken hands on it."

"Have a test drive. I don't think you will change your mind."

The salesman, Alec, sat in the passenger seat and explained the controls. That was all straightforward. He showed Steve how to lower the soft-top and they set off.

"It will take a bit of getting used to," said Steve. "It's a lot lower than I'm used to and this stubby gear lever feels very strange."

"But you do like it?" asked Alec.

"Definitely."

"There are just a few formalities and we'll be finished," said Alec. "If I could just have your signature and the date here and here."

Steve signed the papers.

"Now, all you need is to have a cover note faxed over to me and you can take it away."

Steve hadn't felt so excited for a long time. A lovely, bright red sports car would be his tomorrow!

Chapter 22 - Dinner

Steve climbed out of his new car, pulled up the soft top and locked the car door. Andi came running out.

"Oh, Steve. You've got a new car. It's fabulous. Take me for a ride in it."

"Not now, Andi. I'll be late for dinner."

Andi pouted.

"I'll come around and take you out in it tomorrow if you like?"

Andi was delighted and ran off to tell her Mum and Dad about Steve's new car. Paul came out and had a look.

"Nice one," he said, nodding slowly. He dragged Steve back into the house.

"Oh, just a minute," said Steve, opening the car to retrieve a bottle of wine. "I hope this is okay." He locked up again.

Somehow, Andi managed to snag a seat at the dinner table next to Steve. All the other guests were couples. She may only have been eighteen, but Andi could flirt like a veteran. Steve was very aware that she was touching him more times than could be called accidental. They talked about her art school interview and her aspiration of becoming a fully-fledged photographer. Steve had been through all this himself and could empathise with her.

After dinner, people were making polite conversation. Andi asked if Steve would like to see her portfolio. He should have asked where, because before he knew it Andi had whisked him off up to her bedroom on the second floor.

She spread her portfolio out on the floor and patted the bed beside her for him to sit down. He leafed through the clear plastic wallets and saw her school drawings and paintings, then some photographs and a few examples of Photoshop manipulations.

"What do you think, Steve?" she asked excitedly.

"Very good, he said. You are very talented. I think that you will do very well indeed."

"What about this one," she asked, showing him a close-up photograph of a cricket on a leaf.

"I love it." said Steve. "It's smiling at the camera."

"And this one, this is one of my favourites."

"It's brilliant, Andi, I couldn't have done better myself!"

Andi wrapped her arm around his and leaned over and kissed him on the cheek.

"What kind of photography most interests you?" asked Steve.

"I'd really like to do what you do; reportage," she gushed.

"It's not easy," said Steve. "It takes a lot more than just the ability to use a camera."

"What do you mean?" asked Andi.

"Well, you have to have a nose for a good news story. There is a lot of luck involved too. You have to be in the right place at the right time. Then, there's the nasty side; the elbows in the ribs to the photographer next to you, the pushing to the front. The sticking of your camera up the noses of rich and famous people …"

Andi just smiled and bounced up and down on the bed.

She leaned over and kissed him again, whilst holding onto his arm tightly. The kiss lingered.

Steve turned his head and their lips met.

Just then, Steve heard footsteps on the landing and quickly pulled away. Lizzie, Andi's mother, appeared in the doorway.

"Ah, that's where you are," said Lizzie. "So, what do you think of Andi's work, Steve?"

"I think it's fantastic. She's going to go far, this girl."

He put his arm around her and gave her a friendly squeeze.

"I just don't think that reportage is the right direction though. It's too cut-throat for a timid little girl. Perhaps still-life would be better, or natural history maybe?"

Lizzie waved her hand and went back downstairs.

Andi gave Steve a thump on the shoulder.

"Who are you calling a timid little girl?" she growled.

She pushed him down flat onto her bed and jumped on top of him.

They continued the kiss where they had left off.

* * * * *

"Where shall we go?" asked Steve, sitting in the driveway of Andi's house. "Brighton, South Downs? I haven't had the car on a motorway yet. I haven't really had a chance to see what it can do."

"I don't mind," she replied. "Anywhere."

"Well, let's head south towards the coast and see where we end up," decided Steve.

Lizzie watched them leave from the living room window.

As Steve opened up his new car on the M23, Andi threw her arms to the wind.

"Oh, this is wonderful," she said. "Seventy miles an hour, no, eighty miles an hour in an open-top sports car. Wheee!"

Steve then realised that he was going ten miles an hour over the legal limit and slowed down. It was hard to hear what Andi was saying over the sound of the wind. He slowed down even more.

"What was that Mrs White was saying about a vanishing cow?" she asked.

"I'm not sure," shouted Steve above the wind noise.

"Cows are very big; how can they just disappear?" asked Andi.

"There are things that happen in this world that just can't be explained in logical terms."

Andi put her hand on his knee.

"Yes, I know," she said, smiling.

The car sped down the motorway.

Steve pulled off the motorway into the South Downs. He didn't have any particular destination in mind, but they found themselves in a small car park overlooking sweeping hills.

"It's lovely here," said Andi. "Let's go for a walk."

Steve locked up the car and they headed off down a pathway. Andi took Steve's hand as they wandered through the beautiful landscape. She snuggled up to him as they walked. When they reached a low depression in the ground, Andi pulled Steve to the grass. Steve felt his will being dragged away from him as Andi smothered him in kisses. A few weeks ago she had just been a little schoolgirl, but now...

Okay, so they'd had a snog. Steve was glad that things hadn't got totally out of hand. Andi was all over him, but he had kept it in control. Would he be able to next time? Next time? What was he doing? He was thirty-one years old and she was eighteen. No, it wasn't illegal, but she was Paul and Lizzie's little girl. He felt a responsibility to her and to her parents. He persuaded her to come back to the car. There were other thrills to be had.

When he dropped Andi back home, Steve couldn't see Lizzie peering out from behind the curtains, but he knew she was there. He gave Andi a quick kiss on the cheek and she got out of the car. She held her fingers up to her mouth and ear indicating that she would give him a call. He hadn't given her his phone number explicitly, but it was surely in

Paul's contact list on the studio computer.

Andi rang that evening. Steve wasn't prepared for the proposition.

"Steve, I'd like to come and live with you!"

"Oh dear," thought Steve. "Out of the frying pan…"

Chapter 23 - Bed

Steve didn't return any of Andi's calls, and there were a lot of them. He hid behind his voice mail. Luckily Paul didn't have his land line number, only his mobile. Steve didn't know what to think. Andi was sweet, fanciable even, but he just wasn't ready for this. She was too young, too immature. He was just a crush, that's all, she'd get over it in time. Pushing it to the back of his mind, he picked up his phone and called Marion.

"Steve, I'm so glad you rang. I think someone has been in my office and gone through my papers. I don't want to involve the police. What should I do?"

"You stay there Marion, don't touch a thing. I'll be with you as soon as I can."

Oxford was only an hour away from Steve's flat in Chiswick. He would just have to watch his speed. On his trip down the M23 with Andi he found that the car was doing over eighty at times, and he had to rein back. The last thing he needed was a speeding ticket. He parked in the no-parking bay again and pulled on the quaint brass bell handle. Marion opened the door.

"Oh, thank you so much for coming all this way, Steve. Come in and sit down. I'll make some drinks. Coffee alright?"

"Yes, lovely," he replied.

Pouring the coffee from a percolator, Marion

explained how she had come home to find that files on her desk had been disturbed. The drawers were lying slightly ajar and books had moved on the shelves. Marion was much too fastidious and tidy to leave her room like this.

"Is there any sign of a break-in?" asked Steve. "Broken glass, damaged door or lock?"

"No, that's the thing," said Marion, "there is no sign of forced entry. Whoever it was must have had a key."

"Or been an expert lock-picker," added Steve.

"Did they take anything?" he asked.

"I don't think so. If they did, it wasn't anything of importance. I'll have to check."

"It might be that instead of taking your papers, they just photographed them. They used to have spy cameras, now they just use a phone."

"Who would do such a thing? Why?" asked Marion, half sobbing.

"I have my suspicions," said Steve, sternly.

"Should I report it to the police?" asked Marion.

"I doubt they will be interested, Marion. There's no criminal damage and no theft that we know of. You can't actually prove that anything has happened at all."

"I know what happened," snapped Marion.

Steve made a flutter with his wrists.

"I think that they would need more proof than that."

"It's very disturbing," said Marion. "Steve, you have come all this way, at least let me buy you lunch.

It won't be anything too special, just a University canteen. It's quite good really."

"Thank you, I'd like that."

Marion told Steve over lunch how she had recruited a computer programmer; a University lecturer no less. He would be able to access the serious computing power she needed without too many questions being asked. His name was Brian Harding and he had done something like this before, but it was to do with nations' economies, not missing animals and people.

Steve got back home at about five o'clock. He decided to ring Tony Bishop right away.

"Tony, I'll get straight to the point. Someone has been into Doctor Calvin's study and rifled through her papers. Would you happen to know anything about that?"

"No, Steve. Absolutely not. I don't work like that."

"Are you sure?"

"Steve, I swear. Neither I, nor any of my contacts went anywhere near Doctor Calvin's place. You've got to believe me."

"Who could it have been then?" asked Steve.

"Well, I've been doing some digging and I might have an idea, but I sure as hell don't want to talk about it on the phone. You know where we met last time? Don't say the place, just meet me there tonight at eight."

"Okay, Tony. I hope you aren't annoyed with me for questioning your integrity."

"Not at all Steve. See you later."

Steve drove to Streatham. He didn't want to make the journey home by tube like last time. He parked in a side-street and made sure that there was nothing worth stealing lying in view. He still worried about his soft-top; it was a rough area. Tony was sitting in a quiet corner of the pub.

"What can I get you, Steve?" asked Tony.

"I'll just have a Coke," said Steve. "I've got the new car with me."

"Ah, you got yourself a new one. What is it?"

"Mazda," replied Steve.

"Do you like it?"

"Yes, I love it. Quite a difference from what I had before."

Steve explained about his trip to Oxford and Marion's apparent break-in. Tony just sat there nodding.

"Steve, there are other people interested in the same thing as we are. When I was doing my research, I was only too aware that there were others asking the same sort of questions."

"Do you know who they are?" asked Steve, looking shocked.

"I can't be absolutely certain," answered Tony, "but it smells to me like spooks."

"You mean, National Security?" asked Steve.

Tony nodded and put his finger to his lips.

"You can't be too careful. Steve, yours and Marion's phones are probably tapped. Be very careful what you say. Emails too."

"That all makes sense now," said Steve. "They see a threat to National Security. I know that Marion did speak to someone she knows in the government and they ordered her to keep it all under wraps or risk losing her regular funding – she's a doctor of Anthropology you see."

"Yes, I know. Bastards," agreed Tony. "So, Steve. Be careful what you write or say. Make sure that you aren't being followed too."

Steve found that he suddenly had a new and constant awareness of his surroundings. He looked around before getting into his car. His new car was like the red bullseye on a shooting target. He made a tortuous, roundabout journey home via Wimbledon, his eyes glued to his rear mirror the whole way. He hadn't been home for two minutes when his doorbell rang. A shiver ran down his spine. Who would be calling at this time of night? How he wished that he had a spy-hole in his door. He opened it just a crack, with his foot firmly wedged against it in case anybody tried to push their way in.

"Hello Steve."

"Andi?" gasped Steve. "What are you doing here?"

"Aren't you going to ask me in?" she beamed.

"Do your parents know where you are?"

"I told them I was staying over at my friend Jill's.

"Andi, you little rascal!"

Andi threw her arms around his neck and kissed him. She pushed him backwards into the room and closed the door with her heel.

"I had a phone call from the art school today; they want me in for a second interview. It would seem that I have been shortlisted."

"Excellent," said Steve. "Look, Andi, I'm not sure about this. I mean…" She kissed him again, to shut him up.

"Andi, do you think that you are going to spend the night here?"

She pouted and nodded. He couldn't throw her out at this time of night and such a long way from home.

"Well, you'll have to sleep on the sofa. It's okay; I've slept on it myself several times."

"That's okay," she said coyly. "I would have been sleeping on the sofa at Jill's anyway."

"It's a nice place you have here, Steve. Isn't it a bit big for just one person?"

Steve didn't want to talk about Julie.

"Oh, I like it, and the rent's reasonable for London. I took it over from a friend when he went overseas. Strictly speaking, it's still his tenancy and I'm just flat-minding until he comes back."

Andi got up and had a nose around. She went in and inspected the kitchen and bathroom. She noticed the bedroom, but didn't go in.

"Very nice," she smiled as she went over and sat

very closely next to him on the sofa.

"Can I get you a coffee, or a drink?" asked Steve.

"A drink would be good, what have you got?"

"Not very much, I wasn't expecting guests."

He had a rummage through the fridge and the kitchen cupboard.

"I have lager, some white wine and a bottle of Jack Daniels. Or there is Coke or fizzy water?"

"Oh, some white wine please," she said.

Steve took two glasses from the cupboard, inspected them and gave them a wipe round with a drying cloth. He poured a glass of Soave for Andi and a lager for himself.

Andi curled her legs up under her and leaned against his shoulder. Steve didn't want to push her off, but he was getting a little bit annoyed.

They sat and talked until gone midnight. She did give him an odd peck on the cheek occasionally, but mercifully went no further.

"So, Andi. Is that your real name?"

"Oh, no. The name on my birth certificate is 'Andilyn'."

She stuck her tongue out in disgust.

"Even my parents call me Andi. I think it was my grandmother who insisted on giving me a family name. Hate it! Hate it!"

Steve went and found a spare duvet and pillow in the drawers under his bed and set them down beside her.

"I'll take you home in the morning Andi, but I'll be dropping you off in the next street."

"That's okay," she said, pulling the duvet over her. She puckered-up and closed her eyes. Steve tried to give her a quick goodnight kiss but she threw her arms around his neck and held onto it.

It was about two-thirty in the morning when Steve half awoke and noticed that there was somebody else in his bedroom. He sat up. Andi was standing there in just a pair of skimpy knickers. She pulled back his duvet and slid in beside him. Steve was aghast. The cheeky little minx!

"That sofa isn't at all comfortable," she said. "You have plenty of room in this big, comfy double bed for both of us."

She put an arm around him, snuggled up and fell asleep.

When he awoke in the morning, Andi was still fast asleep. She did have most of a bottle of wine the night before. He dressed and went to the kitchen. He was busy brewing some coffee when Andi arrived behind him. She was wearing one of his shirts with nothing much underneath.

"Good morning," he said. "Did you sleep well?"

"Very well," she grinned.

"Andi, that was very naughty of you. You can't go around jumping into men's beds like that. It can only lead to trouble."

Andi did that thing that she did with her eyes. Where did she learn how to do that? It was so sexy.

"Now, come on. Have a coffee and then I'm

taking you straight home. I have a photo session in Westminster at noon."

Andi gathered up her discarded clothes and took them to the bathroom. She came out ten minutes later ready to go. Steve just hoped that he didn't pass Paul or Lizzie on a road near their home. They couldn't miss him; his car was so distinctive. He would have great trouble explaining what he was doing there.

"Oh, Steve, I forgot to mention. Can you drop me off at Jill's? She has a second interview for art school today too."

Steve gave a sigh of relief. He didn't have to run the gauntlet after all.

"Is this Jill going to back-up your story about staying the night at her place?" asked Steve.

"Oh, yes, she totally knows the score," said Andi, in a matter-of-fact way.

"What?" yelled Steve. "You had all this planned between you?"

Andi smiled and stuck her tongue in her cheek.

"Oh, yes. And I've won!"

"Won?" repeated Steve with a look of incredulity.

"Yes, I was first. She won't know that nothing actually happened, but it could have!"

Steve smacked his forehead.

He dropped Andi off at the opposite end of Jill's street. She kissed his cheek as she left the car and gave a dainty little wave. Steve felt like he had just narrowly escaped from the clutches of a praying mantis. This girl was dynamite. He headed off to find a car park near Westminster.

The next time he heard from Andi was through a phone call to say that both she and Jill had been accepted for places at the art school. He congratulated her warmly and promised they would meet up sometime.

Chapter 24 - Spreadsheet

Tony asked to meet Steve at the quiet pub again. He had some new information. The pub was as dead as usual, the two old regulars making their pints last all day as usual.

"Steve, I think that we should change our venue. I know it's like a graveyard here, but I don't think it is a good idea to keep going to the same place. Any quiet pubs around your way?"

"Not as quiet as this, but it might be okay out in the beer garden. Not many people go out there at night."

"Okay, Steve. This is what I've found out so far." He gave Steve a USB stick. "There's a spreadsheet on there with almost a hundred reports of 'phenomena'. Now, there's no way that they can be verified or corroborated. Some are from local newspaper articles; some are just hear-say. There are a few that are from police reports, but you need to keep those close to your chest."

"Nearly a hundred?" gasped Steve. "I had no idea that it was so common."

"Most of the incidents relate to missing animals, cows mainly. There are some that involve badly mutilated animals – cows, sheep, goats … nasty stuff. Whatever has attacked them didn't manage to drag them through entirely, but managed to rip them apart and take chunks."

"My God," said Steve. "I've heard of unexplained

cattle mutilation. It's been going on all over the world for ages. It has always been attributed to aliens."

"Well, you don't get anything more alien than what we are dealing with," said Tony grimly.

Tony and Steve chatted for about half an hour longer and then went their separate ways, but not before exchanging mobile telephone numbers. New, untraceable, mobile telephone numbers.

Tony's spreadsheet was an eye-opener. This was just UK incidents; he was awaiting many more reports from overseas. He had done a very thorough job. Not only were there dates and place names, he had GPS locations cross-referenced with Latitude and Longitude co-ordinates. There was a brief description of the incident and a code number which related to capture, mutilation or sighting, so apparently, there had been unsuccessful snatches too.

Steve didn't want to contact Marion with the news until she had an untraceable phone. He would buy her one and post it. Cheap, throwaway phones were easy to get in large supermarkets and the sims weren't registered to anyone in particular.

Steve didn't even put a note in with the phone he sent to Marion. All he did was put his untraceable phone number into its contact list. He hoped that Marion would be able to work out what was going on. She called him two days later.

"Hello," she said, noncommittally.

"Hello Doctor Calvin, it's Steve. I sent you the

phone and I'm glad that you worked out what to do with it."

"Steve? Why all this cloak and dagger stuff?"

"I have reason to believe that your phone is bugged. I think that mine is too."

"What? Who would do such a thing?" asked Marion.

"The same people who entered your study and went through your papers."

"But who, Steve? Who?"

"Dr Calvin, you told me that you had discussed all this with a friend in high places and that he told you to keep in under wraps. I think that your friend has passed this along to a National Security agency. It's the government spooks that raided your study and bugged your phone. Heck, maybe they are picking up this conversation with another bug in your room."

"I'm not in my study, I'm in the garden doing some weeding," she said. "I'm not stupid, Steve. I had an inkling of what was going on. Brad warned me about this. Now you have confirmed it."

"I just had to tell you that Tony Bishop has had some fairly spectacular results. Apparently, there have been nearly a hundred incidents in the UK and apparently there have been even more coming in from abroad. I have all his initial data here on a USB stick. How do you want to play it?"

"That's wonderful news," said Marion. "You can't send the file to me, personally. It's too risky. I'll have to think about this and get back to you."

Steve's next call was from Paul Atwood. His phone screen told him so.

"Steve, can I ask you a favour?"

What can you do when somebody says that?

"Don't tell me that it's a reshoot of the reshoot? I've had it just about up to here with cows."

"No Steve, nothing like that," laughed Paul. "Andi has been given her first big assignment. It's called 'Architectural Space'. She reckons that Chiswick House would be a good location with its Capability Brown landscaping."

"Indeed, a good choice," said Steve.

"The thing is Steve, she is very keen to take my good Nikon and my tilt-shift lens. As you probably realise, that is over 5Ks worth of kit. It is insured, but they might be a bit funny if something happened and I wasn't with it. Lizzie and I are going down to Ross-On-Wye for a few days bird watching. Would you be able to play minder for an hour or so on Saturday? You are just up the road and I can drop her off about ten."

"Err, well, yes, of course Paul. I'd be glad to. Does she know what the tilt and shift is all about?"

"Yes, she does. She has used my 5" x 4" Sinar a few times for table shots. She knows her stuff, Steve. No worries on that score. I just wouldn't like some yob seeing a helpless girl with an expensive camera and deciding that he could score a few hits by selling it."

"Yes, understood Paul. I'll see that she's alright."

"Oh, and Steve. I'm going to give her some money to buy you both lunch. She can find her own way home."

"Okay, Paul. See you Saturday."

Chapter 25 - Chiswick

On Saturday Morning, Andi was standing on Steve's doorstep. She had a large camera over her shoulder and a sturdy tripod in her hand. Paul and Lizzie were waving from the car as they moved off.

"Hi Steve," she said, as she walked in and made herself at home.

"Cunning little devil," thought Steve. "She has this all planned. Chiswick House, oh yes, she could find architectural space almost anywhere in London, but she picks the nearest one to me."

"How's art school going?" he asked.

"Oh, good," she replied, coming over and kissing him.

"Oh no, here we go," thought Steve.

"Well, I suppose we had better go and see what state the grounds are in. Do you want help with that?"

Andi handed him the camera bag.

"It's only ten minutes' walk; follow me," said Steve. They headed off towards Chiswick House.

Andi knew the shot she wanted and set up her tripod in the driveway running up to the front door.

Steve realised that she didn't really need a tilt-shift lens for such a low building. There was minimal perspective that could easily have been tweaked in Photoshop.

"Couldn't you just correct the perspective in

Photoshop instead of bringing all that expensive equipment over here?" he asked.

"Oh no. We aren't allowed to use Photoshop. We can only use the features of the camera," she replied.

"Mmm, yes, I understand that," said Steve. "Wouldn't you be better off using a good wide angle lens?"

"That's what I'm planning to use," she said.

"So, what's with the tilt-shift then?"

"I had to bring the expensive stuff so that Daddy would insist that you came too!"

"She's at it again," screamed Steve, inwardly. "The little minx!"

Andi knew exactly what she was doing. She set up the camera at the best vantage points. Steve couldn't have picked them better himself. She understood all about depth of fields and bracketing for exposure. She was already a pro at eighteen. Steve just watched and let her get on with it. She didn't want his help anyway, not photographically anyway.

After taking lots of shots of the house and avenues, Andi decided to go down to the bridge and takes some shots of the wildfowl. She showed some of them to him on the camera's screen. They were good. Sharp, sparkly and very well composed.

"You are doing a fine job, Andi. Have you had enough yet?"

"I probably have all I need," she said. "Know anywhere good for lunch?"

After lunch, they walked back to Steve's flat. He was half expecting, no, totally expecting her to jump on him as she had before, but she didn't. She thanked him for his help and asked for directions to the nearest tube station. It wasn't very far but Steve was a bit nervous about letting her get the tube on her own with all that gear.

"I'll drive you home, Andi. You have a ton of stuff to carry there."

She didn't argue, and tossed the equipment into his car boot.

On the way back, she talked about art school and the kind of projects that were being set. Then, all of a sudden, she changed the subject completely.

"Steve, I've been meaning to ask you for ages. What was all that stuff about disappearing cows at the farm in Dorking?"

Steve didn't know what to tell her. She had asked this before.

"You were asking the farmer's wife, Mrs White, about cows going missing under mysterious circumstances."

"My, you have a good memory," said Steve, still thinking of some story to tell her. "You haven't heard of the vanishing cows of Dorking?" he said with a giggle. "Some farmers were so worried about their cows being rustled in the middle of the night that they camouflaged them with Astroturf onesies. Then, when they went to look for them, they couldn't find them."

Andi punched him on the arm.

Steve quickly changed the subject.

"How is your friend Jill getting on?"

"Oh, still a virgin!" she said, quick as a flash.

"I didn't mean that, I meant with her fashion design."

"Oh, yes, she's doing some quite nice stuff. It's a bit tame though. If I was doing fashion design, I'd want to be more controversial. You know, push the boat out a bit more."

"Yes, I expect you would," smiled Steve.

Steve helped Andi to carry the camera gear into the hallway.

"Aren't you going to put this stuff back in the safe?" he asked.

"I know you, Steve Markham. You are just trying to get me into the darkroom."

"Darkroom? There is no darkroom. Hasn't been since your Dad went digital. Anyway, you have never needed a darkroom before."

Andi fluttered her eyes and ran her finger up and down his jacket collar.

"Oh no," Steve thought worriedly. "Here we go again."

"Stevie, you had me in bed naked beside you and you didn't do anything. Why?"

She tickled him under the chin.

Steve gulped.

However, it seemed that he needn't have worried. Andi just pushed him away and laughed.

"Astroturf onesies indeed. Thank you for the nice

day Steve, and the lift home. I've got to get these shots printed and mounted for Monday. See you."

Steve didn't know whether to laugh or cry.

As he got into his car, Andi was at the living room window blowing a kiss.

Chapter 26 - Sahara

The Toyota Hilux pickup truck bounced heavily across the rocky desert road, its rev counter leaning well over into the red. The sound of AK-47 fire came from the rag-tag group of fighters in the back. More shots came from two other trucks in hot pursuit. A large machine gun mounted on the roof of the cab was totally impotent. It could only fire forwards. The enemy behind also had a disadvantage in that their big gun was mounted behind the cab and could only fire to the back or sides.

The leading truck was slightly less occupied than the two following so had a slight speed advantage, but still, the engine wasn't going to last very long at these revs, nor the suspension.

In the cab, three freedom fighters in camouflage uniforms urged the truck forwards. On the right side the commander, Umair, was yelling instructions into his satellite phone. Sadir was wrestling with the steering wheel. Between them, Hassam was gesticulating wildly to his fighters in the back. They were doing their best, but it was difficult to take an accurate shot at this speed on rough terrain. They were lucky not to shoot themselves.

The three vehicles threw up clouds of dust as they tore along the sand-strewn road. The gunfire continued relentlessly. A soldier in the front truck launched an RPG towards the pursuing trucks. It fell well short and exploded, harmlessly sending rocks and sand flying into the air. The two trucks in pursuit had to swerve around the crater that it had left in the road, the men in it still shooting wildly to no avail. One of the black masked pursuers was hanging out of the passenger window, firing a Kalashnikov with one hand. His aim was no better and left futile pock-marks in the sand. Somehow, a lucky shot from the front truck struck the man in the head. He slumped sideways with a red stain on his black mask.

Around the next dune, Sadir was heading for a group of battle torn buildings. Their roofs were long gone, and their walls largely reduced to rubble. A small group of palms stood nearby that would give cover for them to make a stand. He took his truck down through the gears and slewed around behind a low wall that was still partly intact. Their big machine gun was now pointed in the enemy's direction and its operators feeding a fresh belt of ammunition into place.

The enemy commander immediately saw the imminent danger and ordered his two trucks into depressions in the sand between two small dunes. The men jumped down from the back of the trucks and lay prone along the crest of the dunes. The 'technical' with the heavy, tripod-mounted machine gun, reversed out from cover to give it a clear shot at the ruins. It opened up immediately. A fighter caught in the open was torn to shreds before he could reach cover, leaving the wall behind him peppered with holes and blood. The truck pulled back into safety.

Along the tops of the sand dunes, AK-47s and

larger machine guns laid a steady stream of fire into the ruins. A spray of machine gun fire ripped through the trunk of a palm tree. Its top half buckled and fell over.

Behind a wall, Umair was still on his satphone. He was talking in Arabic interspersed with broken English. His reception was being hindered by the stout, rendered breeze-block wall that surrounded him on three sides. He knew that it would work better in the open. He shifted position to the other side of the wrecked room. Reception improved. A row of new holes pock-marked the wall above his head sending a shower of hot, stinging debris into the back of his neck. He put his hand around it and found that he was bleeding. He wrapped his scarf over the gashes.

Again, the enemy gun truck backed out and opened fire with the heavy calibre weapon. It tore craters in the ruin walls. One fighter was hit with shrapnel in his leg and screamed in agony. Umair's men opened fire with their cab-mounted machine gun as the enemy truck slid back out of sight.

Hassam could see enemy fighters inching closer along the dunes. They would send a steam of fire and then move position. Their black uniforms did little to camouflage them against the white sand. Several of them were picked-off and tumbled down the dunes.

Umair crept through the ruins keeping his head low and found Hassam. He handed his lieutenant his binoculars and pointed at the horizon. Two white streaks arced toward the ground in front of them. The

Hellfire missiles lit up the enemy's two trucks with mushroom clouds of sand and dust. The enemy fire fell silent. A few black shapes slipped away into the desert beyond. Umair's men fired after them until they were out of range.

With damaged suspension, Umair's truck was limping badly. Sadir was coaxing it along as best he could, but he knew that it was just a matter of time before it would give up completely. The desert was riddled with wrecks of trucks. Most had bodies inside, but theirs didn't – yet! A fighter in the back of the truck was scanning the horizon with a pair of high-powered binoculars, watching for trouble. With a near-dead truck, now was not a good time to engage the enemy.

The man with the binoculars banged loudly on the cab roof. Sadir could see him in his wing mirror pointing at something on the horizon. It was a camel train. He headed over a sandy track towards it. The desert people would have some water. His team were almost out. The truck continued to struggle relentlessly with the sand and then with one almighty crack, gave up completely. Its three good wheels carried on spinning wildly, but gave no traction. The tailgate was flung down and the men jumped down to join the three from the cab. They took what they could carry and lobbed a grenade into the truck. It exploded in a fireball as the fuel ignited and burned.

As the group of soldiers approached the nomads, it became apparent that something was clearly wrong. Umair lifted his binoculars. One of the camels seemed to be having a fit and was lying on its side. It seemed to be bouncing up and down. The group of fighters picked up pace, although it was difficult going across the bare sand. Some of the nomad men were firing rifles into the air and Umair watched as the camel floated into the sky and then disappeared completely. As they got closer, Umair could see a mirage in the sky. Mirages were commonplace in the desert, but he had never seen one like this. It rippled and distorted. Two long, black protrusions pulsing with a blue plasma glow emerged from the ripples. Then many more. Another camel lifted off the ground. It was being pulled back towards the mirage. One of Umair's men lifted his RPG and fired it into the middle of the wriggling mass. The camel exploded in a mess of blood and guts. The wriggling arms retracted into the ripples. It faded and was gone.

Umair reached the shocked group of travellers. They were jabbering quickly in a dialect that he could barely understand. When he calmed down, an elder told him that a 'desert devil' had taken his camels. He wiggled his fingers to demonstrate. They all stared at the sky. There was nothing to be seen.

Hassam went over to look at the remains of the camel. There wasn't much left, but among the piles of pulp something was moving. It looked like a black snake. He moved closer and prodded at it with the point of his firearm. It immediately coiled itself around his gun barrel and held on tightly. Hassam yelped and dropped the gun as it gave him a heavy jolt of electricity. The snake continued to hold onto the gun barrel tightly.

Umair took out his satphone and made a call. He was obviously having great trouble communicating with someone at the other end – they couldn't see his hand gestures.

The desert travellers unloaded things from their camel train and pitched camp for the night. Umair and his men had real food for the first time in a week.

Chapter 27 - Sarah

A small white car pulled up at a security barrier. The sign said 'Defence Science and Technology Laboratory'.

"Morning, Sarah," said the uniformed man in the small security building.

"Morning Bob," came the cheery reply.

"Did you have a good weekend?" asked the guard.

"Oh, yes, fine," said the young woman.

They waited.

"Aren't you going to open the barrier then?" asked Sarah.

"I will when you've shown me your identity pass," smiled the man.

"But, Bob, you've known me for three years!" she laughed.

"Might be someone impersonating you," said the guard, not totally seriously.

Sarah muttered something obscene under her breath. Opening her handbag, she produced a plastic card.

The guard leaned over and examined it very deliberately.

"Yes, that seems to be in order," he said, operating a button. "Have a nice day."

The barrier raised and Sarah Frobisher drove through the sprawling collection of buildings to her reserved parking spot.

Dr Geoff Hamilton poked at the strange, long object lying in a stainless steel tray on his lab bench. He was a man in his early fifties with greying hair and wire rimmed glasses.

"Is it still twitching?" asked the white-coated woman looking over his shoulder.

"Not as much as it was when it first came in, Sarah," said the man.

"What is it?" she asked, "some kind of eel?"

"No, it was found in a desert. You don't get eels in deserts. But I have to admit, that's what it looks like. An eel with its head cut off."

Sarah looked closer. She was wearing a pair of safety glasses, as she always did when working with unknown biological samples. A violent twitch and ripple of sparks made her jump backward with a yelp.

"Goodness," she cried. "An electric eel. What do we know about it?"

"It came in from a Special Forces team in The Middle East. The story is that it was picked up by some friendly fighters from a group of nomads. They all witnessed two camels being pulled into a mirage in mid-air by something they call a 'desert devil'. One of the fighters shot it with a rocket propelled grenade and this piece was left behind when it vanished."

"That rings a bell," said Sarah. "I read something in the papers a few weeks ago about something similar that happened at a fête near Cobham in Surrey, only it was a human being that was taken, not a camel."

Sarah was nearly thirty-six, slim and had long strawberry blonde hair that tied back with a clasp to keep it out of her petri dishes.

"Yes, I remember that," said Geoff. "I just didn't make the connection. So, you reckon that this is a bit of, whatever that was?"

"It could be," answered Sarah.

"I'm going to do a section and have a closer look," said Geoff. "I'll remove the ragged end section and do a few fresh slices."

Geoff took off his glasses, peered through the stereoscopic microscope and adjusted the focus.

"I'll put it up on the monitor, Sarah, just a sec."

The cross section on the screen looked like a honeycomb.

"It's made up of hexagonal tubes filled with some sort of jelly. The outer skin is denser and seems to be covered in short hairs. The hairs are still moving, like they are trying to latch onto something."

"That's totally weird," said Sarah. "There must still be some reflex response in there even after it has been isolated from whatever it came from."

"I've seen something like this before in hot-vent organisms from the ocean floor," said Geoff. "I think I'll run a spectrographic analysis on some of this jelly and see what it's made of."

Geoff dissected a sliver from the section under his microscope and took it off to another department in the building. Two hours later he received a phone call from a technician.

"Geoff, this sample you brought down. I'm a bit reluctant to make any rash interpretation of the results I'm looking at here, but I would say that this biology is totally unknown to science. It's an impossible cell structure. I've never seen anything like it. In the visible spectrum, it's just what you see; a honeycomb. When you get up to the ultraviolet end, it disappears. It doesn't reappear until I lower the wavelength again."

"Yes, Sarah's scientific term for it was 'weird'."

"I'll go along with that," said the technician. "In fact, it's really weird'."

"That's why they sent it to us," said Geoff, grimly. "I'd better write a report. There are people higher up the chain looking for answers."

As Sarah was packing up to leave that afternoon, the eel-like shape twitched quite violently. Then again. Her jaw dropped. At its cut end, a small aerial distortion began to appear. It rippled, both in and through the solid stainless steel tray. Sarah jumped back. A blue finger of sheer energy sprang from the ripples and the entire length of the long, tapered object was slowly pulled backwards into them. Then, it disappeared.

Sarah screamed.

Chapter 28 - Kevin

Geoff and Sarah were sitting around a meeting room table with three other people. They all wore suits.

"So, you are telling me that we've lost this specimen," said a stern looking man over the top of his half-moon spectacles.

"I'm afraid so," said Geoff. "Sarah, tell these gentlemen what you saw."

Sarah shared her experience from the previous evening.

"Damn," said the man with the reading glasses. "That was our only chance to find out about this … thing."

"I still have a few microscope slides and we have a very small sample of material in the spectroscopy lab."

The politician put his hand to his forehead.

"I just hope, for your sake, that they tell us something, Doctor Hamilton. I am being pressured for results and I'm not getting any."

"What do you expect us to do with a biological sample that is unknown to man and has the ability to vanish into thin air?"

"Mr Hamilton, please don't tell me what I can or cannot expect. I'll tell you what I expect. I expect you, and your department, to provide some answers. If you don't, and quickly, there might not be a department anymore."

Geoff nodded and gave a quick glance across at

Sarah. She was looking worried too.

"Any ideas Geoff?" asked Sarah.

"At the minute, I'm fresh out of ideas," replied Geoff. "The Right Honourable Ewan Cummings has us over a barrel. All that I can suggest, for the minute, is to get hold of those newspaper reports from Cobham. As I remember, there were some good photos. We'll have to be very careful, Sarah. We can't afford to have any leaks attributed to our department. Do you know anyone who could get hold of them for us?"

"I might," she replied. "Let me speak to somebody. I won't give anything away about what we're doing."

Later at home, Sarah rang her younger brother, Kevin.

"Kevin, how's it going? Yeah. How would you like to earn a few quid? It's nothing illegal; it's just that I don't have time to do it myself. I need to get some prints of newspaper photos. You would just have to go along to a few newspaper offices down in London and buy the prints. If they don't have them in stock, then you would need to order them and pick them up later. No, you can't have them posted to your home. Don't tell them your name, Kevin. Pay in cash too."

Kevin Frobisher was bright enough. He had a good university degree. It's just that a Masters in

Digital and Social Media is not terribly useful when you are looking for a job in the big, wide world and don't even know what you want to do with your life. His only real interest was his motor bike, but delivering pizzas was not a realistic occupation in the long term. Anyway, he wanted a better bike and that would cost a lot of money.

None of the newspapers had the photographs that Sarah had given him the reference numbers for.

He would have to order them online and wait a week. This was going to be tricky. Sarah told him that he wasn't to give his name and to pay only in cash so that his credit card couldn't be traced. That was easy for her to say. He knew that she worked as a scientist in a top-secret government research laboratory and didn't dare to ask her anything else. She wouldn't tell him anyway. The papers wanted an email address. He had lots of those, so that part was easy. A delivery address and credit card? Not so easy. He couldn't ask his girlfriend, Emma. She would want to know all the ins and outs. He was stumped.

Pete!

Pete owed him a favour. He didn't know him all that well, he was a serious biker, but Kevin had been able to source a rare part for his Harley-Davidson online and he was ever so grateful. He knew which pub Pete could be found in most nights, and set off to find him.

"Yo Kev. Have you bought yourself a proper bike

yet?"

"No, Pete, I'm still working on that one. I'm actually here to ask you for a favour," said Kevin.

"Sure, I owe you one. Is it legal?"

"Oh, perfectly legal," returned Kevin. "It's just that I want to buy my better half a birthday present or two and I don't want her to find out beforehand. She is always nosing through my mail. You know how it is?"

"Me, no," grinned Pete. "What do you want me to do?"

"I just need one photo from each of three daily newspapers. You would have to buy them with your credit card online and have them sent to your address. Then, we could meet up again here and I will give you the cash and you give me the photos. Here are the reference numbers and ordering details."

"What kind of photos are they? Why would anyone want them as a birthday present?" asked Pete.

"They are just newspaper archive pictures. She told me a few weeks ago how she would like to have them for her stupid collection. It was probably a hint. I didn't say anything. She will be tickled when I produce them with a bunch of flowers."

"Soppy bugger," said Pete. "Yeah, I'll fix it for you Kev. I'll give you a bell when I've got them."

A few days later, Kevin had the photos. They were still sealed in the envelopes they came in. He opened them. They looked like stills from some horror movie, but what the hell. His sister was going to pay him good money for them, why should he care about her bad taste?

When he arrived on Sarah's doorstep with them, she was delighted.

"Kevin, I can't thank you enough for coming over to deliver these in person."

"I don't mind," he said. "Good chance to open up the bike on an open road."

"What do I owe you Kevin, fifty quid?"

"Fifty quid? You must be joking. You have no idea of the trouble I had getting these."

Sarah smiled and handed him a wad of notes.

"Here's a couple of hundred, don't go squandering it on bike parts."

Kevin slipped the money inside his leather jacket.

"Would you like some Sunday afternoon tea?" asked Sarah.

"Yes, that would be nice. Sarah, can I ask you about those strange photos? Say 'no' and I'll understand."

"Well, they're not a secret, they have been on headline news all over the world," said Sarah." Kevin, how would you like to earn some more money?"

"Yeah I'd love to, what is it this time?"

"I know that you are pretty handy with computers. What I'd like you do is to scour the Internet for any mention of this incident or any others like it. Again, you need to keep it quiet. If you can use library computers or ones that are not linked to you that would be even better."

"Yes, I get it. I've got to cover my tracks. No problemo, Sis. How much is it worth to you?"

"Let's see what you come up with. Don't worry; I'll make it worth your while."

Chapter 29 - Myths

Geoff Hamilton stared at the photos.

"My god, what are we dealing with here?"

"Geoff, have you not read the report that came in with this?" asked Sarah.

"Oh, I took a quick glance at it. It didn't make much sense."

"Yes, it was a bit confusing, but it seems that this phenomenon is well documented in the desert people's folklore. The 'desert devil' or 'sky devil' has many names in Arabic, Tamasheq and Farsi, but they all have this commonality of a mirage in the sky and animals or people being plucked off the ground into it. Many other cultures have similar stories about multi-bodied serpents or nests of worms, but it is very difficult to separate the myth from the fact. Time has a nasty way of melding them together."

"I can't tell the powers-that-be a load of codswallop about mythological creatures. I'd be given the bum's rush on the spot. What we need are some scientific facts."

"You can't deny the photos. They aren't made-up," said Sarah. "Even though we don't have the specimen anymore, we did witness it with our own eyes and you did a spectroscopic analysis on something. Just because we don't know what it is, or have a name for it, doesn't mean it doesn't exist."

"Yes, you are right Sarah. Perhaps I should go back to work on the bits we still have. They do have interesting properties that need to be explored further."

Geoff picked up his laptop and left the lab.

Sarah heard her phone beep. It was a text from Kevin. It was just a bunch of exclamation marks, nothing else. Sarah took it to mean that he had discovered something. When she got home that night, she rang him."

"Kevin, be careful what you say," she warned.

"It's alright," said Kevin. "I'm just going to text you a URL. I think you will find it interesting. It's a research paper done by somebody called Professor Bradley Johnston at Stanford University in California. It is in the public domain, but I suspect that it only tells half the story."

"Myths and Legends of Indigenous North and South American People," she read aloud.

Sarah scrolled down the screen. There was a lot of it, but one heading called 'Snakes of the pool in the sky' caught her eye.

She read on. It all had a ring of familiarity to it. Ripples in the atmosphere, squirming tentacles and animal and human victims.

Sarah copied and pasted the section into a new document and printed it. This would be good ammunition for Geoff. When he read it next morning, he agreed. He quickly assembled a slideshow of the newspaper photos, the spectroscopy report and selected passages from Johnston's paper. He made a phone call.

The three men sitting opposite Geoff and Sarah introduced themselves. They were familiar. The man wearing the half-moon reading glasses, Ewan Cummings, was a politician, but his exact job title was never properly disclosed. Frank Fahey was, of course, their laboratory's top man and their boss. They knew of him, but didn't have much contact at that level. The third man introduced himself as Charles Millar from National Security. He didn't elaborate beyond that.

Geoff started his slideshow. The three men in suits watched with interest. When he had finished, Geoff invited comments.

"Very interesting, thank you Doctor Hamilton," said Cummings. Millar rolled his tongue around his mouth.

"Yes, we know all about this. It's a national security threat, but we don't know what to do about it. We do know about Professor Bradley's work and that of his English counterpart, Doctor Marion Calvin, and her cohort at Oxford. My job, at the minute, is to make sure that all this talk of invisible monsters doesn't scare the bejesus out of Joe Public. So far, we have had to pull the reins on a couple of television exposés and extended coverage of the Cobham fête incident. There were a few YouTube movies too, typical conspiracy theory rubbish. We managed to get them pulled. So, Doctor

Hamilton, the ball seems to be in your court at the minute. I'm sure that Mr Fahey will give you his full support to further your research. I have organised some additional funds from The Right Honourable Mr Cummings here, to allow you to extend your horizons. You are, of course, subject to the Official Secrets Act as usual. All I can do now is wish you every success.

The meeting broke up.

"That went better than I expected," said Geoff, cleaning his glasses. "Thanks for all your hard work Sarah."

Sarah smiled.

"Next thing to do is to contact this Professor Bradley Johnston at Stanford and the woman at Oxford; what was her name?"

"Calvin, I believe," said Sarah. "I'll get right onto it."

"Just remember The Official Secrets Act," said Geoff.

"Oh, did I forget to mention you are booked in for a symposium on Cultural and Social Anthropology at Stanford University next week?"

"What? You know very well that I am a biologist Geoff. I know nothing about anthropology."

Geoff smirked mischievously.

"All you need to know about anthropology, Sarah, is that Professor Johnston will be there. He is top of your hit list."

"I'll be like a fish out of water at an event like that.

What if someone starts asking me questions?"

"Your cover has all been set up, Sarah. Cummings and Millar have taken care of that. You are officially representing the UK Government at the symposium. All you have to do is act like a dumb civil servant. That's not too hard, is it?"

"I suppose not," said Sarah, looking down at the floor.

"Make a chance to speak to this Johnston somewhere quiet, and get him talking about his 'other interest'."

"You are not suggesting that I try to seduce him?" said Sarah, with a startled look.

"He's old enough to be your grandfather, but that's up to you," said Geoff, smirking.

Sarah bit her lip.

"Okay, Geoff. Leave it to me."

"I might add," continued Geoff, "you have been given a generous 'entertaining' allowance."

She sighed.

"I'm not very good at this kind of thing."

"You'll be alright," said Geoff. "Go for it!"

Chapter 30 - Stanford

Sarah stood in the main quad at Stanford University. As far as the eye could see were low, sandstone, red-roofed buildings with rows of arches like cloisters in a medieval abbey, but not quite so grand. She struggled to identify the architectural style; a strange mixture of Spanish Colonial and Art Deco.

Sarah was looking for Building 50, that's where she was supposed to report to register. It wasn't hard to find. At reception she was given her symposium welcome pack, which had a timetable, a map and a clip-on identity pass. It even had her photo on it and described her as a researcher for HMG Cabinet Office.

"That's a timely promotion," she thought. "I just hope I can act the part."

Sarah was directed to go back out through the Memorial Court and turn right. The Wallenberg Hall was just a few minutes' walk. The area was much greener and more spacious than any similar facility she knew of back home.

Inside, she was directed to a hall where coffee was being served. People with clipboards were passing among the guests and writing down notes. Sarah was trying hard to keep out of their way, but eventually she was accosted by a young man. She panicked a little, but tried not to show it.

He read her identity badge.

"Ah, you're from England. Welcome to Stanford University, Doctor Frobisher. Can I ask, what is your particular interest?"

Sarah's mind went blank. She had read a book on the plane over from England to prepare her for such questions – 'How to bluff your way in Anthropology'.

"The British Government is particularly interested in the interaction between early British settlers and the indigenous American people," she spouted.

The young man looked down at his clipboard and ran his pen down a list, then back up again. He flipped over to the next sheet and gave a slight shake of his head.

"Mmm. I'm sure that you will find the symposium of great interest," he said, noncommittally.

"I am a particular fan of Professor Johnston. Is he here today?" asked Sarah.

"Professor Johnston has retired from the faculty now and he's not in the best of health. He doesn't speak at events like this now," he informed her.

Sarah's heart sank.

"I have seen him in the department a few times recently, he still drops in on the odd occasion, but he is looking very frail."

Sarah spent most of the day at the symposium. It was of little interest to her. She decided to make her way back to the Building 50 reception.

"Are you enjoying the symposium?" asked the dark-haired receptionist.

"Very interesting," lied Sarah. "I was rather hoping to meet Professor Johnston. I have always admired his work."

"He doesn't come here much these days. He's not very well."

"Yes, I know that. Have you any idea when he will be in again?" asked Sarah.

The receptionist typed something on her keyboard.

"He usually comes in to meet up with an old student of his, Rachael Hartmann. She's post grad now. If I can establish her movements, I will have his."

Sarah waited as the girl flicked through pages on her computer screen.

"It looks like Rachael is due in the day after tomorrow," she said, pointing at an item on the monitor. "So, Brad might be in, if he is well enough."

Sarah thanked her and left. She knew there was a shuttle bus back to her hotel in Palo Alto, but took a taxi.

Chapter 31 - Brad

Sarah attended the second day of the three-day symposium. She was more interested in the slick organisation of the event than the subject, but still found some of it fascinating.

On the third day she signed in, but left immediately to go back to the anthropology department. The receptionist recognised her and remembered who she was looking for. She suggested that Sarah go to the library to wait. She didn't know what Rachael looked like, but she had seen a photo of Professor Johnston. He had a beard and had lost most of his hair on top. He would surely stand out among all the young people that milled about, being mostly students. The few older people must have been staff, or administrators.

Sarah flicked through some newspapers. She read the international news headlines and moved on to a Californian paper. Something caught her eye at the bottom of the second page. It was a small piece about a strange sighting by some climbers at Mount Shasta in Northern California. It reported that they witnessed a strange distortion in the air, like the ripples on a lake. It remarked that mirages are uncommon at that altitude, but it didn't say very much other than that and there was no mention of loss of life.

Sarah noticed a woman with small oval spectacles and craft-knitted top come into the library. She took a seat at a table along from her, opened a laptop and started to type. After about twenty minutes, an older man joined her. It was him! She recognised the man in the photograph that Geoff had given her. He was well built with a short grey beard and moustache.

The professor gave who must have been Rachael Hartmann, a friendly hug, and sat down beside her. She was showing him something on her laptop.

"Shall I go and confront him now or wait until he is alone?" she pondered. She didn't want to make a fool of herself.

Finally, she plucked up the courage to go and talk to him.

"Professor Johnston?"

The old man looked up at her with puzzlement on his face.

"My name is Doctor Sarah Frobisher and I would love to have a chat with you, if you don't mind. We have an interest in common."

"You're English," he said, with a hint of interest in his voice. "I'd love to talk to you. But won't you give me a clue what's it's about?"

"Err." Sarah was unsure about Rachael's involvement." It's about certain phenomena, like the one described here."

She laid the newspaper article down in front of him. He adjusted his spectacles, read it and looked up at her.

"Yes, I know about this," he said. "Why is it of any interest to you?"

"I think it is a common interest," said Sarah,

glancing over towards Rachael. The professor knew what was she was asking.

"Oh, don't worry about Rachael, we are in this together. In fact, she is just back from Oxford, England."

"Doctor Calvin?" suggested Sarah.

"Ah, you know Marion?" asked Johnston.

"No, not personally," said Sarah. "We move in different circles, but I have heard of her."

Sarah was still wearing her symposium identity card and Bradley noticed it.

"Ah, you are an anthropologist too?" he said.

"Not exactly, Professor," said Sarah. "I'm a research biologist, actually."

"Oh," said the Professor, nodding. "A biologist? And what does HMG mean?"

"Her Majesty's Government," explained Sarah.

"So, you are a British government scientist," nodded Johnston.

Sarah was beginning to panic, Official Secrets Act and all that.

"What part of England are you from?" asked Johnston.

"Wiltshire," said Sarah.

"Wiltshire? Wiltshire? I've heard of it. Where is it near?" asked the professor.

"You've heard of Stonehenge?"

"Stonehenge, yes of course. Oh, that Wiltshire."

He banged the side of his head.

"It might be an idea to go somewhere more private?" whispered Johnston.

Sarah realised that he was on the same wavelength.

"Come with me," he said standing up. "There is an office that I can still use. You don't mind if Rachael comes too?"

Sarah agreed, and they headed off down a corridor and around a corner. The professor opened a door with a key and beckoned the others inside.

"Thank you, Professor," said Sarah, but had hardly finished the sentence when he put his hand up to stop her.

"This is California, Sarah. We don't do titles. My name is Bradley, or Brad if you like. 'Professor' is just something they stick on in front to annoy me."

"You aren't a professor then?" asked Sarah quizzically.

"Yes, I am," he said, flapping his hand in dismissal. "It doesn't matter. Now, can we get down to business. What can I do for you?"

Sarah took out her phone and opened her photo app. She held up a newspaper photo of the Cobham fête incident.

"You know about this?"

"Yes, yes, of course. You didn't come all the way from England to show me this?"

Sarah swiped her phone screen.

"I bet that you don't know about this?"

Johnston stared at the picture of a long, black object. His eyes opened wide.

"Is that what I think it is?" he asked, in shock.

Sarah nodded.

Johnston took the phone off her and pinch-zoomed in on the object in the tray.

"How did you come by this?" he gasped. He passed the phone over to Rachael.

"A British Special Forces team got hold of it from some freedom fighters in the Sahara Desert. Whoops, I shouldn't have told you that. I'm not used to this 'Official Secrets' stuff. You won't mention it to anyone?"

"Of course not. It won't leave this room."

He looked over his glasses at Rachael. She nodded.

"So, do you still have this?" asked Johnston.

"Not exactly," said Sarah, with a hint of embarrassment. She explained how the specimen had extricated itself from this world in front of her eyes in her lab.

"You actually saw this happen?" said the Professor, excitedly.

"Yes, some blue glow dragged it into a pool of air above my lab bench and disappeared."

"It's all gone?" asked Johnston.

"Except for a few slices on a microscope slide and a tiny fragment of, what I can only describe as marrow that we had in the spectrometer."

"This is fascinating," said the Professor. "No, it's more than that…"

Rachael butted in.

"Does Marion know about this?"

"No, I work in a place that is classified as 'Top Secret'. Only my boss, Geoff Hamilton and a few higher-ups in the Government know about this. Geoff is under great pressure from the powers-that-be to come up with results. That's why I am here. He sent me."

"This changes everything," said Johnston, looking into space.

He pulled the newspaper article back in front of him.

"I would love to know more about this," he said. "Sarah, how do you fancy a scenic drive through California?"

"Brad, you are not suggesting that you are going to go to Mount Shasta? You are not well. It's a long drive," said Rachael.

"I didn't offer to drive," said the professor. "You have a nice big car."

"But Bradley, you are only just recovering from a stroke," pleaded Rachael.

"A mini-stroke. As long as I take my medication, I'll be just fine."

"Well, I don't mind driving," said Rachael. "Are you sure that you will be okay?"

"Sitting in a car is no different than sitting in my living room. I told you, I'll be fine!"

Chapter 32 - Legends

Next day, Brad and Rachael picked Sarah up from her hotel. It was a four-and-a-half-hour drive, but the Americans thought nothing of it, as if it was just five minutes around the corner.

During the long drive, Brad told Sarah about his side interest. It all spawned from his research into Native American mythology. Tales of horses and buffalo being pulled into the air by a horde of snakes were not all that common, but significant enough to grab his attention. He later found that similar stories were told across the globe and spanning the ages. It became his life's mission to explore these legends.

The four-and-a-half-hour journey seemed to pass quickly. They stopped twice for coffee, but Brad's stories were riveting and embellished by Rachael, who had heard them all before. She filled in the bits that the old man had forgotten.

As Mount Shasta came into view in the far distance, he explained how the volcano, called Úytaahkoo or "White Mountain" by some local Native American tribes, had long been the subject of legends. It is supposedly inhabited by The Spirit of the Above World, Skell, who would fight with his enemy from the Spirit of the Below World, Llao, in fierce battles using hot rocks and lava as missiles. The fact that both spirits lived on volcanoes might have had something to do with it, but sometimes, Llao would help himself to a few animals on the lowers slopes. Tales of the creatures being pulled-through into 'The Spirit World' were abound.

Mount Shasta was also the name of a small town at the foot of the mountain. Brad was looking for the local newspaper office. It wasn't hard to find. It was a small, single story building down a street full of touristy stores.

Brad introduced himself and asked if it was possible to speak to the reporter responsible for the 'mountain climbers' story. An internal phone call brought a young woman into the reception area. She told Brad that her name was Juanita Mendez and invited all three of them into a small meeting room with glass partitions. She offered them a drink from a filter coffee machine, which they accepted graciously.

"Your story of what the climbers saw in the mountain didn't have much detail. I wonder if you have any more information?" asked Brad.

"I spoke to the three climbers; it was about a week ago. They weren't local, not sure where they were from. Anyway, they told me how they saw an apparition just below the snow line. They described it as like the surface of a pond with ripples on it and twigs sticking out. The only thing was that the pond was vertical in the air, not flat against the ground as you would expect.

"And did anything else happen?" asked Rachael.

"No, it was only there for about thirty seconds, then dissolved into nothing and was gone."

"Have you ever heard any similar stories, Juanita?" asked Brad.

"No, I haven't been here very long. I came up from Los Angeles about six months ago for the job. I do know that the mountain is supposed to be sacred to the Native Americans and that there are, apparently, all kinds of spooky things going on up there. Myself, I put it down to…" She put her thumb and forefinger to her lips, indicating smoking something.

Brad smiled.

"How far up the mountain can you go by car?" he asked.

"The Everitt Memorial Highway will take you up to Panther Meadow Trailhead. That's about as far as you can go by car. After that, it's stout boots all the way."

"No, I think I'll pass on the boots," grinned the professor.

"It's not going to erupt, is it?" asked Sarah.

"It hasn't erupted for over two-hundred years," said Juanita. "It must be due for one any day now," she laughed. "Where are you from? I don't recognise the accent."

"England," said Sarah.

"Oh, of course," said Juanita.

"Well, I reckon we'll find somewhere to stay for the night and have a look tomorrow morning. Can you recommend a good hotel, Juanita?"

Juanita told them of a couple of places to try. It was too early for the skiers, so the lodges would have room. There was also a three-star Best Western and a few smaller motels.

"A motel would be fine," said Brad. "No point in wasting money."

They thanked Juanita for her help and left to find a place to stay.

Chapter 33 - Shasta

"Your motels are a lot better than the ones we have in England," said Sarah, in the cafe at breakfast.

"Yes, I wasn't too impressed with your hotels in England," said Brad. "They are either very expensive or small and filthy."

"Oh, I don't know," said Rachael. "I stayed in a lovely little place in Oxford. Totally charming it was."

"Yes, there are good places if you know where to go," agreed Sarah.

They climbed into the car and took a drive along the foothills of Mount Shasta. Every now and then they would see a group of teepees.

"Are those Native American camps?" asked Sarah.

"No way," laughed Brad. "Hippies. New Age Hippies. You won't catch the tribes living in tents these days. They are all rich casino owners."

"Not all of them," corrected Rachael. "They are still considered second-class citizens. There is a lot of poverty, and the associated drug problems."

As Mount Shasta loomed above them, its top shrouded in clouds, Brad wound down the car window and started taking photographs with a compact camera.

"It is beautiful," said Sarah. "It reminds me of the French Alps."

"I think I prefer the French Alps," said Brad.

From behind their car, they could hear a loud whooping sound. Rachael looked in the rear-view mirror. She could see two police motorcycles followed by an ambulance with flashing blue lights. She pulled into the side of the road to let them past.

"Must have been an accident on the mountain," she said.

They continued along Everitt Memorial Highway as far as they could go and eventually came to a bare car park. There was just a sign and a few rocks to stop the cars from going any further. The sign, still dripping with raindrops, said 'Panther Meadows Trailhead - Shasta Trinity National Forest'. They could see the ambulance stopped in the middle of the car park with its back doors open. A number of people were crowded around and a policeman was talking frantically into his motorcycle radio mic. Rachael pulled over into a parking space, wound down her window and spoke to an onlooker.

"What's happened?" she asked.

"Not quite sure. There are a couple of people over there with blankets around them. It looks like they are wearing riding gear."

Brad climbed out and walked over to a policeman, who was taking down notes.

"The horses," said the woman, "they took the horses."

"Who took the horses?" asked the policeman.

"Not who," she replied. "What. It was horrible. There were four of us on horseback just riding along when all of a sudden there was a peal of thunder and the horse and rider in front were grabbed by something. Then they just disappeared into a kind of whirlpool in the air. I thought it was a localised tornado at first. Then another whirlpool appeared and took Marianne and Swift. Only it wasn't a tornado; it had arms, tentacles, I don't know what they were. We immediately got off our horses and started running. Two more whirlpools appeared and took both of our horses. I don't know what happened back there. I just don't understand.

With that, she passed out.

The man sitting on the step of the ambulance with a blanket around his shoulders was shaking uncontrollably.

"They are both in shock," said the paramedic. "We'd better get them back down to hospital."

Rachael and Sarah were now out of the car. A policeman was doing his best to hold the onlookers back.

"Back off now, there's nothing to see," he said. "Would you folk kindly get back into your cars and leave the car park?"

Rachael, Brad and Sarah reluctantly got back in and headed back down the mountain highway.

"Mmm," said Brad. "Never been so close to an actual incident before."

"It's really terrifying," said Rachael.

"Now perhaps you understand what I went through when that … 'thing', disappeared into a hole above my lab bench," said Sarah, shivering.

"Well, it puts one theory to rest," said Brad. "Marion thought there was only one of these exopods. Looks like she was wrong. If we can go by what that shocked woman said, there were two or more of them."

"Exopods?" asked Sarah.

"Yes, I made that name up," said Brad, smiling. "We can't keep calling them 'things'. I just joined 'exobiological' and 'cephalopod'. It's an octopus that's out of this world."

"Exopod means something different in zoology," said Sarah, "but I can see what you're getting at."

Brad lived alone in a medium-sized house in Woodside, about fifteen miles from Stanford. He showed Sarah and Rachael into his large living room. Every available space was covered in statues and pictures from places all around the world.

"Looks like you have travelled a lot," said Sarah.

"One of the perks of the job," said Brad.

Rachael agreed.

"Do you like Piri Piri chicken?" asked Brad. "It's my speciality."

"Sounds lovely. It's not too hot, is it?" asked Sarah.

"Too hot? What's too hot?" said Brad with a serious look. "Do you mean too hot for a Californian or too hot for an English rose?"

"Too hot for me," replied Sarah. "I can't eat Mexican food."

"Well, we won't know that until you have tried

it," smiled the professor. "Besides, Piri Piri is not Mexican, it's Portuguese."

"Sorry. All that I know is that it is hot. Chicken Korma is hot to my taste."

"Oh, if you find Chicken Korma too hot then I will make something else. My Piri Piri will definitely blow your head off. Rachael has had it. What do you think, Rachael?"

"It's too hot! Your taste buds are shot, Brad."

"I think that I had better take you out then. Anything I make will have chillies in it. Can't get enough of those chillies."

"We have been driving for nearly five hours, why don't you let me make something," said Sarah. "I can cook; it just won't be hot. What's in the fridge, Brad?"

Sarah was overwhelmed by Brad's kitchen. It was easily as big as her entire house, with an island unit in the middle complete with bar stools. It would take ages to explore all of the cupboards.

He had a huge, well-stocked fridge and a separate matching freezer beside it. Sarah knew that she was no cordon-bleu chef, but she could get by. She found some steak, flour and mushrooms, so decided to make a traditional English steak and mushroom pie.

"Do you have any potatoes, Brad?" she asked.

"You mean those round, knobbly things?" Brad shook his head. "There are some frozen French Fries in the freezer."

"How about vegetables, fresh vegetables?" she emphasised.

"Well, I have red and green peppers, jalapeños, chillies, poblano, habanero and red onions."

Sarah tapped her foot.

"Carrots? Leeks?"

"No, nothing like that I'm afraid," he shook his head. "How about maize?"

"Oh, you mean sweetcorn? Yes, that will have to do."

He pointed at the freezer.

"Do you want me to help?" asked Brad.

"No Brad, just go and sit down."

"Why don't I open a bottle of wine?" he suggested.

"That's a good idea," said Sarah, as she started to make the pastry.

While the pastry was resting, Sarah cubed the steak and seared the sides. She spotted a chip fryer, but didn't have a clue how to use it.

"The fryer, Brad. How does it work?"

"Ah, it's a low-fat model. It just needs a tablespoon of oil in the compartment on top."

He brought Sarah a glass of wine and leaned on the side to watch her working.

"I don't usually have my steak cut up for me," he quipped.

"It's an English favourite; we tend to make our meat go further."

"What do you do for fun, Sarah?" asked Brad.

"I read, play a bit of tennis, that kind of thing," said Sarah.

"Have you been to California before?"

"No. I've been to Florida on holiday," she volunteered. "Nowhere else."

"Tomorrow we will drive over to the Pacific coast. It's lovely there. Rachael will put you up at her place for the night. She doesn't want to drive you back to Palo Alto after drinking wine. She lives nearby. I want to talk to you some more about your work."

Brad opened his bottle of pills and swallowed two with a sip of wine.

Chapter 34 - Pacific

The Pacific coast was not at all what Sarah had imagined it would be. She was thinking Baywatch, this was big and wild.

"So, tell me more about your experiments on the sample," said Brad.

"I rang Geoff this morning from Rachael's place. He has been working on the marrow-like substance. It seems that it reacts to electrical stimulus. It increases in mass when a small voltage is applied."

"Is that how a cephalopod's tentacles work?"

"I'm not a marine biologist Brad, but from the little I do know, they are just muscular. There is a difference between tentacles and arms. Most of them are referred to as arms. An octopus only has arms; they have suckers along the whole length. Squids have eight arms and two tentacles. A tentacle only has suckers at its tip. Interestingly, a nautilus has about ninety tentacles with no suckers. Go figure."

"So, if it has no muscles, how does it move?" asked the professor.

"The arm is about forty millimetres at its thickest. It has fine hexagonal channels running its length. These channels are filled with this marrow substance. I can only assume that it moves by applying electrical stimulus to the stuff in the hexagonal tubes, causing it to expand and contract. This warps the entire mass, much like muscles would. The outside of these … arms … are coated with fine hairs. We don't yet know what those are for. I can only assume that they do what the tentacles' suckers do – fix onto the victim. It is much more like a plant mechanism than an animal one. The other thing that was mentioned was that the slivers in the microscope slides became invisible in ultra-violet light."

The professor shook his head.

"Damnedest thing."

"Okay, never mind the biology. It is clearly not of this world," said Rachael. "Where does this thing come from?"

"You know, our ancestors didn't have to answer questions like that," said Brad. "They were quite content to attribute anything they didn't understand to 'spirits'. I suppose that some folk still do. Spirits, gods, call them whatever you like – they are the lazy way of thinking. Just blindly accept what your parents and peers ram down your throat no matter how nonsensical it is. The world is full of it. I can look back at all those idols, all those graven images from the past that I've seen. Their worshipers are long gone, yet humanity lives on without them. At one time, civilisations revolved around them and still we have 'true believers' beating the shit out of one another because 'my god can lick your god', just like a five-year-old might boast about his Paw. I was rather hoping that in my lifetime this nonsense would finally sort itself out. Unfortunately not. Bob Dylan sang a song fifty years ago that included the words – 'even the Germans had God on their side'. He had the right idea. Everybody and nobody has God on their side."

Sarah listened to the old man. He was a scientist. He asked questions and accepted nothing as gospel.

"I'm afraid that I am feeling a bit tired now and I'm ready for my bed. Sarah, I am very happy to have met you. I hope that you have a pleasant flight home tomorrow. Please email me when you get back. I'd very much like to keep in touch."

"Me too," said Rachael. "You have my email address."

Sarah gave Brad a big hug.

"Lovely to meet you, Brad. You have been a great help. Now, I have a very long report to write for my boss. If we find out anything more interesting, I'll let you know."

Sarah and Rachael drove off, waving goodbye.

* * * * *

Sarah had a bad case of jet-lag when she got home. She took some paracetamol and went to bed. When she awoke in a daze next morning, she remembered the report she had to write. Geoff would be wanting it urgently, but she wasn't in the mood for report writing just now. Instead, she went for a walk.

When she got home, Sarah opened her laptop to start the report. She noticed an email from Rachael and was expecting another 'nice to have met you' message. It wasn't.

'Dear Sarah, I'm most sorry to tell you that Brad had another stroke this morning. This time, he didn't make it.'

Sarah read it over and over again. She closed her laptop, put her head in her hands and cried.

Chapter 35 - Mongolia

Ghazan had looked after his herd of Mongolian cattle since he was a boy. The steppes were a harsh environment for cattle and humans alike, with temperatures swinging from -50°C in winter to a scorching 35° in summer. His way of life was leisurely, nothing much ever happened. A few times a year he would make the hard, thirty-five-kilometre trek into the nearest conurbation, Erenhot, to stock up on luxuries. That included just about anything that wasn't water, milk or beef. He would take with him goods to sell – wool, cashmere yarn and hides from the slaughtered livestock on which he fed himself and his family. He didn't get much for them, but then, he didn't have much need of money. He lived off the land. Unlike some of the nomadic people who took their homes with them, Ghazan and his family had a fixed abode made from stone rendered with cement and pebbles. It kept them warm in winter, and cool in summer.

This region of Inner Mongolia was famous for two things; dinosaurs and its greatest son, Genghis Khan. At one time, the Mongol Empire was the greatest in the World. Now, Inner Mongolia is just a remote autonomous region of The People's Republic of China, and most of its inhabitants, like Ghazan, toil in the endless grasslands.

It was a cold morning in the short and dry spring. Heavy sandstorms would sweep the more arid regions, but here in the steppe, Ghazan's cattle had a bountiful supply of lush, green grass. He sat on the grass and dreamed of the far off lands and wondrous sights that he saw in magazines. He would always buy a few magazines in town to take home to show his children. How else could they learn that there was something beyond all this grass? He dozed off.

Ghazan didn't know how long he had slept, it didn't really matter. He was awakened by frantic mooing and scrabbling nearby. One of his cows was thrashing on the ground, and the others were running away from it. He got up and walked towards it. As he got closer, he saw what he thought were ropes wrapped around the animal's midriff. How could there be ropes out here? He didn't bring any. What he saw next made his stomach churn. In a flurry of sparks, parts of his cow were being ripped off its body, leaving fountains of blood spurting and innards suspended in the air. He pulled out his mobile phone and starting taking photos. In a few seconds, there was little left of the poor animal. He watched, as most of it disappeared into a pool in the sky. He kept taking pictures until his phone memory was full. He moved forward cautiously, with one eye on the remnants of his cow on the ground and the other on the sky, where the rest of it had just disappeared. He flicked though the photos on his phone screen just to assure himself that he wasn't still asleep and dreaming. No, they were real. He grabbed his stick from where he had been sleeping and ran for home as fast as he could, looking over his shoulder every few seconds in case something was following him.

Breathless, he squeezed through the door of his house, slammed it shut and put the bar across. That was something he almost never did. He showed his wife the photos and, between deep gasps, tried to explain what had just happened. She didn't understand his rantings. She made him sit down and insisted he ring the authorities right away.

Two hours later, a police 4x4 arrived outside his door. He undid the bar and beckoned the men in. Without wasting any more time, he showed them the pictures on his phone. They turned the phone sideways and upside-down, but the images made no sense no matter which way up they were. Ghazan jabbered on. All that the policemen knew was that he was very distraught.

Much to his dismay, the police insisted on taking his phone back to base. They promised that they would send it back when they had retrieved the photos from it. That would take days. How could he possibly herd his animals without a mobile phone?

Chapter 36 - Report

"Did you have a good time at Stanford?" asked Geoff Hamilton.

"I did, until I got home," answered Sarah.

She gave a brief summary of her trip and her meeting with Bradley Johnston. She broke down when it came to the morning's email from Rachael.

"I'm so sorry, Sarah. Do you want to take the day off? We can wait another day for your feedback. It's not a problem."

Sarah shook her head.

"No, you need to read this," she said, pushing across a sheaf of paper.

Geoff looked at it quickly.

"Sarah, go home. I'll read your report and we can talk some more about it tomorrow."

"No Geoff, it's too important. Read it now. There's a file on this USB stick if you want to pass it on."

"I'm not passing it on until I've read and digested it, Sarah."

As Geoff read through the report, Sarah continued to talk.

"Brad was a lovely man. I only knew him for a few days but he was kind, insightful and very intelligent. I will never forget him."

"What about this Rachael Hartmann, was she in on all of your discussions?"

"Yes, she was. I liked her too. She will dearly miss the professor."

"Do you think that she is a security risk?" asked Geoff.

"No, of course not," replied Sarah. "What are you suggesting, Geoff? That we get an MI6 agent to go over and knock her off so that she won't talk?"

"Don't be melodramatic, Sarah. I know that you are upset. I just think that I'll edit her out of the report. She doesn't figure in the main narrative and I think it's best that we don't mention her up above."

"Whatever you say, Geoff. You're the boss."

"Wish I was," said Geoff, looking up at the ceiling. "The real boss might not be quite so understanding."

Geoff reached the part about Mount Shasta.

"My God, you were actually there when this happened?" he exclaimed, whacking the paper with the back his hand.

"I didn't witness the occurrence personally," replied Sarah, "we arrived half an hour too late. The police and ambulance were already on the scene. I heard someone give her account to the police, but she was in a state of deep shock, there was no chance for any discussion."

Geoff read on. He set the papers back down on the table and cleaned his glasses.

"So, these events have been happening all over the world, and across the centuries. All this time they have been passed off as myths and superstition."

"Yes," said Sarah. "It's hard to believe. If somebody other than Brad had told me that, I would have written them off as certifiable. Now, he won't know what happens. It's such a shame. By the way, Brad had a name for the thing. He called it an 'exopod'."

Geoff pondered.

"Not totally accurate, but clever. It will have to do for now."

"There is a brief mention here of Doctor Marion Calvin from Oxford University. Where does she fit in all this?"

"Geoff, remember that she is another one of the people you asked me to contact. I got the impression that she and Brad were old friends, maybe even more."

"Yes, speak to her by all means but remember…"

Sarah nodded out the words.

"Official, Secret, Act. Yes, I know. I just want to ask her some questions, that's all. I'll be careful."

"I see you have a theory here about the hexagonal tubes and marrow, or 'sap', as you are suggesting?"

"Yes, it only came to me as I was talking to Brad. What do you think?"

"I think you have a very valid observation there. Yes, plants do use such a capillary mechanism, ones that move anyway."

"The insectivores and carnivores?"

"Yes, exactly," said Geoff. "Not sure that it is triggered by electrical means. I think it's more chemical, or maybe hydraulic. You would need to talk to a botanist about that."

"Good idea. We must have a tame botanist in the facility somewhere; I'll find out."

After lunch, Sarah met with Geoff again.

"I think I've found our botanist, he's coming over tomorrow."

"Ah, good," said Geoff. "And, have you spoken to Doctor Calvin?"

"No," said Sarah. "She's gone to California for a few days. I can guess why. I have emailed Rachael Hartmann to ask her to not make any mention of my visit. I do hope that she gets it in time."

Chapter 37 - Funeral

Marion Calvin sat beside Rachael Hartmann in the crowded chapel. She looked around. "Looks like Brad was very popular."

"Yes, he was," replied Rachael. "I recognise most of the mourners here, they're students and faculty staff. There are a few I haven't seen before. They might be family. Brad never spoke about his family."

Marion sobbed into a handkerchief as Brad's coffin slipped behind the curtain. Rachael put her hand on hers.

"He was a good friend, Rachael. We had some great times, Brad and I."

Marion managed to stop herself from bursting into tears completely.

"Come on Marion, let's go to the wake. I need a stiff drink and I'm sure that you could do with something yourself."

Marion nodded and held on tightly to Rachael's arm as they walked towards the waiting car.

Back in Marion's hotel room, she opened up to Rachael.

"Brad and I met in New Zealand back in nineteen-sixty-six. I went abroad, mainly, to get over a broken relationship. He was studying Maori tribal mythology. We hit it off straight away. We did have a short fling, but I wasn't ready for it so soon. He went back to Stanford and I went to Oxford. We wrote to each other regularly for years. He invited me out here to stay at that lovely big house of his. It was a wonderful few months. Yes, I think I overstayed my welcome, but we got on like a house on fire. I think Brad had that effect on everybody. Of course, it helped that we both worked in the same field, but there was more to it than just work. We had a relationship. Oh, I don't mean that kind of relationship. It was friendship. We were soul-mates. Kindred spirits swept along on a tide of mutual admiration – and the odd joint," Marion added smiling. "It was the sixties."

Rachael was amused at the idea of Marion and Brad smoking pot. She had never seen Brad smoke anything.

"After that, we both got more involved with work and university pressures and I didn't hear from him for a while. Twenty years to be exact! Then one day, out of the blue, he rang me and said that he was in London for a conference. I was on the next train to Paddington. I met him at his hotel for dinner and he told me about this side interest he had. It was unexplained phenomena that he connected to Native American myths and legends. I was fascinated. When I got back to England, I started looking for parallels in European cultures. I found quite a few. So we continued to share notes, and I pulled in a few friends and colleagues. We formed a sort of 'secret society'. I suppose that you must have joined it too?"

She had.

"When our incident at the Cobham fête made

all the headlines, we hadn't been in contact for a few months. Then I found out about his stroke. He seemed to recover from it quite quickly, but he didn't have the same energy as before. I think that that's why he sent you over to see me. He didn't relish the long journey himself, but he wanted a first-hand account, or as near as possible, of that terrible event. You know the rest of the story."

"Well, I have some news for you Marion," said Rachael. "It was only a week ago that something happened at Mount Shasta, in Northern California. Brad asked me to take him up there, even though he wasn't really fit for it. We went to the local newspaper, but they weren't of much help. They did, however, direct us to a location – a car park in the foothills. We found that two horses and riders, and two other horses on their own, had been whisked off into oblivion only half an hour before we got there. Sarah and I stayed in the car while Brad tried to glean more information from the policeman."

"Sarah?" asked Marion.

Rachael bit her tongue.

"Oh, she was a student that went with us to share the driving."

"I'd like to know more about this," said Marion. "Did it get any news coverage?"

"It's funny you should say that. I haven't seen any. I think it was deliberately hushed up."

"By whom?" asked Marion.

"I don't know," said Rachael, "but there must be people in this country who don't want it to get out.

Whether they are worried that it will affect the tourist industry or national security, I just don't know. Anyway, the news just evaporated like the event never happened. I think I'll ring that reporter woman in Mount Shasta. I can't think of her name. Something Hispanic or Latino. Juanita Mendez, that was it."

Next morning, Rachael rang the newspaper offices in Mount Shasta. Juanita Mendez was there and said that she remembered her visit a few days ago. When Rachael asked about the horse incident, Mendez went quiet.

"I'm afraid that I don't know what you are talking about. I know nothing about this."

"But…"

The phone was put down.

"The police," thought Rachael. "They were there. They will have a record."

She rang the Mount Shasta police, introducing herself as a post graduate student from Stanford working on a thesis.

"No, I don't have anything on the system like that," said the officer on the other end of the line. "What did you say the date was?"

Rachael told him the date.

"Ah, yes. Here's something. Two riders had horses out from the local horse rescue centre. A thunderclap spooked them and they bolted, throwing their riders off. An ambulance was called, but they weren't hurt badly, just a bit shaken. That's all I can tell you. I can only read what's on my screen. I shouldn't even be telling you that."

Rachael thanked the officer for his trouble.

"That's not what happened. I was there," she said to herself. "This is a cover-up."

* * * * *

"How long are you staying?" asked Rachael.

"Just a few days. My department in Oxford won't run itself," said Marion.

"You can come into the faculty then? There are some people that would love to meet you."

"Yes, I'd like that," said Marion. "It's a while since I've been to The Farm."

Marion was embarrassed by the applause that greeted her when she entered the small common room. There were six people standing clapping.

"Oh, I don't know what to say to all this. Thank you. Thank you very much."

Rachael stepped forward and addressed the small assembly.

"Dr Calvin has kindly graced us with her presence. I just need to explain to her that you are not anthropology students, you are a 'special interest' group."

"Thank you for your warm reception," said Marion. "I'm sure that you will all understand that I am still recovering from the sad news of Professor Johnston's death. I am not my usual, bubbly self."

"Are you prepared to answer a few questions?"

asked Rachael.

Marion sat down at the table.

"I'll do my best."

Several of the group raised their hands. Marion pointed to a man who looked to be Chinese.

"Dr Calvin, my name is Lu Chen. I am a theoretical physicist here at Stanford. I would be particularly interested in your theories about where this thing comes from, and goes back to."

"Just a minute," interrupted Rachael. "Things, not thing. We have established that there are more than one of these."

Marion's jaw dropped.

"How so?" said Marion. "I was always of the opinion that it was one creature that moved back and forth in time. How can you be sure that there is more than one?"

"Ah, the incident at Mount Shasta. A witness clearly saw at least two, perhaps three, attacking the horses and riders."

"Oh my," gasped Marion. "That puts a completely different slant on things."

For the benefit of the others present, Rachael related her experience in the Mount Shasta car park. She also told them about the apparent cover-up.

"So, the government doesn't want news of this event to get out," said Lu Chen, "I can't say that I'm surprised. It would cause mass panic. Stock markets would crash. There would be pandemonium."

"Exactly, that's what happened at Cobham in England," said Marion. "All hell broke loose across the country, but a week later it was all passed off as just a freak tornado. Society is far more resilient than you'd think. Now, getting back to your initial question. I, and some others, are of the opinion that this thing has the ability to manipulate a rift in the fabric of time and space. It can open a portal and reach into our world from the other side. It only puts a few arms through, so we have no idea what the rest of it looks like. I hate to think what would happen if the whole thing came through."

Another from the group put her hand up excitedly.

"I am Justine Baker. I'm not from Stanford, I'm from UCLA and I'm doing a doctorate in quantum physics. You may know about the ability of some particles to appear to be in two places at once. Is it possible that this creature, whatever it is, has the ability to be in multiple locations at the same time?

In other words, there is just one, but it can generate other instances of itself."

"Now you have me," said Marion. "Justine, was it? These ideas have never occurred to me. I'm going to have to think about them. It's an interesting idea."

Another man raised his hand.

"Howard Landry, I'm, err, an exobiologist, for want of a better word. I study the biology of things that are not of this world. Now, before you tell me that we haven't yet found any examples of extra-terrestrial life, I can tell you that we most definitely have. It's just that they are all dead and fossilised inside meteorites. In the not too distant future, I hope to be looking down a microscope at a wriggling Martian trilobite, and other living things on comets and asteroids. I don't expect to be communicating with them any time soon, but I do believe that they are there. Now, my question, Doctor Calvin, is this. Is it possible that your phenomenon could be extra-terrestrial in origin? Could it be from another world in our universe?"

"Mr Landry, your work sounds intriguing. I'm afraid that I just can't answer your question. In the absence of hard facts, all I can do is guess. I can't even claim that it is an educated guess because, even though we are all academics, it is still all supposition. Sorry that I can't be more informative."

A woman with a floral headscarf stood up.

"Hi, my name's Ruth Emmett. I'm not a scientist like the rest of you folk, I'm a lecturer in humanities. I know that y'all like to examine everything logically and analyse it to the nth degree, but I have another perspective that you might want to consider. While you are all taking about these highfalutin' scientific theories, did it ever occur to you that you are ignoring the spiritual aspects…"

Marion put her hand up like a traffic policeman.

"Ms Emmett, can I just stop you there. This is a scientific discussion; how did you get in here?" She glanced across at Rachael.

"It's okay Doctor Calvin, Ruth is a friend of mine," said Rachael. "I invited her along today myself. Perhaps we should just open our minds a little and hear what she has to contribute?"

Marion waved her hand for Ruth to continue.

"I'm not an anthropologist like Rachael, I have studied Native American cultures more at a roots level. I have Sioux blood in me. The stories that I was told as a child all had a common thread – the spirit world. I know it's not very hip to talk about such things in polite circles, but I believe in it. I know there are things beyond human comprehension that just cannot be explained scientifically, and I also know that the thing you are discussing here today has long been told of in our folklore. Do not dismiss the spirit world just because you don't understand it."

"Yes, Ms Emmett, I will not deny that the line between science and folklore is a fine one, but I would call it pseudo-science. The difference is that, in science, someone postulates a theory and then breaks their back to prove it. In folklore, spiritualism, whatever you want to call it, someone postulates a theory … full stop, or period, as you put it. You have your beliefs, fine, I have mine too. This 'thing' that my good friend Bradley Johnston dubbed 'exopod' is not a spirit, it is real. The carnage that it leaves in its wake is real. No, we don't understand it, as you suggest, but the universe is cram-packed full of things that we don't understand. I, personally, am content with the fact that there are things that I don't understand, but I would much rather be in blissful ignorance than submit to the vagaries of 'a belief' and stop questioning."

For a few moments, the room was in utter silence. Then more hands shot up in the air.

The questions and answers would have gone on for longer had the room not been booked for another meeting. They all shook Marion's hand enthusiastically. Marion asked if they would each leave their contact details with Rachael, but she had them already. They all went their various ways until only Rachael remained.

"I think that went very well," said Rachael.

"Yes, I have just had more thought-provoking ideas thrown at me in the last two hours than in five years at Oxford. I need some time to get my brain around all this. It is quite disturbing to have your beliefs sorted, chewed, consumed, digested and then spat out again in such a short period of time."

"So, in what direction are you going back home in this respect?" asked Rachael.

"I have been persuaded, by a photographer no less, to try to plot sightings and encounters by date and location. We plan to build a four-dimensional computer model and see if there's any pattern that might allow us to predict future incidents and confront the thing with … well, we haven't got that far."

Marion and Rachael went out into the quadrangle. Marion wanted a last, probably final, look around before heading for San Francisco and an early morning flight back home.

Chapter 38 - Botanist

Oliver Langham peered at the specimen through Geoff's stereo microscope.

"Does it look botanical to you?" asked Geoff.

The botanist adjusted the microscope's back lighting.

"I can't say I've ever seen anything like it before. What is it?"

"Truth is, we don't know, said Sarah. "It's a slice of a specimen that was sent to us by people in the Sahara Desert."

"Ah, a desert species?"

He continued to fiddle with the microscope.

"No. It's not like anything that I've come across before."

"Dr Langham, can you explain to me the mechanisms that make plants move; carnivores, that sort of thing?"

"You are thinking of Dionaea Muscipula, the Venus Flytrap, right?"

"Yes," said Geoff.

"That is complicated and not well understood. As I understand, it is all about the movement of hydrogen ions lowering the pH in the cell walls. There is a water flow by osmosis, that causes the cells to collapse."

"So, there is nothing electrical involved?" asked Geoff.

"Don't think so, not what you would call

neurological pathways anyway."

What about plants that always turn towards the sun?" asked Sarah.

"They are called heliotropic or phototropic flowers," explained the botanist. "The light from the Sun causes the plant's cells on the shady side to elongate and twist the head to face the sun. What I'm looking at in the microscope here, is definitely not from plants. It looks more like a crystalline structure to me. The nearest I've seen is in graphene nanotubes. I do wish you could tell me where it came from?"

"As I told you, it came from the Sahara Desert. I don't know any more than that. Thank you for your help, Doctor Langham. We are slowly making steps in the right direction."

As soon as Oliver Langham had left, Geoff closed the door.

"Sarah, I've had a phone call. We are expected at Whitehall tomorrow morning; can you get here for seven?"

* * * * *

Sarah had not been to the large Ministry of Defence building in Whitehall before. The sumptuous entrance lobby had marble floors and walls with two rows of black leather seats, with small tables between them. She was surprised to see the large modern paintings adorning the walls, which were a little incongruous in the neo-classical setting.

Geoff gestured for her to sit down.

"They know we have arrived. Someone will be down to meet us shortly."

Ten minutes later, a woman in a pencil skirt arrived and led them to a lift. They were taken through a maze of corridors to a grand meeting room with a large, oval mahogany table and paintings of military dignitaries around the walls. They were offered coffee as others began to join them, one by one.

Sarah recognised two of the men from earlier meetings back at the lab. Ewan Cummings was the sour-faced politician from the cabinet office. Charles Millar, she knew to be from the National Security Agency. The third man was introduced as Toby Fanshawe, from GCHQ in Cheltenham. Cummings chaired the meeting while the woman in the pencil skirt took notes.

"I'm sorry to spring such an early meeting on you," said Cummings, looking around the table, "but my day is choc-a-bloc. Mr Hamilton, I believe that you have something to report?"

Geoff opened the folder in front of him and passed around some documents.

"Gentlemen. As you know, our specimen managed to extricate itself from our … existence, but I did manage to take some slices for microscope analysis before it disappeared. Having run all the tests at our disposal, I can say with some certainty that what we are dealing with is neither animal nor vegetable – which leaves mineral. If it is mineral, it is not any mineral known to man. So, my prognosis is that what we have here is non-terrestrial. Note that I didn't say 'extra-terrestrial' as that suggests that it came from somewhere in outer space. We don't know much about extra-terrestrial materials but we would expect it to conform to the laws of known physics. What I have under my microscopes, and in my spectrometers, does not adhere to our laws of physics at all. If you look at the photograph, 'Fig 1', you will see a cross section of this 'arm'. It is made up of a collection of hexagonal tubes, all the same size. A cross section through a plant stem would have circular capillaries of differing diameters depending on their function. These would be separated by a pith to provide packing and keep them apart. Our specimen here has perfectly tessellating hexagons right up to the outer skin, which you will notice, is covered in short hairs. The individual hexagonal tubes are filled with a jelly-like substance, which, I have established, expands and contracts with electrical stimulus. This, I suspect, provides the muscle substitute that allows the thing to move as the hexagons elongate on one side and shorten on the other."

"What do you think the hairs on the outside are for?" asked Charles Millar.

"My best guess is that they behave like the hairs on a gecko's foot. They create adhesion, much like the suckers on an octopus's arm would, to hold on to its prey."

"Very interesting," said Millar, looking around the

table for support. There was none.

"Now, we have a very interesting discovery made 'in the field', as it were, by my colleague Doctor Sarah Frobisher. I will let her explain."

Sarah told them of her trip to Stanford University, about Professor Johnston and their visit to Mount Shasta. She recounted the story told to the policeman by the rider who saw two or three of these apparitions grab two horses and riders, and other riderless horses.

"So, there's not just one of these things. There are no other reports of them hunting in packs, but this is a completely new revelation."

There was silence.

"I have something to report," said Toby Fanshawe." We have a team at GCHG tasked with monitoring the airwaves and the Internet for any mention of this anomaly. It has become clear that any initial contacts, in any country, are quickly suppressed by their governments as they realise the security and public reaction implications. We were fortunate enough to be able to monitor a local television report from some place in Inner Mongolia – that's part of The People's Republic of China, by the way. It seems that some rural herdsman was able to take some photos of one of his cows being ripped to shreds by one of these things. Here, look. I warn you, it makes gruesome viewing. The quality of the cheap phone photos has been enhanced by our back-room boys."

He rotated his laptop for all to see. The sequence of photos showed the cow being butchered by the flailing limbs and the individual pieces being drawn back into the distortion in the air.

"Look," said Geoff, "see how the pieces of the animal stick to the limbs. It doesn't wrap around them, it just touches the cow and pulls. I think that confirms my suspicion about the hairs on the outside having an adhesive property."

"Notice also," said Fanshawe, "that there are two limbs that do nothing but hover above all the working ones. I believe that these are its eyes. If they are not optical, then I think that they must be electromagnetic sensors of some kind. They were also the last things to be retracted before the distortion vanished."

"Good," said Cummings. "We seem to be getting somewhere at last. I think that our task now, is to find some way to eliminate this potential threat to society. I am going to propose to the cabinet that we set up an international committee so that we can consolidate our efforts and pool our resources. These things must be stopped!"

Chapter 39 - Visitors

Rachael Hartmann struggled to get her key in the door. The large brown bag of groceries under her left arm wasn't helping. She stepped into her hallway and tried to kick the door closed. She couldn't, there was a foot in it. Two strange men pushed her door open, came in and closed it.

"Miss Hartmann, we need to have a word with you."

"Who are you?" she gasped.

"We'll ask the questions if you don't mind, Miss Hartmann. Don't be concerned, we are not here to harm you or rob you. We just want to talk."

Rachael put down the heavy bag of groceries.

"What's it about?"

One of the men flashed an identity card. It had his photo in the middle and an official-looking seal on the left side. He didn't give her time to read any of the text.

The men looked around Rachael's living room. One wandered across into the kitchen.

"Is there anyone else here?" he asked.

"Em, no. I live by myself."

The man held out his hand indicating that Rachael should sit down on an armchair. They sat on the sofa.

"I believe that you have been asking questions about something that happened on Mount Shasta last week. Is that correct?"

"Yes, I did," admitted Rachael. "Not that I got

many answers."

"Miss Hartmann, whatever your motives are, you are not to pursue this line of enquiry any further. This issue is not to be discussed or disseminated in any way. Is that clear?"

"Why?" asked Rachael.

"We cannot go into that, Miss Hartmann. All that we can tell you is that your activities have to stop now. Whatever you were told, forget it. Nothing happened up there. Do you understand?"

Rachael nodded meekly.

"If we hear of any further such activity on your part, you could be spending some time in a very unpleasant place."

He waved his finger back and forth to make the point.

"We would be having this same conversation with Professor Bradley Johnston, but I believe that we are a little too late?"

"He passed last week," confirmed Rachael.

The two men got up and went to the door. One was looking back and wagging his finger as they left.

Rachael was flustered. She knew that they had obviously made a similar dictate to the people at the newspaper and the police in Mount Shasta. Now she was being shut up too. Dare she risk talking to any of the others? Maybe her every movement was being watched? She was frightened.

* * * * *

Rachael decided to go into the university. That's what she would do normally anyway. She headed for the physics building, looking all around to see if she was being watched or followed. It didn't seem so. She headed to where she knew she would find Lu Chen. He was exactly where she expected.

"Chen, is there somewhere we can talk privately?"

Chen looked around, and then beckoned her towards a storeroom door. They went in and closed the door behind them. The room was stacked with filing boxes, printer paper and ink.

"What's all this about Rachael, is a man not safe around here?" grinned Chen.

"This isn't funny, Chen. I had two men come to my home earlier today doing their best to scare me off researching the phenomena. Have you had any such warnings?"

"Not yet. I knew that there was a cover-up going on, but this is getting a bit too close to home for my liking."

"What do we do?" asked Rachael.

"We will just have to be more careful. These guys could be monitoring our emails and phone calls. I suggest that we form a society, something innocuous and boring."

"A knitting circle?" asked Rachael.

"No, something innocuous, boring and believable."

"I know," said Chen, "genealogy. A genealogical society. I am already doing some family research and if everybody else signed up to the same web site that I use, we could pass coded messages between ourselves – dates, locations, names. It would all look to be above board."

"That sounds good to me," said Rachael. "My family were mostly wiped out in the concentration camps in Poland during World War 2. I could research Europe in that period without any suspicion."

"And my family came from China," said Chen. "I can go back centuries. Leave it to me. I will contact the others and tell them to sign up and how to phrase their messages. They will appear online for all to see, but only the chosen few will understand."

"Brilliant," said Rachael. "I'll go home and sign up right away."

"And," continued Chen, "I'll put a notice up on the main pin-boards inviting students to join our family research society. That will give us credibility to book meeting rooms and so on. They won't know the underlying purpose. I don't think that we can all join the site in one lot. Best to spread it out over a couple of weeks, that way our new members will be mixed up with thousands of others."

"And I will get in touch with Marion and Sarah in England, though I'm not sure how to do that yet if my phone and emails are being monitored."

"Get a cheap, throwaway phone," suggested Chen. "I'll get one too."

"Excellent idea," smiled Rachael. "You have all the answers Chen, don't you?"

Chapter 40 - DragonMan

Sarah got a cryptic text on her mobile. She didn't recognise the sender and it didn't have a normal English dialling code. It just said 'Out of Area'.

The text instructed her to sign up to a genealogy web site and subscribe to forum messages from 'DragonMan'. The message was signed '-R'. It all sounded very fishy, some marketing scam no doubt.

A few seconds later, she received a second text.

"Hope everything was okay when you got back? -R."

Sarah replied to the text.

"All was fine, -R. –S."

In return, she got a 'thumbs-up' emoticon."

So, it was Rachael that was asking her to sign up to a genealogy web site. She must have a good reason for that.

Later, at home, Sarah signed up. She found her way to the forum with thousands of requests from people looking for information about long lost family members. She entered 'DragonMan' into the forum search box. There were only three posts with that search term. One was from somebody with the nickname 'FarmGirl'. The girl from The Farm could be Rachael. Sarah used the nickname 'EnglishRose' to sign up for the forum. They would understand that. She posted a message in reply to the 'DragonMan' thread.

'Hey DragonMan, I think that we have a common relation from the Bradley family. -S'

It was half an hour before she had a notification in her inbox telling her of a reply to her forum post.

'Hi EnglishRose, yes, I can confirm that there are Bradleys in my tree. You can download a PDF of my tree here, to check against yours.'

Sarah downloaded the PDF. It was a family tree diagram with the Bradleys at the top and branching off into various families. When she discounted the name 'Bradley' from the husbands, wives and children, she was left with a list of names. She recognised 'Hartmann' and 'Frobisher', but none of the others rang any bells. She suspected that this was a list of the real names of Brad's group of like-minded people and that they must be using the forum as a cover for their communications. She then posted another request for information.

'Anyone know a family called 'Mendeth' in Northern California?'

She was careful to spell 'Mendez' phonetically with a Spanish 'th', just in case anyone else was searching for the newspaper reporter. She also didn't want to use the term 'Mount Shasta' explicitly.

In a few minutes, 'FarmGirl' replied, 'Mendeth connection severed. Extremely disgruntled!' The 'grunt' part was highlighted in red.

Oh, this coded messaging was frustrating. Sarah took it to mean that Juanita Mendez couldn't be contacted. Why was 'grunt' highlighted? 'Grunt'? That's the noise that pigs make. 'Pigs', could that be referring to the police?

Finally, Sarah realised that the police in the USA were instrumental in hushing everything up. That tied in with what she learned at the meeting in Whitehall. Reports of phenomenal activity were being stifled. Everywhere!

* * * * *

Marion Calvin's phone notified her of an incoming text. It was just a phone number, a Californian phone number. She typed it in and after a few seconds of ringing, someone answered.

"Hello?"

"Hello, this is Marion Calvin, who is this please?"

"Marion, Hi. It's Rachael. Rachel Hartmann. This is a throwaway phone number. I can't talk on my usual phone or send you an email. I think I'm being bugged."

"Aha, my dear, I'm way ahead of you on that one. I have a 'throwaway phone' too, do you want the number? Have you got a pen?"

"Okay," said Rachael, "I'll ring you straight back."

Rachael told Marion about the visit from the 'agents' as she called them. Marion told her that they were called 'spooks' in England. They both understood what they were talking about. Rachael then told Marion about the genealogy web site and how to use it for their purposes. Marion listened attentively. She was in her late sixties, but using the Internet didn't cause her any problems.

"So, subscribe to the thread 'DragonMan', that is Lu Cheng, the theoretical physicist that you met here. I am 'FarmGirl'. The rest you will get to know. By the way, do you know Sarah Frobisher?"

"No, I've never heard of that name. Who is she?"

"She works at a government research facility in Wiltshire. Oh, I wasn't supposed to tell you that. Would it be okay if I gave you her 'throwaway' number? You can contact her directly without any reference to me."

"Yes, I'll do that. Thank you so much. I'll be in touch. Bye."

Sarah was very surprised to get a phone call from Dr Calvin. She was on her list of people to contact but she hadn't got around to it.

"Dr Calvin, I was just going to contact you."

"Hello, Miss Frobisher. It is Miss, isn't it?"

"I'm 'Doctor' too, but no matter," joked Sarah. "Plain Sarah is just fine."

"Look, Sarah, I don't want to discuss things over the phone. It is supposed to be an untraceable phone but I never trust these things. Can we meet up? I'm in Oxford and you are somewhere near Salisbury, I believe. Can we meet somewhere in-between? Do you know Newbury? That is about half-way."

"Yes, of course. It will have to be at the weekend though."

They agreed to meet at a pub restaurant that Marion knew on the following Sunday.

Chapter 41 - Bugs

"You knew Brad?" asked Sarah.

"Oh yes, Brad and I go way back," said Marion.

The pub restaurant was busy providing Sunday roast dinners. They were lucky to get a space in the small courtyard garden. It had a vine growing all the way up one wall and across their heads, suspended on a trellis.

"It was so sad seeing him disappear behind that velvet curtain," sighed Marion.

"You were at his funeral?" asked Sarah.

"Yes, I was. I owed it to him. How did you know Brad?"

"I was with Brad for most of last week," said Sarah.

"You were?" said Marion, with an acute look of surprise.

"Yes, I was sent across by my boss to talk to him. He was a lovely man."

"Wait a minute," said Marion, "you're not the Sarah that went with him and Rachael to Mount Shasta?"

"Yes, I am," said Sarah, looking a bit puzzled.

"Rachael mentioned a 'Sarah'," said Marion, "but when I asked who Sarah was, she said that was just a student that came along to share the driving."

"Yes, that is my fault. I told Rachael that she wasn't to mention my presence. It's all that Official Secrets stuff. I never know what I can say and what I can't, so I tend to say nothing most of the time."

"Are you able to tell me what your involvement is in all this?" asked Marion.

"I could go to jail," said Sarah, smiling and looking all around. "I am a biologist working for a government research laboratory in Wiltshire. All our work is classified 'Top Secret' on the pain of being tied up with red-hot chains in the Tower of London for the next two-hundred years."

A faint smile crossed Marion's lips.

"I wouldn't like that to happen to you. At least, not until you tell me all you know."

Sarah looked around again. There were lots of families with screaming brats. No MI5 agents.

"We were sent something by a Special Forces team instructing freedom fighters in the Sahara. It looked, to me, like an eel that had its head chopped off. My boss took some slices to make microscope slides and some gooey stuff oozed out. While he was studying these samples, I was left in the lab with the remains of it. What did it do? It promptly wriggled itself back into a hole in the air and was gone. Pfft! It took Geoff a lot of boot-licking to not have the department closed down. Anyway, he was ordered to do more work and come up with results."

Sarah went on to tell Marion about the meeting at Whitehall and the photos of the cow being dismembered.

"Ugh, I don't need so many details when I'm eating roast beef," said Marion, putting her knife and fork back down across the edge of her plate.

"Have you been invited to join 'DragonMan's' genealogy forum?" asked Sarah.

"Yes, Rachael told me about it on the phone. I haven't signed up yet. I will, later."

"You are using a phone?" asked Sarah in surprise. "Do you realise that this is 'topic of the month' down at GCHQ?"

"It's okay, I have an untraceable phone," replied Marion.

"I wouldn't count on that, Doctor Calvin," said Sarah. "I wouldn't make a call from an 'untraceable phone' if the spooks were watching me."

"I am very careful," said Marion. "I never use it indoors or in my car."

"They could break into your house and fit a bug inside the phone itself. I've seen them, they are tiny."

"I did have a visit from 'someone' a few weeks ago. They rifled through my papers. It was after that that I got the throwaway phone. Obviously, it is time to throw it away and get a fresh one."

"Good plan," said Sarah.

"I'll tell Rachael to do the same," said Marion.

"What, Rachael has had a 'visit' too?"

"Oh, yes. She told me all about them bursting into her home. I would have been petrified."

"Well look, I'll get myself one of those phones at the supermarket and hide it away. I'll find some way to get the number to you surreptitiously, via Rachael perhaps. I do believe that we have to pool our resources before this all gets out of hand. If we leave it to the politicians, anything could happen. They are likely to call in the army and try to blow the thing up, like the rebel fighters did in the desert. Who knows what would happen if we were to use explosives on a rift in space? Maybe open it permanently and have God knows what pour through."

Marion shivered at the thought.

"Now, I am still supposed to have an 'official' meeting with you," said Sarah, "I have to write a report for Geoff and those above him. Can we agree now on what we will, and will not, discuss?"

"I'll tell you what we mustn't talk about," said Marion, "just so that the conversation doesn't drift in that direction. I have commissioned a 4-D computer model plotting incidences by time and place. I have quite a lot of the data already. When there is enough of a spread to do something meaningful, we will run the program and see what we come up with. Hopefully, we will spot a pattern and be able to predict where the thing will turn up next."

"If only you could include the GCHQ data, it would be very helpful. I don't think that they will be producing any 4-D models.'

"How could we do that?" asked Marion. "GCHQ are not going to pass that data over to me, or anyone else."

Sarah's eyes glinted.

"Maybe I know a way."

Chapter 42 - Fanshawe

Sarah showed her pass at the barrier into the GCHQ car park and the attendant directed her to the appropriate parking area. Her meeting with Toby Fanshawe was at eleven and she was a few minutes early. At eleven o'clock on the dot, Fanshawe came to reception to collect her personally. The inside of the building swept in a huge curve. There was a deck along the outside wall and another against the inside wall. In between, a circular well punctuated with palm trees acted like the common floor space in a shopping mall.

"I expected to see banks of servers and satellite dishes," said Sarah.

"Oh, we have plenty of those," said Fanshawe. "This is the iconic 'Doughnut' building. When GCHQ is mentioned in the press, you always get a photo of this place but it's only a small part of the organisation. I'm considered to be an administrator, so my office is here. They crossed a walkway over the well between the outer and inner rings.

Sarah didn't like the way he took every opportunity to touch her as they wove between the open-plan work spaces.

"Here we are, Sarah. Go in and have a seat. I'll be with you in two ticks."

Fanshawe's office overlooked the large, inner green-space. Sarah stood by the window and admired it. He came back in with two plastic cups of coffee and set one down in front of her.

"Oh, this is very nice," said Sarah. "Quite different from the dump where I work."

"I find it a bit soulless myself," said Fanshawe, "glass and concrete is not my thing. Anyway Sarah, what was it you wanted to talk about?"

Sarah took a sip of the coffee. It was horrible and had sugar in it, but she tried not to show her disgust. She set it down.

"It's a bit delicate," she continued, "The Right Honourable Ewan Cummings and his sidekick Charles Millar are leaning on my boss, Geoff Hamilton, to bust his gut on this remaining material we have in cold-store at the lab. I can see that it is beginning to take its toll on him. I don't like those bully-boy techniques, especially when we are up against something that is way beyond our comprehension."

Fanshawe stroked his chin.

"What could you possibly want of me? I couldn't intervene, even if I wanted to."

"Those photos that you got from Inner Mongolia. Is there any way that you could let me have copies?" asked Sarah. "I mean, high resolution copies, not prints. You said that your people had enhanced them, or something. Geoff wants to study them really closely."

"Sarah, all you had to do was put a request through normal channels. You didn't have to come down here personally."

Sarah scratched her nose.

"Okay, but there's something else. Could you let me have the time and location of any other incidents that have come in?"

"Wait a minute, hold your horses," said Fanshawe agitatedly, "that is highly classified information. I could lose my job, or worse."

"Oh dear," Sarah said to herself, "looks like I'm going to have to play my trump card."

Sarah eased her skirt up over her knees.

"I would be ever so grateful," she said, with a pout.

Fanshawe loosened his collar.

"How grateful?"

Sarah rolled her tongue around her lips. She had never had to do the seductress thing before, never having had any trouble attracting handsome young men. Her secretive demeanour must surely have been a turn off though, because none of them ever stuck around for long.

Fanshawe was in his mid-forties, had a beer belly and pock-marks on his face. Not what you would call 'catch-of-the-day'. Had he been younger and more fetching, her ploy might have backfired, but she thought she had him summed up just about right, a 'dirty old man'.

"Well, I'm sure that we can come to some … arrangement … Sarah. Give me a few days to put some things together. You can come down here again and pick them up and maybe I could buy you dinner?"

"That would be very nice," she said with a

straight face. "Why don't you give me a call when you're ready?"

She ran her finger slowly along his desk while looking him straight in the eye. She had seen it being done in the movies many times. The hardest part was to stop herself bursting out with laughter.

She felt quite proud of herself as she drove back down the A40. She thought that she had played the 'femme fatale' part to a tee. When she saw the road sign saying 'Oxford', it reminded her that she must get back in touch with Marion.

When she got back to the lab, she told Geoff that she had managed to get the Mongolian photos and that they would be emailed to his encrypted mailbox from GCHQ. Somehow, she forgot to mention the rest.

There was a text on her phone when she reached home that night. She assumed it had been sent by Rachael, from the 'Out of Area' in the 'From' box. It was just a number, broken up into small groups. It didn't look like a telephone number; the sequence and spacing weren't right and it was a mixture of numbers and letters. After a few seconds, she realised that it was a mobile telephone number. It had been entered backwards with letters in between each number pair. This was pure Enid Blyton. That wouldn't fool any real code breaker. She wrote it down the right way around, omitting the letters, and deleted the text from her phone. When she rang the number, Marion was on the other end.

"Hello," she said, hoping that Marion would recognise her voice without her having to explicitly say her name.

"Oh, lovely to hear from you my dear. How are you? I haven't seen you for ages."

"Marion, you are good," she said to herself.

"Auntie, I have those old photographs and drawings I promised to get you."

"Really, that is marvellous. You must pop around for tea."

"I can't make it this week, Auntie. I'll give you another call next week."

"I can't wait to see you again. I'm looking forward to it."

Sarah hung up. If anyone was listening in at either end, the conversation was not going to give anything away. She remembered that she had to get a pre-paid phone from the supermarket.

Chapter 43 - Ratface

The Mongolian photos arrived next day in Geoff's encrypted mailbox. He and Sarah spent a couple of hours looking at them blown-up on the big screen in the meeting room. Geoff did some amateurish sketches in a notebook and started writing notes around them. They agreed that the two limbs with small blobs on the end were likely to be eyes, or something that served the same purpose. They tried to count the other limbs. There were about eighteen, but they couldn't manage an exact number as they twisted and mingled, changing from shot to shot. The area around where each limb protruded looked very much like a meniscus curve, as seen on the surface of water and caused by surface tension.

"It reminds me of looking though a bullseye pane in a leaded window," said Geoff.

"Yes, I see what you mean," agreed Sarah.

"Well, I think that we have exhausted the possibilities now," said Geoff. "I can't see anything else that adds to our comprehension at the minute."

Sarah was having lunch at her desk, as she often did, when her outside line rang.

"Hello Sarah, it's Toby. I have those figures that you wanted. When will you be able to come and collect them?"

"Is Friday alright for you?" she asked.

"Yes, Friday is perfect. Don't come to the

headquarters though; meet me at the Coach and Four Inn on Bath Street. Half past twelve?"

"Yes, that's fine," see you then.

"Oh my God, what have I got myself into?" she said to herself. "He will probably have the bedroom upstairs booked already, dirty sod."

"Kevin," she called down the phone.

"Hello ratface," he taunted back.

"Ever the old Frobisher charmer. You never change, Kev."

When they were children, Kevin came across the term 'ratface' somewhere and used it on his sister. It produced a violent reaction, so he continued to use it mercilessly. Over the years, the actual words became meaningless, just an intimate expression of love for his sister.

"You only ever ring me when you want me to do something for you," said Kevin, accusingly.

"Now, you know that's not true," said Sarah, sounding hurt at the suggestion.

"So, what is it this time?" he asked.

"How would you like to make a couple of hundred towards that new bike?"

The line went quiet.

"Make it three hundred and I'll do anything," he replied. "As long as it doesn't involve drugs, I'm through with that shit."

"What?" shouted Sarah. "You … drugs?"

"Forget it, what do you want ratface?"

"A little job that involves a pub. Interested?"

"Keep talking. Which pub are we talking about?"

"The Coach and Four."

"In Salisbury?" asked Kevin.

"Err, no. Cheltenham."

"What? That's miles away."

"It's not all that far, and you do enjoy a trip on your bike, my dearest brother."

Sarah knew that any form of sloppiness was as repugnant to him, just as the term 'ratface' would be to anyone else.

There was another brief silence.

"It'll cost you another fifty for petrol."

Sarah was about to scream but she was in a troublesome situation and knew she had little choice.

"Okay then, you little robber. Now listen very carefully, here's what I want you to do…"

Chapter 44 - Bubbly

Sarah took a last look in her bathroom mirror. She flicked her long hair onto her shoulders. It was usually clipped-up at the back for work. She squeezed her lips together to spread the bright red lipstick. She hardly ever wore lipstick, only the slightest hint of eye liner. With her hands, she smoothed down her short skirt. It was years since she last wore it, in her rollicking student days. The skin-tight, low-cut top she had never worn before. She bought it in a sale once, on a whim. She tried it on when she got home, and decided that it was much too immodest for her.

"Wow, Sarah Frobisher. You are a stunner. Even though I say so myself."

Sarah had told Geoff that she had a meeting with Dr Calvin in Oxford. That was partly true, but that was for later. Now she had the part of a leading lady to play.

Half way to Cheltenham, she started having second thoughts.

"I know what's going to happen," she said to herself. "Cheap bottle of fizz, fish and chips and then upstairs for a quick game of 'hide the sausage'. Oh, I know your type Mr Toby Bastard Fanshawe."

She drove past the pub, turned into a side street and found a vacant parking space. One more glance in the car mirror and she was ready.

No, she wasn't.

"No, no, no. I don't want to do this," she thought. However, she then quickly and resolutely grabbed her purse and got out of the car, locking it behind her before she could change her mind.

Fanshawe was already sitting in the veranda dining area working his way through a bottle of Prosecco Spumante. He stood up and waved her over.

"Oh, poppet, you do look wonderful," he said, leering up and down her body and undressing her with his eyes.

"Hello Toby. Nice to see you again."

She gave him her best smile and a quick peck on the cheek.

Yuck!

"Here, have a glass of bubbly," he said, pouring the wine into a long flute glass.

She sat down on the cushioned, wrought iron chair.

"How are you my dear? I must say, you do look absolutely ravishing. Now look, I have something here for you."

He opened his wallet and slid a micro SD card out of a credit card pocket. He placed it on the table, pushing it down hard with his finger.

"This is for you … later," he said, running the tip of his tongue over his top lip. He set his glass down on top of the memory card.

Sarah could see it through the clear base of the

glass. So near. So far.

"I didn't realise you were such a … bobby-dazzler, Sarah. You looked such a Plain Jane in your work clothes."

"Thank you very much," said Sarah, indignantly.

"Oh sorry, I didn't mean that, Sarah," he said, patting the back of her hand. "It's just that the transformation is quite remarkable."

A young waitress interrupted with menus. Probably just as well, as Sarah had enough of the lecher already.

"What's actually on the memory card?" she asked.

"Just some spreadsheets. Dates. Locations. That sort of thing."

He lifted his glass momentarily to let her have a tantalising peek.

"It's for you. Afterwards," he smiled.

Sarah stuck her forefinger into the glass of wine, and put it into her mouth provocatively.

"I think that we are going to get along just fine," said Fanshawe.

He shook off a slip-on shoe and put his foot against her inner leg under the table. She jumped.

"Sorry, did I frighten you, poppet?" he asked. "My apologies."

Sarah smiled sweetly. This was all going too fast.

Fanshawe was sliding his glass around the table with the memory card trapped inside its base. He would move it towards Sarah tantalisingly, and then pull it away again.

He stared at her. She felt a shiver run down her

spine.

Just then, a loud voice came from behind.

"Hey mister, what you doing with my tart?"

Fanshawe swung around to see two bikers in heavy, studded leather jackets bearing down on him. He stood up to face them.

"Fuck off," he said waving them away.

The big biker with the tattooed face went nose to nose with him. He froze.

"What was that you just said, pigface?"

Fanshawe backed away, tripping over his chair and sprawled across the floor. There was a gasp from the other diners. A waitress rushed over to help him to his feet but recoiled when she saw the burly bikers looming over her.

Sarah seized the opportunity. She moistened her finger again, picked up the micro SD card with just a touch, and slipped it into her purse.

The two bikers then lifted Sarah off her chair unceremoniously and manhandled her towards the door.

"Home, bitch," said the smaller one, still wearing his helmet. He turned around and pointed his finger at Fanshawe menacingly.

"Toby, Toby, help me!" shouted Sarah, in her best damsel-in-distress voice. She could hear Kevin sniggering, even through his helmet.

Fanshawe was not interested. Tackling two brutes in studded leather gear was not his game.

The memory card!

He suddenly realised that he couldn't see his

precious micro SD card. He instinctively patted his pocket, but realised that that was plain silly. He lifted the glasses, the coasters underneath and everything else that was on the table. It wasn't there. He pulled out the chairs and got down under the table on his hands and knees, patting the floor with both hands. The floor was grooved wood decking with narrow gaps between the planks. Fanshawe tried to look down though the gaps. It was no good. There was no way he was going to retrieve his tiny memory card from down there. Nobody else could either, not until they refitted the pub anyway. Even then, it was so small and thin, nobody would find it.

He brushed himself down and made a quick exit. The waitress ran after him.

When Sarah got back into her car, she took some wipes from her glove compartment. She couldn't meet Marion Calvin looking like that; she would get the wrong idea. She retrieved a jacket from her car boot to cover up the skimpy top, and put it on. She clipped her hair back, like it usually was.

There, semi-respectable.

* * * * *

Marion opened her front door and promptly pulled it closed behind her.

"Ah, my dear niece."

Sarah did a double take. "Niece?" Then, she remembered that she had called her 'Auntie' on the phone.

Marion took her by the arm and led her over to the car park.

"Where are we going?" asked Sarah.

"I promised you a cream tea," said the smiling doctor.

"Lovely," said Sarah. She only had two sips of wine for lunch and was feeling a bit peckish.

"Maybe just a sandwich."

"It's lovely to see you again, Sarah," said Marion.

A little doorbell tinkled as they entered the quaint tea shop.

They sat down at an empty table.

Look, I have something for you."

Sarah handed Marion a paperback romantic novel across the small table.

"What's this?" asked Marion, in surprise.

"Open it," instructed Sarah.

Marion flicked through the pages of the book and then back again. She stopped at a page that had a slit through it, holding the small memory card. She pushed it lightly with her finger.

"I'm not sure what this is," said Marion. "Is it a SIM card?"

"No, it's a micro SD card. It has some spreadsheets on it with the details you were looking for."

"I don't think that my old computer can handle these. I'll have to give it to my programmer chappie, Brian. He's the one that's coding the 4-D model."

"I haven't seen what is on it myself," explained Sarah. Then a horrible thought occurred to her. What if it was blank? What if Fanshawe was expecting to do the dirty deed and leave her holding an empty memory card? She wouldn't put it past him. Then other disturbing thoughts crossed her mind. What if she had to sit in a business meeting again with him? What if he rang and wanted her to conclude her part of the deal at a later date with threats of blackmail. She shivered.

"Are you all right, Sarah? It's not too cold so near the window?"

"No, I'm alright," replied Sarah. "Just someone walking over my grave."

"With this new data, and what I have already from other contacts, I think that we will be able to do some preliminary testing with the modelling software. After we've had our afternoon tea, I will take you over to meet Brian.

* * * * *

As Marion and Sarah strolled through the computer lab, there were rows and rows of desks with blank screens on them. A few had students tapping at the keyboards, but it was empty for the most part.

"Doesn't look very busy," commented Sarah.

"It's nearly five o'clock, they will all be down at the Student's Union bar by now. I hope that Brian is still here."

She tapped on a door. Brian opened it.

"Hello Brian, is it safe to talk?"

"Yes, Doctor Calvin, come in."

"This is Doctor Sarah Frobisher. She is a biologist and is helping me with my little project."

Brian shook Sarah's hand limply.

"Can you deal with one of these?" said Marion, handing him the small memory card.

"Micro SD, yes, I think that I have an adaptor somewhere."

He went over to a drawer and rifled through it.

"Here we are. Not much call for these around here. They are normally only used in consumer cameras."

Brian slipped the card into an adaptor and plugged it into a USB socket on a computer on his desk.

"What are we expecting to find on this?" he asked.

"Spreadsheets," said Sarah.

She breathed a sigh of relief when the files appeared on Brian's screen with the .XLS extension. Brian clicked on one. It took a while to open.

"Large file," said Brian, "here we are."

"I think that this spreadsheet has been generated by some sort of database program. It isn't formatted as I would expect for a spreadsheet. Don't worry, I can massage it and import it into my database as a comma-delimited file."

"What is on it, Brian?" asked Sarah.

"You mean that you don't know?" asked the programmer, looking at her quizzically.

"Does it have dates, locations, things like that?"

"Oh, yes. GPS locations, Longitude and Latitude co-ordinates, timestamps and what seem to be cross-referencing indices. There also seems to be a lot of text."

"That's what I was hoping for," sighed Sarah. So, Fanshawe had fulfilled his end of the bargain! There was hope for him yet. Bastard!

"Just leave this with me," said Brian. "I should have something workable in a few days. It's just a matter of stealing some processing time."

Chapter 45 - Whitehall

Sarah drove straight home after her meeting with Marion and Brian. It had been a trying day. First thing she did was to have a long, hot shower. Fanshawe hadn't touched her, but she still felt dirty.

Sitting in her living room in her bathrobe with a towel wrapped around her head, it occurred to her to ring Kevin. He had played his part on-cue, and with relish.

"Yo Bro," she said. "Thanks for your help today, I owe you."

"Hi ratface. Yes, you do owe me. Three hundred and fifty smackers if I remember correctly, and I want it in cash."

"Yes Kevin, whatever."

"Who was that bloke?" asked Kevin. "I think that Colin scared the shit out of him."

"So, that was your friend Colin? Looks like a hard man."

"Ah, no. Colin is a pussy cat. Would you believe that he works in a florist's?"

"Um, no," said Sarah. "Really?"

"Naw, I'm just kidding. He doesn't work at all. Lives on benefits."

"Now that I do believe," she replied. "I'll get your cash on Saturday. You can pop around on Saturday night or Sunday for it."

"Can I come for dinner?"

"I suppose, it's as easy to make for two as one,"

she said.

"Can you make for three?" he asked.

"You're not planning to bring Colin are you?"

"Oh, no. My new girlfriend, Suzie."

"Another new girlfriend, Colin? That's the third in a few weeks."

"Ah, that's the Frobisher charm that we were talking about. Works every time. No, this time it's the real thing."

Sarah sighed as she rang off. Every one of Kevin's girlfriends had been 'the real thing'.

* * * * *

"Morning Sarah," said Geoff Hamilton. "Don't take your coat off; we have a meeting at Whitehall at twelve. We are cutting it a bit fine."

"Oh no, thought Sarah, "That Fanshawe man will be there. Maybe he's been rumbled, passing on restricted data to a third party."

She worried about it during the whole drive into London. Luckily, Geoff was driving in his big Merc and they made it with fifteen minutes to spare.

When they were shown into the meeting room, she expected to see Fanshawe leering at her as usual. He wasn't there. Beside Cummings and Millar was a new face. A woman.

"This is Sandra Tomkins from GCHQ. She has taken over from Toby Fanshawe," said Cummings.

"What happened to Mr Fanshawe?" asked Sarah.

"Toby Fanshawe is no longer with the

department," said the new woman. "He was arrested on Friday trying to rip up the flooring in some pub. He seems to have flipped completely. We won't be needing him anymore."

Sarah let out a deep breath.

"What this meeting is about," said Charles Millar, "is that we have agreed with a number of other nations, that all future sightings, reports of takings, or mutilations, or any related activity, will be handled by their respective National Security agencies. We are also putting pressure on countries that have not agreed to the clamp down to do so as quickly as possible. It's not easy to get a truly international agreement on anything, but this is in everybody's interest. Last thing we want is for some loonies with placards calling for hands off this rare, protected species. We really don't know what we are dealing with here. It turns up completely at random, kills people and livestock and skedaddles back to wherever it comes from. As far as we are concerned, there is no such place. It is totally beyond human comprehension."

"Do your biologists have anything to add?" asked Cummings.

Geoff straightened up.

"As far as we are concerned, it is not biological. There are no signs of cellular structures, no DNA. It could be a machine for all I know."

"I don't think that we had considered that possibility," said Millar, looking over at Cummings. "Interesting thought. Maybe we need engineers rather than biologists?"

"Or quantum physicists?" suggested Sarah. Then she realised that one of Rachael's team in the USA was one. She didn't want to go there.

"Yes," nodded Cummings. "I'll look into it. Anyway, Doctor Hamilton and Miss Frobisher, thank you for your contribution, it has been immensely helpful. You can go back to your normal work now, there's nothing more you can do on this case."

"Damn," thought Sarah. "So I've been fired. Just when I thought it was getting interesting too. My excuses to talk to Marion and Rachael are not going to wash from now on. Have to be careful."

On the drive back to Wiltshire, Geoff admitted that he was glad that the responsibility had been passed on to some other department. He was fed up with getting nowhere with a whip at his back. Sarah said that she had enjoyed the intrigue while it lasted, but would be happy to get back to normal. That wasn't true, she was going to get even more involved than she could possibly imagine. They may try to cover things up, but sooner or later, it would all come to a head.

Chapter 46 - Suzie

"Hello Suzie," said Sarah." So lovely to meet you."

The small, overweight, black-haired girl had more face-furniture than Sarah had ever seen outside a horror movie. Rings and piercings everywhere … and that was only the visible parts of her body! She was dressed mostly in black. Black top, with the 'Triumph' logo across it, black leather jacket, black tights, black boots and a short red tartan skirt. The lapel of her jacket was covered with 'metal' badges – skulls, spiders and bike logos. Had there been a few witches on broomsticks, it could have been a tribute to Halloween.

"Hi Sarah," said the girl. "Kev's told me lots about you."

From behind her, Kevin crossed his fingers over his mouth and wiggled them, twitching his nose at the same time. Sarah knew damned fine what he was getting it. Ratface, indeed! She hated that name, but it had become a term of endearment as far as he was concerned, but not to anyone else in earshot.

Kevin put the two motorcycle helmets down on the hallway floor and gave Suzie a sneaky kiss.

"You like lasagne?" asked Sarah.

"Is that like pizza?" asked Suzie. "Yeah, nice."

"No, it's not pizza Suzie. It's sheets of pasta with Bolognese and Béchamel sauce in between and melted cheese on top."

"Oh, yeah, think I've had that. Nice. I don't want

any of that salad stuff though. You can give that to the rabbit."

She snorted at her own joke.

"You mean the rat?" giggled Kevin.

Suzie looked around at him with a baffled look.

"Would you like a glass of wine?" asked Sarah.

"Got any lager?" asked Suzie.

"I'll have a look," said Sarah scornfully, looking in the fridge.

"I have some lager in the cupboard, but it's not chilled," she said.

"Don't matter," said Suzie, through her gum chewing. "It's okay like that."

Sarah fetched a can of lager and gave it to Suzie, along with a glass. Suzie looked at the glass as if she had never seen one before, put it down, pulled the ring-top and drank from the can.

"I'll have a glass of red wine please, Sarah," said Kevin.

"You know where it is, Bro. Help yourself."

Kevin headed for the fridge.

"If you want red, Kevin, it won't be in the fridge." She pointed to the cupboard.

"I always keep red wine in the fridge, what's wrong with that?" asked Kevin.

Sarah rubbed her forehead and didn't answer. She had never known Kevin to drink wine of any colour. He was just trying his best to impress Suzie, but his ploy was completely wasted. Suzie didn't have a clue – about anything.

Sarah couldn't understand how Suzie could eat with all the lip-rings and the tongue stud. She was clearly well practiced and quickly put her portion of lasagne away, without it touching the sides.

"Would you like some more?" asked Sarah, when she spied the empty plate. "There's another portion left. The dish is meant to serve four and there are only three of us."

Suzie looked over at Kevin.

"I'll share it with you," he offered.

"That must be love," thought Sarah.

Sarah served them half of the remaining portion each. She absent-mindedly passed the salad bowl across to Suzie, but it was pushed aside as she washed the last forkful of lasagne down with a slug of lager from the can.

"Nice!"

Suzie got up from the table and pulled another can of lager from the cupboard without asking. Sarah ignored her rudeness. Suzie crashed down on the sofa and carried on drinking.

"Got any fags?" asked Suzie.

"Sorry, I don't smoke," replied Sarah.

Suzie raised her eyes.

"Kev's stopped smoking, you know" she said.

"I didn't know you smoked?" Sarah asked Kevin.

"Not really, just the odd spliff. Just to be sociable, you know how it is."

Sarah shook her head in dismay.

"So, what are you guys up to this weekend?" she asked.

"Springvale Rock festival, over near Swindon," said Kevin. "We have tickets and we are dying to see the headliners, 'The Deadly Dark Destroyers'."

"What? Where do they get these names? What kind of music is it anyway?"

"Thrash Metal," said Kevin. "They're the top band."

"Great," said Sarah, trying to feign enthusiasm, but not with a great deal of success.

"Have you got my wad?" asked Kevin.

"Wad?"

"The three-fifty you promised."

"Oh, yes Kevin. I have."

She pulled a roll of banknotes from a biscuit tin in the cupboard.

"Don't go spending it on silly things," she said.

"Don't refer to Suzie like that, it's not nice," he laughed.

Suzie scowled and slapped him around the head.

"I hope you are going to share that with Colin?" asked Sarah.

"Oh, yes. I'll slip him a pony."

"Twenty-five quid, you are very generous," she said sarcastically.

"You think that's too much?" said Kevin, grinning. "If you ever need any little jobs like that doing again, you know where I am."

Sarah folded her arms and grimaced.

"Well, I hope that the weather is alright for your festival," she said, "those things so often turn into mud baths."

"Nothing wrong with a bit of mud," sneered Kevin. "Come on Suzie. Bring a couple of cans with you from the cupboard."

Sarah raised her hand to complain, but then thought better of it. These two were made for each other. She glanced over at the heap of dirty plates and dishes on the draining board. Sighing, she shook her head and collapsed into an armchair, exhausted both physically and emotionally.

Chapter 47 - Festival

The thump of a bass guitar could be heard a good two miles from the Springvale Rock Festival site. As festivals go it was not a large one, yet there were easily a couple of thousand standing around the three sound stages. It wasn't raining, but the clouds above looked ominous.

Kevin and Suzie pulled into the secure motorcycle paddock. They didn't want to be carrying their helmets around all day so left them at an enterprising cloakroom van and got receipts. The only things they were carrying were cans of lager.

Kevin pulled a program from his inside pocket and scanned it. He handed it over to Suzie.

"I've never heard of any of these bands," she complained.

"There won't be any bands that you've heard of until later in the day. These will just be warm up acts. They'll be playing for free I reckon, just so they can say that they've played live at a rock festival."

They wandered around the site. The three stages had huge television screens at each side showing close-ups of the performers on stage. Only a lucky few got anywhere near the front of stage and the sound levels were painful. Kevin could feel the low bass shake his entire body, just as if he was sitting astride some heavy machinery. People all around them were standing shaking their heads up and down to the beat. Some were playing air guitars as the lead guitarist broke into a screeching solo.

"He's quite good," said Suzie. "What's the name of the band?"

Kevin looked at his program.

"That must be 'The Heavy Babies' according to this. Have to watch out for them."

On the next stage, three people were playing synths with a heavy techno beat.

"Aaagh," said Kevin. "Call that rock? That's bloody techno pop. If I wanted to hear that, I would go to a disco."

"Disco?" asked Suzie. "Do they still have discos?"

"Oh, believe me, they do," scowled Kevin. "There was one every Christmas at my school. I bet they still have them."

He stuck his tongue out as far as it would go.

"Let's see what's in those tents," suggested Suzie.

As they went off to explore, the drizzle started.

"Mike and Ian," shouted Ken through his headset microphone, "get those cameras covered up. I think we're in for a downpour."

"Way ahead of you there, Ken," replied the camera operator.

"I'm at the side of the stage, won't get rained on here," said Ian.

The rain got heavier. The bands played on. Only a few festival goers headed for the tents, the rest just braved it and head-banged on.

Ken and Maggie were in the control van with rows of monitors above them and a large mixing desk in front. Dougie, the director, paced up and down behind them. The rain was only just apparent in the close-ups, the longer shots showed its full ferocity, as diagonal lines against the spotlights.

"I'm glad we're not out there," said Maggie. "I think I need a notch on the sound feed to filter out the rain noise."

"Difficult to filter out that," said Dougie. "White noise spans the full audio frequency spectrum."

Maggie twiddled with the knobs on her audio mixer.

"That's a little better," she said.

"It's really throwing it down, now," said Dougie, edging the production truck door open just a crack. "It's got very dark too."

Kevin and Suzie were in a beer tent. It wasn't to buy beer; they still had three cans each remaining from their six-packs.

"It's getting very muddy out there," he said.

"You told Sarah that you didn't mind a bit of mud," grinned Suzie.

"That was when I wasn't up to my knees in it," he replied.

A flash of lightning was followed by the reverberation of thunder five seconds later.

"That was a mile away," said Kevin.

"How do you know?" asked Suzie.

"Five seconds for every mile, didn't you learn that at school?"

Suzie smiled her 'are you mad' smile.

"Must have been off that day."

"You were off most days," said Kevin.

She gave him a shove.

The beer tent was getting very full.

"If you aren't buying beer, outside," said a gruff voice.

Kevin and Suzie were pushed through the tent flap into the rain and were instantly soaked.

"Oh, my new boots," moaned Suzie. "They'll be ruined."

There was another flash of lightning. The peal of thunder followed two seconds later.

"It's getting closer," said Kevin. They could see lightning bolts arc across above the trees in the near distance.

Back in the production truck, Dougie was getting worried.

"The thunderstorm is headed towards us," he said. "If lightning hits one of those lighting rigs, we're in big trouble. I've seen it happen before. Melted the bloody thing to a slag-heap and took out all the generators too."

"Shouldn't they shut down until the storm passes?" asked Maggie.

"They should, but they won't. It would take The Ride of the Valkyries to stop a rock festival."

"Listen to that, the static in the air is playing havoc with the sound system," said Maggie.

"What's that screeching noise?" asked Dougie, "are the sound crew having problems with feedback?"

"I can hear what sounds like screaming through the crackling in my cans," said Maggie. "I think there must be a lot of people frightened by thunder and lightning out there."

Ken looked up at a monitor above him. The outside broadcast cameras showed lots of terrified faces.

"Look at them. I've never seen anyone so scared of a bit of rain."

Just then, one camera swung around to give a wide shot of the crowd. Some people were pointing into the sky and others were trying to run, but not getting anywhere because of the mud and mass of people.

"What the hell's going on?" asked Dougie, opening the production truck door. There were two lightning flashes in quick succession accompanied by an ear-splitting bang. In the illumination of the lightning, he saw something unbelievable. Hanging above the crowd were a number of rippling haloes, too many to count. Things like whips were coming out of the haloes and lashing at the crowd. Bolts of lightning rippled along their lengths and arced between them. The whips were hitting the people below and causing them to collapse. However, before they could even hit the ground, they were being whisked up into the air. They were disappearing into the sky.

"Mike, Ian, Chris, are you getting this?"

The music suddenly stopped.

The monitors were full of close-up and wide shots of the carnage outside. Festival goers were being yanked off their feet and whisked into oblivion.

"My God," said Maggie, "what the fuck is happening?"

"I've no idea," said Ken, wrestling with his vision sliders.

The monitors were giving fleeting glimpses of the wet ground and the dark sky. In between, was a crowd in sheer panic, with people running about in all directions. Long black shapes whipped through the air, wrapping themselves around terror-stricken people. A woman's face with red welts across it filled a monitor briefly and was gone. Another was dangling upside down in the air, long shapes slithering around her legs. She then vanished into a hole in the sky.

A blood-curdling scream came over Ken's headphones. In the monitor showing Mike's camera feed, a writhing mass of black snakes and blue sparks hauled the camera and its operator upwards. The monitor flashed and then briefly showed an unidentifiable setting. The camera feed died. There was a strong smell of ozone.

Ken put his hands over his head.

"Whatever those things were, I think that they got Mike."

Maggie fainted in her chair.

* * * * *

Sarah saw that the phone call was from Kevin and answered.

"What's wrong Kev, getting wet? I saw on the weather forecast that there were thunderstorms headed for the Swindon area."

"Sarah," came the breathless voice on the phone. Kevin never ever called her 'Sarah', so she knew that something must be wrong.

"That thing in the photos I picked up for you, from the Cobham fête, it was here with its mates. Dozens of them. They electrocuted lots of people and snatched them off the ground in front of my eyes. It was horrible."

He started crying.

"Are you alright?" asked Sarah. "Are you and Suzie okay?"

"Yes, we are fine. The thunder and lightning has passed and the things in the sky are gone. It's such a mess here. There's mud and bodies all over the place."

"Bodies?" gasped Sarah.

"Well, not bodies, it's bits of human beings, to be more accurate. They were literally ripped apart, those that weren't taken. We've headed back for the bike. It's hard to move. Everybody is heading out at the same time. The turn-styles have been pushed over. Cars are stuck in the mud. It's utter mayhem."

"Kevin, you get back here as fast as you can!"

Sarah rang off.

"Let the bastards try to hush this one up," she whispered.

Chapter 48 - Interviews

The Springvale Festival site was empty of rocking people. Most of the spotlights were switched off. A few roadies humped heavy amplifiers towards flight-cases in the wings. A fleet of ambulances and police cars were parked around the periphery in the dark.

In the television truck, Ken and Dougie were reviewing the footage.

"We need to get this edited quickly and put on the uplink," said Dougie. "The police want us off the site immediately."

"But, we can't show people being killed," said Ken as he fast-forwarded through some clips.

"No," said Dougie. "Let me see the interviews."

Ken scrolled through the clips quickly and stopped at a shot of a man with a microphone stuck in front of him. He pressed 'play'.

"It was utter carnage," said the man, "whatever those things were, they had a feeding frenzy. People were just plucked into the air screaming, and then vanished from view. I didn't know what was happening. It was like being in a real, live horror movie."

"Right, we'll have that one," said Dougie. "Any more?"

A sobbing girl stood in front of a microphone, biting her fingernails nervously.

"My friend Janine was standing beside me. Next thing, these black tentacles wrap around her and she was pulled upwards. I don't know what happened to her. One minute she was there, the next she was gone. I think I'm going to be sick." She turned her head around and retched onto the muddy ground.

"Trim off the vomiting, the rest is good," said Dougie. "What else?"

A couple of very muddy goths were propping each other up in front of a microphone.

"It was crazy," said the male. "I've never had a trip like it."

He staggered. The girl was more forthcoming.

"There were these ripples in the air. They were like the surface of water. I saw a mass of wriggling black snakes come out of them and latch on to people in the crowd in front of me. I didn't know where to run, they were everywhere. I saw this bloke with a television camera. They got hold of him and his camera, and wrenched him up into one of the ripples. They must have pulled him inside. I saw the camera cable snap and fall to the ground."

"Oh, Mike!" said Ken. He looked around at Dougie.

"That's good," said Dougie. "It's in."

Ken marked the clip and went on to a wide shot of people in panic. A few shimmers floated above them, but nobody was being visibly taken.

"Okay, Ken. Get that lot on the uplink as soon as you can," said Dougie, and left the truck.

Ken put his hand across his forehead. This wasn't right. They had just witnessed a sickening cataclysmic disaster and all Dougie had on his mind was ratings.

* * * * *

Steve Markham's phone rang.

"Hello? Oh, Tony. How's it going?"

"Steve," said Tony Bishop, "have you seen the evening news?"

"No, Tony, I've been watching a movie."

"You had better have a look at the News Channel. Now, Steve!"

Steve picked up his television remote control and flicked through to the 24-Hour News Channel. He could read the captions running across the bottom of the screen before he understood what was going on.

'Slaughter at Springvale Rock Festival. Dozens dead and missing.'

Then, there was a very brief shot of a crowd of panicking people. Just above their heads, there were writhing tentacles.

"Oh, no! Not again."

Chapter 49 - Aftermath

"Marion, I've just seen the news. It was terrible. That's the second incident within a month. Why England?"

"Yes Rachael, our country is in shock. You ask 'why England?' I think it is to do with the density of population. These 'incidents', as you call them, are happening all over the world every day, but the vast majority go unseen and unreported."

"I think that the whole world is in shock. Governments have been stifling reports on national security grounds so we can't see the full picture. Is Swindon anywhere near you?"

"It's about fifty miles away. It's a place I tend to go past rather than through."

"Those poor people. I just don't know what to say."

"Yes, and here was me arrogantly postulating that there was just one of them," said Marion.

"Do you know how many there were?"

"No. Ten, twenty, thirty, reports vary wildly."

"And the number of victims?"

"They are just saying 'dozens'. They don't even know yet. It could take weeks to account for all the missing people at an event like that. Then, there are the body parts. They will have to use DNA profiling to identify those."

"So, what's going to happen now?" asked Rachael. "Are you getting anywhere with your computer model?"

"I have quite a lot of sighting data, and now this one. We'll be running the program in the next few days. Brian reckons that he has finished writing the program but he is having problems squeezing in the processing time on the clusters. He's having to do it behind the department's back, it's not official University work you see. Although, I suppose that might change now."

"Marion, I'd very much like to come back over to the UK and be part of all this. I feel a responsibility to carry Brad's work forward. He taught me all I know and it's the least I can do. Could you contact that guest house I was in last time, Mrs Todd's, and see if she can fit me in for a week? It was lovely, but if that is booked up, something similar would be okay. It doesn't really matter."

"Yes, of course, Rachael. Mrs Todd is a good friend of mine. I'll see that she finds a room for you even if she has to throw somebody else out. Just let me know when you get your flight booked and I'll fix it up."

Marion had only just rung off when her disposable phone rang again.

"Sarah. I've just been on the phone with Rachael at Stanford. She's coming back over in the next few days because of the developments. I'm sure that she would love to see you again."

"That's great. I'm sure that Geoff won't mind if I snatch a few days' holiday at short notice. Yes, that incident at the rock festival was devastating news.

Truly awful. My brother, Kevin and his girlfriend were actually there and saw the whole thing."

"Oh no! Poor children. An experience like that will scar them for the rest of their lives."

"You don't know those two," said Sarah. "They live a pretty wild lifestyle."

"I'd love to have a talk with them," said Marion.

"Errm, I don't think that is such a good idea," replied Sarah.

"Why not? I am broad minded."

"They are a bit … peculiar. Nose rings, tattoos, that sort of thing. They came back to my place late last night, having rode forty miles on a motorbike in the dark and the worse for wear from drinking, God knows, how many cans of lager."

"I think that an experience like that would soon sober you up," said Marion.

"Anyway," continued Sarah, "we sat up most the night while they told me all about it. They were still in shock. They went over it again and again. I don't think that they left out any detail, no matter how sordid."

"Your brother and his girlfriend must be very brave," said Marion.

"I wouldn't call it bravery, more like crass stupidity knowing those two," said Sarah.

"Well, look Sarah; I'll give you a call when I know when Rachael will be here. We can all meet up for a good old chin-wag."

"Yes, I'd like that," said Sarah. "Now, I'd better go and get those two up and cram some strong coffee down them. Bye."

Suzie was curled up on the sofa and Kevin was wrapped in a sleeping bag on the floor. As soon as Sarah entered the living room, Suzie sat up and rubbed her eyes. She was a mess, having obviously zonked-out just about sunrise. She jumped up and headed for the bathroom.

"Kevin … Kevin, it's time to get up," called Sarah.

Kevin just moaned.

"Kevin, I've made a jug of coffee, it's in the kitchen. I have to go out; I've got shopping to do."

He very reluctantly unpeeled the sleeping bag and got up onto his knees. He gave his head a good shake and slumped onto the edge of the sofa.

"Are you alright?" asked Sarah.

"Yeah, I'll be okay in a minute."

As the mist cleared in his head, the images came flooding back. He rubbed his forehead.

"Ohhh," he groaned.

"Kevin, have some coffee. It will wake you up," said Sarah.

"Don't think that I want to wake up," whimpered Kevin. "Where's Suzie?"

"She's in the bathroom," answered Sarah.

Kevin got up and went over to the bathroom door.

"Hurry up, Suzie. I need the loo."

There was no answer.

Kevin opened the door. Suzie was putting on eye shadow, lots of eye shadow. He went in and closed the door behind hm.

Sarah looked at the state of her living room and sighed.

Chapter 50 - Firmament

Rachael was wheeling her baggage trolley towards the departure gate when two men stepped out in front of her. It was the same two that had come to her house a few days earlier.

"Miss Hartmann, a quick word if you don't mind?"

They took her to an alcove at the side.

"Nothing to be alarmed about, Miss Hartmann, we won't keep you for long."

"What is it now?" asked Rachael.

"We know where you are going, and why. It's not a problem, but my boss would very much like to talk to you when you return."

He handed Rachael a business card. She gave it a quick glance and put it in her top pocket.

"Yes, okay," said Rachael. "I'll be in touch."

"Have a pleasant trip, Miss Hartmann," said the talkative one, waving goodbye.

Rachael was a little shaken, but heard the call for her flight and headed straight for the departure gate.

While she was waiting for the plane to take off, she took the card from her top pocket and read it again.

'Daniel Malloy, Director, United States of America Homeland Security.' It gave an address in San Francisco. She slipped the card into her handbag. If they knew where she was going and why, and didn't stop her, they must be planning to use her as a spy. Did that matter? This was a worldwide security threat, not just a national one.

Rachael looked out the window as they passed over Golden Gate Bridge, banked, and headed eastwards. It would be a ten-hour flight and Rachael had some serious reading to do.

* * * * *

It was strange to be landing in London nearly four hours before she had taken off. It was going to be a long day. From Heathrow, Rachael took the bus to Oxford. It was a lot more convenient than going back into London to catch a train. Marion had told her that after her first trip, and it made sense.

Sure enough, Marion was there waiting for her at Oxford Bus Station, as she said she would. Marion was in a zip-up jacket, tight jeans and black canvas shoes. She dressed like a much younger person.

It was only nine o'clock in the morning in Oxford, so they took a cab back to Mrs Todd's B&B so that Rachael could drop off her luggage and freshen up.

"I could do with a walk to loosen up after that long flight," said Rachael.

"We could have a stroll around the town," suggested Marion. "It's a lovely morning. Then we can have some lunch."

Marion pointed out the various Oxford colleges and told Rachael their history.

"The difference in architecture between this and

Stanford is quite remarkable. Is that sandstone?"

"No," said Marion. "That is St George's Tower. It's eleventh century, considerably older than Stanford. The stone is called 'ragstone' and it was quarried locally. Other buildings around here are faced with Bath or Portland stone."

"Let's sit down for a minute," said Rachael. "You must need a rest?"

"Huh? I do this walk almost every day. We can sit down if you like, but I don't need a rest."

They climbed a short set of steps and sat down on a bench.

"Marion, have you every studied Hebrew astronomy and cosmology?" asked Rachael.

"Not Hebrew specifically, but I do know something of biblical cosmology," said Marion.

"So, you understand the meaning of the word 'firmament'? It is a translation of the Hebrew 'raqia' meaning to beat or spread out, as you would do with a metal worker's hammer. The ancient Hebrews believed that the sky was a solid dome and the Earth a circle, floating on a mystical sea. The stars and planet were simply embedded in this dome and sparkled like the jewels in a crown."

"My understanding of 'firmament'," said Marion," is from Genesis. It is the structure that separates the waters above the Earth from those below. Some Greek philosopher believed that there was a series of eight concentric orbs with the Earth at their centre. The outermost orb contained the celestial bodies and this is what is referred to as 'the firmament'. The inner seven were referred to as 'the seven wanderers of the sky', the planets that gave us the names for the days of the week. Why are we discussing Hebrew and Biblical cosmology?"

"It's just," said Rachael, "that our ancient forefathers had little grasp of science. They tried to explain what was unexplainable with the knowledge that they had at hand. Most cultures have concepts of 'parallel existences', spirit worlds, places where humans can't go in their Earthly guises, but the spirits can visit us. It's all one way. Here we are in the twenty-first century with something equally unexplainable, yet people are spouting out their moronic theories – monsters from another galaxy, time squids and denizens of the mystic seas. Those are only the ones I saw in newspaper headlines back home."

"Yes, we've had something similar here. They are bringing all kinds of so-called experts onto news and talk shows on television – politicians that glibly make promises that everything is under control, military people that say that it is nothing that they can't handle, scientists who really haven't a clue and try to explain it away as mass hallucinations or tricks of the light. Then there are the usual loonies predicting the end of the world, again!"

Rachael gave a grim smile.

"I have my own theories," continued Marion. "But I've had to update them. It didn't occur to me that there could be more than one of these things, but now I seem to have been proven wrong. Two or three at Mount Shasta, 'dozens' at Springvale Farm at Swindon, yet I still have this sneaking suspicion that I might have been correct the first time. There is just no way to prove it one way or the other."

"Marion, how could there be only one of anything? It doesn't make sense. You need at least two to procreate."

"Not so," said Marion, "there are creatures that are asexual. Most lower life forms multiply by simple cell division, but there are fish and reptiles that can produce offspring without any mates. It is feasible that this creature can regenerate itself ad infinitum."

"Have you any idea what size it is?" asked Rachael.

"I have no idea what is beyond the portal. Judging by the relatively small amount that it consumes, it can't be massive. On the other hand, we don't know if it has other hunting grounds beyond our world."

"So, what is your basis for thinking that there is only one? We have seen a multiplicity of them on television at the rock festival."

Marion tried to think of a way to explain her theory. It wasn't easy.

"I think that what we were looking at were multiple instances of the same creature. It has the ability to manipulate time and space. As such, it is quite possible that given the abundance of prey, it takes the opportunity to gorge when it can, by sidestepping what we understand to be 'normal physics'. It can be in multiple places at the same time. I can't prove it; it is just a hunch. I also suspect that the electrical storm over the festival might have had something to do with it. I think that it was able to harness energy from that storm and use it to make additional selves. It sounds ridiculous, doesn't it? Rachael, dear. I hope you are able to humour the rantings of a barmy old scientist. Call me 'mad' if you like, I don't care."

"I think that you are very insightful, Marion. I can see how you and Brad got on so well."

"I don't know about you," said Marion, "physics or no physics, I'm ready for an early lunch. I was up early this morning, but then, so were you. Did you get any sleep on the plane?"

"Just a catnap," said Rachael. "But my body tells me that it is dinner time."

Chapter 51 - Video

Deep in the bowels of the Ministry of Defence building in Whitehall, four people were staring at video monitors in a darkened television suite.

"This is all the raw footage that we got from Swindon," said Charles Millar. "Eric, here has been all through it in detail and has edited out the less interesting stuff. I warn you, what is left is both gruesome and distressing. Parts of it are devastating in implication."

Ewan Cummings spoke.

"Yes, we are not looking at cows this time, these are human beings. Can you roll the tape Eric, in slow-mo?"

Vivian Tyler had forsaken his usual white coat for a suit and tie. He had been briefed on the Rock Festival incident and on the others on record. He dismissed the idea that he was 'an expert', but he was the most distinguished government scientist that there was. He found the images on the monitor quite sickening.

"I've sat through films of concentration camps and the aftermaths of battles, but those had an element of detachment. This is in our own back yard."

They sat in horror as the ripples manifested themselves out of nowhere. The two eye-stalks came through quickly and were followed by a mass of limbs coiling themselves around arms, legs, necks and torsos. Some that didn't get a good hold, pulled back, taking with them clothes, headgear – and body parts. Each victim was pulled back into the rippling maelstrom that divided this world from another. Again, and again the black whips lashed out, like a swarm of serpents, engulfing their helpless prey and taking it into oblivion.

"Just a minute," said the government scientist, "could you just wind back a few seconds?"

Eric turned his jog-shuttle dial and the footage began to scrub backwards.

"Stop there," ordered Tyler.

The picture became a high resolution still.

"Look, see how that limb is shorter than all the others. It seems to be damaged, it has a ragged end to it. I've noticed that in a few other shots too."

"Maybe it is normal for those creatures," said Millar. "We haven't a clue about their anatomy."

"But remember the specimen that was sent from the Sahara, blown off by an RPG and subsequently examined by our biologists in Wiltshire?" asked Cummings. "What if that is what is missing here, the same limb piece?"

"Yes, but why would the same damage feature on multiple creatures?" asked Tyler.

"I'm afraid that I have no answer to that," said Cummings, brushing his lapel.

"Eric, wind forward to the bit where the television cameraman is captured," instructed Millar.

The monitor showed the flailing limbs in a harrowing close-up. Part of the cameraman's bloodied face flashed into view for a few frames and was gone.

"Now, watch carefully what happens next," said Millar. "The camera is being taken through the vortex and for a brief moment you can see what's on the other side before the signal is cut off. Ultra-slow please, Eric."

"It wasn't shot in slow motion," explained Eric, "so it will be a bit jerky, and it's not very clear."

The sequence of still images showed the base of the thrashing arms surrounding a hexagonal mouth with six triangular flaps that opened and closed. The cameraman was dragged towards the mouth, stuffed inside and disappeared. The arms seem to be attached to a wide, light coloured dome. Could it be a head? It was impossible to make any sense of it.

"This could have been the result of a camcorder being eaten by a giant squid," said Cummings.

"No," said Tyler, "a squid has a definite beak, like a bird, and it certainly doesn't open and close like that. Undoubtedly it is a feeding orifice of some kind, but not like anything I've ever seen."

"And what about this 'dome', for want of a better word?" asked Millar, "The arms seem to be attached to it around the mouth."

"I can only guess that it is the part of its anatomy that produces the rift in space and time. Don't ask me how it works," said Tyler. "It must be surrounded by a dish-shaped body because there is a definite cavity between that and the visible distortion. It's only slightly more than two metres deep, judging by the size of the victim. I suspect that the cavity expands and contracts to allow the arms to reach out beyond the distortion and then pull back, giving it room to draw its prey into the buccal cavity. There don't seem to be any teeth; the sticky arms can rip the victim apart into bite-sized pieces before they are consumed. This expansion and contraction of the cavity could explain the ripples on the surface."

"I have never seen anything so abominable," said Cummings. "How are you going to deal with this, Mr Millar?"

Millar shrugged.

"I think that it's going to take someone a lot smarter than me!"

Chapter 52 - Nanuq

Noël Gauthier zipped down the flap of his tent. Outside, there was a crystal-clear view out over the Hudson Bay. Adrienne, his wife and assistant, rolled up their double sleeping bag and moved it to the corner of the tent.

"The snow storm has subsided. It looks like it's going to be a wonderful day."

He sucked in the fresh, cold air.

"What equipment do you want to take today?" asked Adrienne.

"Take all we can manage on the sled," replied Noël." I don't think that we are going to get many more chances before the weather comes in again and I do want to get some decent shots of that mother polar bear and her two cubs."

Noël and Adrienne Gauthier were well-known in wildlife photography circles in Canada. Through sheer patience and tenacity, they always managed to get the shots demanded of them by their commissioning editors in Montreal. The female bear 'Nanuq' was reported as having two new cubs the previous November – perfect subjects for a profitable photo opportunity.

Noël loaded up the sled with photographic equipment, some food and a small white hide tent. He threw a tarpaulin over the top and strapped it down firmly with nylon webbing. The sled was hooked up to a 2-up snowmobile and was ready to go.

After breakfast at their campsite, they tidied up, closed the zipped flap and set out across the snow. Every year, the polar bear population was diminishing. Habitat loss was the main reason, but that had a knock-on effect as bears, especially the large males, found it increasingly difficult to feed themselves and would resort to cannibalisation of other bear family's cubs.

Both riders scanned the shoreline for sight of a mother bear and two cubs. The bears' off-white camouflage made them difficult to spot with the yellow sunlight on the snow, but the two photographers were looking primarily for movement in a vast field of still, frozen ground.

Adrienne spotted an Arctic fox slinking along in a depression in the landscape, most likely stalking some hapless seabird. She pointed it out to Noël, but he didn't stop. He wanted to photograph the bears; nothing else mattered. The noise of the snowmobile's four-stroke engine would be audible to animals at a great distance in the still air. The fox was already inquisitive as to what the racket was, but soon lost interest and carried on with its stalking. Noël didn't want to frighten off the polar bears and eased off on the throttle. The engine's brapp, brapp died down to a slow putt, putt. It was still too loud, and smelly. Polar bears have an acute sense of smell for detecting seals. Petrol fumes would carry for miles. The wind direction was favourable, carrying the smell and noise in a perpendicular direction.

In late summer, the sea was not yet frozen. A thin strip of seaweed-covered rock separated the land and sea. A seabird landed there and found something of interest to peck at.

When they eventually caught sight of the bears, they were a long way off. Noël knew that they would have to abandon the tracked vehicle and pull the sled by hand for the rest of the way. He longed for a team of dogs, but their barking would spook the bears too. It took the two of them the best part of half an hour to drag the equipment sled within long-lens distance of Nanuq and her cubs. They lifted off the tarpaulin and opened the large equipment box. Adrienne took out two SLR cameras with long lenses and attached them to two stout tripods. Noël was already watching the animals through powerful binoculars. His SLR had a long telephoto, while Adrienne's had a 500mm zoom. Between them, they had the shoot covered. Noël wound his tripod centre column up to its optimal height. Adrienne decided to take her camera off the tripod and try to shoot hand-held. The bright landscape gave her plenty of available light to set a fast shutter speed.

"I can't see one of the cubs now, it's in behind the mother," said Noël. Adrienne lifted her camera to her eye and zoomed-in fully.

"I can only see one cub," she said. "Are you sure that it's behind the mother?"

"It was as we were setting up," he answered. "It seems to have disappeared. Did it fall into the sea?"

"No, they're not all that close to the sea," said Adrienne. "It's just your telephoto playing tricks with perspective. Look, is the mother bear covered in seaweed, or something?"

Noël refocussed his long telephoto.

"It can't be seaweed that far from the shoreline. Hey, it seems to be moving."

As both photographers watched through their cameras, the large mother bear stood on its hind legs, its front ones flailing wildly. It seemed to be pawing at the air. Its back legs left the ground, kicking.

"What's happening?" asked Noël. "The bear seems to be fighting something that we can't make out."

Nanuq appeared to levitate for an instant and then was gone.

"What just happened?" asked Adrienne. "There is only one cub there now."

Noël let go of his camera and took his binoculars out again. As he focused on the bear cub, it became entwined in something black. It shot into the air and vanished too.

"Sweet Jesus," said Noël, wrestling with his focusing ring. "They've all gone. All three bears."

They continued to watch where the bears had just been, but only the waves in the distance made any sound or movement.

"Noël, it seems very much like what happened in England two days ago at that rock festival. You don't think…?"

Chapter 53 - Brian

"Sarah is coming over this afternoon," said Marion.

"It will be good to see her again," said Rachael.

"I meant to ask you, Rachael, how are you getting on with Elsa Todd?"

"She's looking after me very well," said Rachael, "but she never stops talking. My mother would call her a 'yenteh'. She's the kind of person that always finishes a sentence with another sentence. There are no periods!"

Marion laughed, "Yes, that's Elsa. She was vaccinated with a gramophone needle."

"A what?" asked Rachael.

Marion waved her hand, "Oh, never mind. You are too young."

When they heard Sarah's car pull into the courtyard parking area, they both went out to meet her.

Rachael gave Sarah a hug.

"Are you well, Rachael?" asked Sarah.

"I am, but I think that I'll be putting on the pounds with all these cream teas that Marion keeps feeding me."

"A little of what you like does you good, Rachael," piped Marion.

"Plenty of time to lose weight when you go back home," said Sarah.

"Do come in Sarah," said Marion. "We have so

much to talk about."

Sarah told the sad story of Kevin and Suzie's experience to Marion and Rachael. Marion was especially shocked when it finally it sank in. There were multiple creatures. She was very confused.

"I just don't get it," she said. "There has never been a mass sighting like this before."

"Kevin made an interesting observation," said Sarah. "The distortions always remained on the same plane. They never twisted around to face their prey; they appeared to be sticking to the same invisible wall. They could move from side to side and up and down, but they never went in front of one another."

"I can't imagine why that would be," said Marion. "Maybe they are bound to what is, essentially, a two-dimensional surface."

"I don't think so," argued Rachael. "I believe that it was only because there was a gang of them working together. We already know that they can tilt from looking at the Cobham photos. That one was almost horizontal."

Marion produced a quiche and some salad for lunch. When they had finished, it was time to go to meet Brian at the computer lab.

Brian was nowhere to be seen. Marion peered through windows in doors trying to track him down. A computer lab assistant saw her looking in and opened the door.

"Can I help you?" he asked, in a tone of voice that

sounded more like, "what the hell do you want?"

Marion recoiled.

"I'm looking for Brian Harding, actually."

The technician looked at his watch.

"Probably still in the canteen. Wait here, I'll go and get him."

"Thank you," said Marion.

The three women stood in the corridor looking around at the complex charts on the walls. A few minutes later, a man rounded the end of the corridor.

"Dr Calvin," he said, offering out his hand.

"Hello, Brian. I hope that you don't mind, I've brought two colleagues along to meet you. This is Rachael Hartmann, another anthropologist from Stanford University in the States."

"I'm delighted to be here," said Rachael, shaking Brian's hand.

"And this," said Marion," is Sarah Frobisher, or should I say, Doctor Sarah Frobisher, who is a biologist." No mention was made of her place of work.

Brian and Sarah shook hands.

"Now Brian, I would love to know what progress you have made with your modelling software."

Brian led the group to his small office. He had to go and find another chair.

"Can I ask you something?" said Rachael. "I'm an anthropologist, not a mathematician. Why a 4-D model? I understand the fourth dimension to be time, but the surface of the Earth is essentially flat isn't it? There is no vertical component."

"Ah," said Brian. "I think it is generally accepted that the Earth's surface is a sphere. There are those who still won't accept that," he grinned, "but my model is based upon a three-dimensional sphere plus the time element."

"Of course, silly me," said Rachael.

"Now, I will just try to explain the principle. You are obviously all well-educated ladies so I won't dumb it down too much. No doubt, you are all familiar with the term 'interpolation' – that's with an 'o' not an 'e'? Well, my model takes the data points we have, and tries to deduce a pattern. It then applies that pattern back to the data and fills in any gaps. I've had to eliminate a lot of the data because it was too incomplete. For instance, a time that is too vague or a location that covers too large an area. I have ignored any data over ten years old as I am just not confident about its accuracy. So, taking what we know to be fairly reliable, I have produced this…"

Brian brought up an image of a spinning sphere on his computer monitor. The sphere was covered with coloured dots, each representing a sighting, a mutilation or a taking. The stronger colours related to actual data and the more pastel tints, the interpolated ones. As the points came and went, a numerical readout at the bottom of the screen showed the hours, days, months and year. When the running time display reached the current date, the spinning sphere froze.

"That is incredible," said Marion. "Now, last night I received another spreadsheet from Steve in London.

He was the photographer who took the photos at the fête in Cobham and he has had a researcher scouring the world's newspapers for reports."

She handed Brain the short list.

"Okay. We have a few more data points here. They give us an opportunity to cross reference a few interpolated points," said Brian, running his pencil down the list.

He changed the computer monitor to display a database instead of the graphic, and scrolled down through it.

"Yes, there are two interpolated points here exactly where they should be, according to this new data. I'll have to ignore the rest as being too far away from the expected results."

He made two alterations to his database.

"Excellent, so that shows that the model is fairly accurate."

"How did you handle the multiplicity of takings and mutilations at that rock concert in Swindon?" asked Marion.

"I think that that was a freak occurrence," replied Brian. "I only counted it as a single incidence."

Sarah raised her hand slightly to ask a question.

"You stopped the model at today's date. What happens if you let it continue on into the future?"

"I was coming to that," he said, half-smiling. "Understand that very few incidents have actually been reported. There must be many more that have happened in remote regions of the world that went unseen. A few have been reported as mutilations, but many more were not witnessed at all, and if there were any takings, they were probably animals that nobody missed. So, in projecting forward, I have to filter for incidents that are likely to happen in populated areas."

"Have you done this?" asked Marion.

"Yes, I have. I must warn you, the projections are devastating!"

"We need to tell somebody about this," said Marion. "But who?"

"I can answer that," said Sarah. "I know the people at the top. I don't have their details with me though, they are on my computer at work and I can't access it remotely. I need to go back to Porton, now!"

Chapter 54 - MOD

"What?" Charles Millar screamed down the phone. "Who is this Calvin woman anyway?"

"She is the one person in the world who knows more than anybody else about this phenomenon," explained Sarah. "She has made it her life study, and is surrounded by other academics from all over the world who are collaborating with her. Up until now they have had to work in secret, thanks to all the cover-ups and threats made by people like you."

"I only have the nation's security at heart, Doctor Frobisher. You must surely realise the consequences of leaving this information unmanaged?"

"And where did it get you, in the end?" said Sarah, angrily. "It left you with egg all over your face after what happened in Swindon."

"I don't have to take this from you, young lady. What's your interest in all this anyway? Your department have been removed from the project. It's none of your business now."

"It is very much my business, Mr Millar. My young brother was at the Springvale Rock Festival with his girlfriend. They survived, but they have been left emotionally scarred. I don't know what's worse, dying or having that inside your waking and sleeping head for the rest of your life."

"I'm sorry, Doctor Frobisher, I didn't know," said Millar. "Look, I have to meet these people ASAP. I'll make myself available any time, just as soon as you can get them all together here at Whitehall. Please liaise with my secretary."

"Right, I will do that," said Sarah.

"And thank you, Doctor Frobisher, for bringing all this to my attention. I might not sound appreciative, but I am. Very!"

Despite saying that he would make himself available at any time, Charles Millar's secretary had other ideas. She was going to schedule a meeting ten days away. Sarah insisted that the secretary talk to Millar and get back to her. The meeting was brought forward to two days hence. The greatest problem was Brian's data. He couldn't bring a cluster of thirty computers with him, and there was no way he could run his simulation on a desktop or laptop. The best he could do was a sequence of screenshots. It would have to do. It was the only way to get his information across at such short notice.

The meeting took place in a conference room. There were several dozen people there. Sarah only recognised Millar and Cummings, apart from Marion's team and her boss, Geoff, who had rekindled his interest when Sarah broke the news of the meeting. Ewan Cummings chaired the meeting from a small stage. Beside him sat Charles Millar and Marion Calvin. He introduced Marion to the others.

"Dr Calvin is a research anthropologist from Oxford University. She has been following the occurrences of this phenomena for many years along with a Professor Bradley Johnston, from Stanford University in California. Unfortunately, Professor Johnston is recently deceased, but is represented today by his colleague, Rachael Hartmann."

Rachael stood up and nodded to the assembly.

"The purpose of today's meeting, is to explore what we know about this creature, or creatures, which isn't very much. First, I will call upon Professor Vivian Tyler to give a brief synopsis of our findings. The more detailed report is available for you to collect on the table by the door."

Tyler came to the lectern with a folder and opened it.

"Ladies and Gentlemen," began Tyler, "the terrible incident that we saw on television last week, and, you will recollect, another lesser one that happened at a church fête down near Cobham made the front-page news. There have been many other incidents like these, not just locally, but all around the world going back into the mists of time. What we are dealing with here is beyond our comprehension. What we do know, is that it is not of this world, but we don't know if it is extra-terrestrial or something else. Our biologists tell us that it is not biological, in the accepted sense, nor is it botanical. It doesn't fit in with any known cellular structures. Other tests that we have done demonstrate that it does not even conform to our understanding of universal physics. Well, what do we know about it? Let me show you a photograph."

On the large screen behind him, one of Steve's

photos from Cobham showed the rippling distortion in the air and the protruding limbs. The image changed to a still from the rock festival.

Tyler used a laser pointer to pick out specific aspects of the photo.

"The aerial distortion would seem to be a curtain that the creature can pass though, partially. We have never seen anything other than these arms, or tentacles, but note, these two limbs are terminated with bulbous features. We believe that these organs allow it to see. They are not necessarily eyes, but serve a similar purpose, to allow the creature to identify its prey. Our military aircraft have many sensors that use non-optical means to identify their targets and work beyond the visible spectrum. So, these things come through first, spot the targets and then the rest of the arms follow. You may notice that they have a black velvet texture. This is cause by a myriad of tiny hairs that work like geckos' feet. They create what's known as the 'Van der Waals effect' to create adhesion."

Tyler then showed the slow-motion clips taken by the video camera at Swindon as it entered the chamber behind the ripples. He pointed out how the arms terminated against a dome and surrounded some sort of hexagonal mouth aperture. He speculated that victims would be pulled apart by the adhesive arms inside this inner chamber, before being passed into the mouth. He also pointed out that he didn't think it could handle anything much larger than a cow or a camel, because there just wasn't room.

Marion gasped inwardly. Most of these revelations were new to her. She certainly didn't know about the 'eyes' or the chamber behind the ripples, but it made sense. She was the next to be called to the rostrum.

Marion gave an overview of her involvement and told how she had been collating information about the incidences. She explained about Brian's computer model and how it had successfully filled in some of the gaps in the data. Brian's sequence of screenshots was used to illustrate the concept of location and time.

"But now," said Marion, "we come to the pivotal part. The projection of these incidences into the future. Where will the thing strike next?"

The auditorium fell hushed.

The next image showed new data points spread all around the globe.

"Some of these locations, in the next month, are in remote places in Africa, Australia and The Antarctic. We are more concerned with places that have a sizeable population or are here in the UK. They are marked in red. We will, of course, pass this information on to the countries concerned and let them deal with it as they see fit. What are more interesting are the next two projections for the British Isles. The first is in Snowdonia. It's wild and sparsely populated, except for cattle and sheep. The second is much more worrying. It's smack-bang in the middle of a city. Glasgow!"

The auditorium was in uproar. Ewan Cummings tried his best to restore order. Questions were fired at the stage, but were lost in the clamour. Eventually, Cummings banged his microphone and waved his hand for people to be quiet.

"I know that you have a lot of questions and we will try to answer them in due course. I think that the most important question is; how are we going to deal with this? At the moment, I have no answer. It is not a simple matter of firing a few missiles from an attack helicopter as you might think. We have considered that. Let me pass you over to Doctor Calvin again, she will explain."

Marion stood up to the lectern again.

"What I am about to tell you is sheer speculation on my part. Well, that's not entirely true, I've had some of the best brains at Oxford, Stanford and UCLA thinking about it, so I can't take all the credit. You have seen what Mr Tyler describes as a curtain, a pass-through curtain. This, I believe to be a rift in space and time that the creature is somehow, able to manipulate at will. I am very concerned about what would happen if we were to bombard this rift with high explosives. At best, it would close the rift at that particular location, but not at any others. In a more cataclysmic scenario, it could open the rift even further. I shudder to think of the consequences if that were to happen. I will leave that to your imaginations. Using weapons of any kind is just too unpredictable and dangerous. We have to find another way, but we simply don't know what that might be at this time."

A few more hands were raised, but Marion left the stage.

Cummings stood up.

"Thank you, Ladies and Gentlemen, that's all we have for you today. Please remember to take the documents waiting for you by the door. They will tell you more than we could cover here. If you have any ideas, any at all, please email them to me for consideration. Good day."

The auditorium emptied.

Outside the Ministry of Defence building, Marion hailed a taxi. The three women climbed into the back. Sarah fully expected Marion to instruct the driver to take them all to Paddington Station. She didn't.

Chapter 55 - Malloy

Sarah admired the bright red sports car sitting outside the pub as they went in.

"Oh, what a delightful old pub," said Rachael. She looked around at the drab flock wallpaper and nicotine-stained ceiling. There was a smell of stale beer. Marion saw someone sitting with a pint of lager in the corner.

"Hello Steve," she waved.

"Dr Calvin," he said, standing up.

Marion introduced Sarah and Rachael. Rachael was still enraptured by the real English pub.

Can I buy you ladies a drink?" asked Steve.

"No, I'll get them," insisted Marion, and went over to the bar with the order. She brought the tray of drinks back to the table.

"Steve, I just had to tell you that the information you got for me was invaluable. More than that, actually, but I don't think I can talk about that."

"That was a terrible disaster at Swindon," said Steve. "That's not far from Oxford?"

"Fifty miles," said Marion, "That's what I call a safe distance. But Sarah's brother was at that event. She looked over at Sarah. "Wasn't he?"

Sarah had to tell the sorry tale yet again.

"So, what brings you all to London?" asked Steve. "Apart from me offering to buy you a drink."

"Official business," was all that Marion would offer. Steve knew that that was all he was going to get, so turned his attention to Rachael.

"How are you liking London?"

"Oh, I adore London," said Rachael.

"First time?"

"Oh, no. I've been here many times, but I just love it."

"Where is Stanford University?" he asked.

"Palo Alto, that's near San Francisco," replied Rachael.

"Oh."

He then started asking Sarah about her involvement.

"Sorry, I'm afraid that can't talk about it," smiled Sarah. Marion could say all she liked. She wasn't bound by the Official Secrets Act. Yet! Thankfully, she had the good sense not to say too much.

"Well, you did say that we should meet up for a drink the next time I was in London," said Marion. "Thanks for making the time. How is your work going?"

"A bit of an anti-climax after my scoop at Cobham, but I'm getting by. A few bob here and there."

From the way he said it, Marion got the impression that he wasn't doing all that well. Rachael bought the next round and they chatted on for the best part of an hour. Then Marion announced that it was time to go for the train. They all shook hands with Steve and wished him all the best before going outside to look for a taxi. Sarah was dropped off at Waterloo and the other two continued on to

Paddington.

* * * * *

Rachael's week passed so quickly. She and Marion talked into the wee small hours every night. Luckily, Mrs Todd's B&B was only ten minutes' walk and she had given Rachael a key. Rachael would much rather talk to Marion than Mrs Todd. As they said their goodbyes at Oxford Bus Station, they both held back their tears.

On the flight back to San Francisco, Rachael searched for a pen in her handbag and came across the business card given to her as she left a week ago. This was something she had to do.

Daniel Malloy was more affable that Rachael had imagined. For a director of Homeland Security, he was uncharacteristically pleasant. Likeable even. Rachael expected the 'bad cop' to appear any minute, but he didn't. They established at the outset that they were both expected to use first names.

"So Rachael, I won't beat around the bush. I know that you were at a top-level meeting at the Ministry of Defence in London. Can you tell me what happened there?"

"You didn't have anyone in that meeting then?" asked Rachael facetiously.

"No. Tickets were sold out," joked Malloy. "What did they talk about?"

Rachael fished for clues about how much the man

knew already. He knew more that she had imagined. He had seen the same photos and television footage that she had. His team had been through the same process of analysis. All that was missing was Marion's insight and the information about the creature's inner chamber from the snatched camera, which had never been made public. Malloy took notes.

"And you saw this footage from behind the ripples?" asked Malloy. "Can you describe what it was that you saw?"

Rachael told him that all she saw was a series of blurry still frames. The details had come from the presenter, Vivian Tyler. Malloy wrote the name down.

"That's an 'a' not an 'e'," said Rachael, "It's a man."

"And the details of the future attacks?" he prompted.

"You will be given that information through regular channels," replied Rachael.

"When?" he demanded.

"I don't know exactly," said Rachael. "All I know is that they said they would be contacting the nations concerned. They didn't even say which ones."

Malloy tapped his pen on the table.

"Thank you, Rachael, you have been very helpful," smiled Malloy. "You are free to go."

As Rachael made her way back to Palo Alto, she realised that there had been no need for a bad cop. The good cop had all the information he wanted from her. The truth was that she felt too intimidated to hold anything back. She just hoped that they would stop following her.

Chapter 56 - Microscope

Geoff Hamilton looked perplexed when Sarah went into work the next day.

"What's wrong Geoff?" she asked.

"There's nothing 'wrong' exactly," replied Geoff. "I've just had a call from The Right Honourable Ewan Cummings. He wants us to continue our work on the samples where we left off; a complete about turn. He thinks that we might find some sort of 'Achilles' Heel', as he put it. He thinks we might find some vulnerability in the creature that we could exploit. He doesn't realise how little we have of this material. I can't do anything meaningful with those few scrapings."

"From what I remember, you discovered that the samples reacted to ultra-violet light and to electrical stimulus," said Sarah. "Is it not worth exploring those properties further?"

"No, I hit a brick wall on that," he answered.

"Is it okay if I have a go?" asked Sarah.

"You go ahead, Sarah," said Geoff. "I hope that you have better luck than I did."

"Can I read your notes first?"

"Sure, they are by the window in my notebook. I didn't get around to typing them up. There didn't seem much point when we were stood down."

"You should always write up your notes," said Sarah. Horrified, she suddenly realised that this was her boss she was criticising. Before she could apologise, Geoff broke in.

"Yes, Sarah, you are right. I was so annoyed about the whole thing that I just said to myself 'sod it', and did nothing."

Sarah took the notebook from the shelf and started leafing through it.

"You didn't actually do the spectrometry tests yourself?" asked Sarah.

"No, that's what Colin is here for. He's the expert with that equipment."

"I think that I'll have a word with him," said Sarah, picking up the notebook and heading off down the corridor.

"Colin, Geoff asked you to do some tests on the material from the specimen that came from the Sahara, right?"

"Why, yes, Sarah. Then he told me to stop, that the project had been cancelled."

"That's right, but it's back on again. Tell me exactly what you did."

Colin opened a file on his computer to remind himself.

"I wish that Geoff had written up his lab notes on the computer instead of using pen and paper," said Sarah. "I find his handwriting very difficult to decipher."

"I don't know anybody in our business that has decent handwriting," said Colin. "Too many years of scribbling notes at university."

Colin scanned his notes.

"Yes, standard spectrometry tests, results inconclusive. Broad spectrum analysis, odd properties at higher wavelengths. Electro-stimulation reaction tests, positive."

"Yes, I've read all that, but you were of the opinion that the material was inorganic?"

"Definitely," said Colin.

"If it is not organic, why would it want to consume flesh?" asked Sarah. "It just doesn't make sense."

"None of this makes sense, Sarah. I can only assume that however its metabolism works, it needs protein. It is an inorganic carnivore. Maybe it needs flesh, maybe it's something else – brainwaves?"

"Did you do any qualitative chemical tests?" asked Sarah.

"No, that would have been next on my to do list. The only issue is that we have so little material to work with. The sample we have is so small, and chemical tests are destructive, others less so. Could you find me any more material?"

"No, there isn't any more Colin. That's all we have."

"Not much I can do then," he shrugged.

"The electro-stimulus test isn't destructive, is it?" asked Sarah.

"Can we run that one more time? I'd like to see that."

"Geoff, why are you keeping these samples in the freezer when we know that they are not organic?"

asked Sarah.

"Force of habit," said Geoff.

"I want to run the electro-stimulation tests again," said Sarah.

"Be my guest," he said, gesturing towards the lab freezer.

She took the microscope slide container back to Colin in the other lab. He removed it and put it into his high-powered digital microscope. A polarised image of the jelly appeared on the computer monitor.

"There are two electrodes mounted on the glass slide and a small piece of the jelly substance is bridging the gap between them."

He attached two crocodile clips to the electrodes and plugged the other end into a variable power supply.

"Now, watch what happens when I tickle it with ten microvolts," said Colin.

The jelly twitched.

"That's the reaction I would expect from organic cells, but the spectrometer can't find any indications of organic molecules."

"What happens when you increase the voltage?" asked Sarah.

"Let's try," said Colin, switching his power supply to a higher range. "Look at what happens at 100 volts."

Sarah watched the microscope image on the monitor. The tiny speck of jelly enlarged, and then split in two.

"It's like cell division," gasped Sarah.

As Colin increased the voltage, the specks got no larger. Instead, the separation between them increased. The higher the voltage, the further apart they got.

"Now I'm beginning to understand what happened in that lightning storm at the rock festival," said Sarah.

Colin switched off the power supply. Instead of staying apart, the two pieces of jelly collapsed into one, as if they were connected by rubber bands. It shrank back to its original size.

Colin brought up his notes and appended the observation.

"Colin, can we re-do the ultra-violet test?"

"Yes, it will take a few minutes to hook up the UV light source, bear with me."

As Colin fiddled with the equipment, Sarah read Geoff's notes.

"It says here that the specimen disappeared under ultra-violet light."

"Yes. If anything, I would have expected it to fluoresce," said Colin. "But as long as it was in ultra-violet light, it just ceased to exist."

He switched on the UV backlight, and then off again.

"See, it comes and goes."

"Let me have a look through the eyepieces, the resolution on the monitor sucks," said Sarah.

She looked down through the stereoscopic eyepieces and turned the turret to a higher magnification.

"Keep turning the UV light off and on," said Sarah.

"I think I can see what is happening. As the light comes on, a tiny aerial distortion appears and the specimen disappears into it. It is going back into its other existence, on the other side of a micro-rift."

Colin had a look.

"Yes, I think you are right. This is incredible. There might be a Nobel Prize for you in this," he smiled.

"I'm not looking for a prize," said Sarah, "I'm looking for a weakness. Let me get Geoff."

Chapter 57 - Fishing

With the entire world now aware of the incident in Swindon, the pretence of a national security clampdown had now diminished. Messages on the genealogy site tailed off and became just straightforward requests about family trees. Sarah felt it was safe to communicate with Marion and Rachael by open email, but still made a password protected PDF of her lab notes and sent them to both. She phoned them on her throwaway phone to explain what she had done, and give them the password, '0urLev1athaN%'.

An hour later, Marion was on the phone to her.

"Sarah, I think that this vindicates my theory about there only being one creature. Using high voltage electrical power, it can temporarily make aliases of itself. There were thunderstorms at Mount Shasta and Springvale when multiple sightings were reported."

"Well, I think that rules out electrocuting the thing," said Sarah.

"So, we can't use explosives and we can't use electricity. Our options are diminishing by the day," said Marion. "Its next appearance is projected for just over a week away, in North Wales. We had better warn Mr Millar what not to do. I don't know if they have come up with any other options, but I wouldn't want them to do anything stupid!"

* * * * *

"It was an idea sent to me in an email," said Ewan Cummings. "It sounds so totally ridiculous that at first, I thought it was a joke. Yes, I've had quite a few suggestions that were less than serious."

Charles Millar looked at the printout.

"You're not serious," he said. "Fishing?"

The badly drawn diagram showed a horned animal tied with a piece of rope to the winch of a truck.

"If we put a bull out in the open, connected with a metal hawser to a powerful winch, the thing will spot the bait and try to pull it in. We know that when it has latched on to something, it can't let go. When we start up the winch, I reckon that one of two things will happen. At best, it will haul the entire thing out of its hidey-hole onto the ground. Clear of the aerial distortion, we can hit it with all the firepower we can muster. I can have a couple of fully tooled up Apache helicopters on standby."

"You said that there were two possibilities?" asked Millar.

"Yes, the other one is that it will rip those arms off, leaving it a cripple. It needs those arms to feed, as far as we know."

"There are other outcomes that I can think of," said Millar. "One is that it pulls the truck and its occupants in through the distortion. Another is that the wire ropes could simply snap."

"We can anchor the vehicle to the ground with chains and stakes," said Cummings. "If the ropes snap, which is unlikely as they are the same ones used on heavy-lift cranes, someone has lost a prize bull, no big deal. At least there won't be any human casualties."

"Well, personally, I think it is a lunatic idea," said Millar. "There are just so many things that could go wrong."

"I've passed it by a couple of our top generals," said Cummings. "They think it is an excellent example of good old British military divergent thinking, and are all for it. I've given them the go ahead to set it up – unless you have any better ideas?"

Millar shook his head.

"In that case, I'm going to recommend to The Cabinet that we go ahead with it."

Charles Millar had an email from Marion waiting for him when he returned to his desk. It warned of the follies of using explosives or electricity on the creature. He had deduced that for himself, but thanked her politely for her input. The fishing idea was insane, but he didn't have any other options. Maybe it would work. If it didn't, Glasgow would have to be evacuated. His phone rang. It was Daniel Malloy, his counterpart with USA Homeland Security. Malloy explained who he was, Millar already knew.

"I've just received a list of projected attack locations in the United States, thank you for sending those across," said Malloy. "The USA is a big place. Apart from a few densely populated areas, it's mostly prairies or wasteland. None of the locations on this list are particularly worrying. Only one is near a town in Arizona and we will keep an eye on that."

"You realise that those projections are only for the next month?" said Millar. "I don't yet have co-ordinates for after that. The UK is a lot more densely populated than the USA. Our first location is, luckily, in an area that usually only has hikers and sheep. The one after that is in the middle of Glasgow City. We don't really want that to happen."

"So, what is your battle plan?" asked Malloy.

Millar reluctantly told him of the plan that Cummings was lining up.

"My God," said Malloy. "You gotta be kidding!"

"That was my reaction too," said Millar. "I don't want anything to do with it."

"My idea was to pick one of these remote locations here and hit it with low-yield nuke," said Malloy, "but our scientists here are in touch with yours and tell me that that is a big no-no."

"Correct," said Millar, "that's only likely to make things worse."

"You know, I've had some ridiculous suggestions too," said Malloy. "There was one Native American academic from New Mexico who claims to have found evidence that his tribal legends tell of braves fighting off one of these things with spears and arrows."

"I wouldn't like to confront this thing with only a

bow and arrow," said Millar. "Besides, arrows could only affect the tentacles; nothing can pass through the rift unless it is pulled in. There is no way to target whatever is on the other side of the distortion."

"Yes, that's what I'm told," said Malloy. "I'm beginning to think that your fishing pole idea is not so mad after all."

Millar sighed.

"It's been signed off at the very top level. Who am I to argue?"

Chapter 58 - Camouflage

Sarah was flabbergasted that Millar was being so frank with her. It wasn't so long ago that everything was all so very hush-hush, and now he was discussing things of national importance with a humble biologist.

"I hope that you dissuaded him from using nuclear weapons?" said Sarah.

"I think that your friends at Stanford had already put him straight on that one," said Millar.

He then told Sarah about the fishing trip. A fishing trip where the anglers were a crack team from the army, and the bait was a live bull. He told her that as farcical as it sounded, it had been given approval at Cabinet level and would be implemented in a week's time.

Sarah was utterly lost for words.

"Unless your people can come up with something better?" said Millar. He was effectively passing the buck onto Sarah and her friends.

"Oh yes, I hear you," said Sarah. "You expect me to ring my mad professor friend, the one with the inter-dimensional gunship, and tell him to go in there and blast the thing to kingdom come. Fine. I'll do that now."

"Seriously, Doctor Frobisher, if you can think of anything, I'd really like to hear it."

He hung up.

* * * * *

"Hello Steve," said Marion, cupping her hand over the phone. "It's Marion Calvin. Now look, I have something to tell you, but you didn't hear it from me. There is going to be an attempt to attack and destroy the creature a week from today. Our computer predictions show that it will materialise in the Snowdonia National Park around noon. It would make a very good photo opportunity, if you know what I mean?"

"Blimey," said Steve. "I could use another scoop. Can you tell me exactly where?"

Marion gave him the precise GPS co-ordinates.

"But, I warn you," said Marion. "The place will be crawling with soldiers. You do need to be very careful."

"I'm not so worried about the soldiers, it's all those flailing arms that bother me."

"You will be a good way off; I wouldn't worry too much on that account. You have a good, long lens, no doubt?" asked Marion.

"Not that long, but I can hire one for a few days."

Marion outlined the attack plan. Steve found it incredulous.

"Fishing? Hey, I suggested that once as a joke," he laughed. "One way or the other, that is going to make some interesting headlines."

"Yes. Just remember, Steve. You didn't hear about it from me."

Steve pondered the problem. He needed a long zoom or telephoto lens. He had a 50 to 400mm zoom, but wanted something more powerful. The professional hire shop would have one but it would be expensive to hire, especially by the time the insurance was added on. He also needed some camouflage gear.

Paul!

His old boss was a keen birdwatcher on the side. He would have some camouflage gear, in fact, Steve remembered seeing it stowed on a shelf in the studio the last time he had visited. He got on the phone.

An hour later, Steve was sitting in Paul Atwood's driveway. He got out and rang the doorbell. Andi answered the door.

"Oh, Hi Steve, I haven't seen you around for a while. What have you been up to?"

"Nothing very exciting, but I have this assignment next week in North Wales. I need to borrow Paul's camo-suit and hide."

"Not celebrities this time, then?" asked Andi, cheekily.

"On the contrary," smiled Steve, tapping his nose.

"Who?" she demanded.

Steve put a finger to his lips.

"Oh, you!" said Andi, slapping him. "Dad told me to tell you to help yourself."

"How are you getting on at art school?" asked Steve.

"It's great, really enjoying it," said Andi.

"And what about your friend, Jill? Has she, you know, yet?"

Andi put on a serious look.

"It is an art school, what do you think?"

Steve collected the birding gear from the studio.

He was going to give Andi a quick 'thank you' kiss as he left. She had other ideas.

Chapter 59 - Brainstorm

Rachael entered the meeting room. There were sixteen people there.

"Goodness!" she said. "I wasn't expecting so many people."

She sat down on a chair waiting for her at the head of the table. Having nothing more solid to use, she knocked on the table with her knuckles.

"Hi. Hi everybody. For those that don't know me, my name is Rachael Hartmann. I was a student and good friend of the late Professor Bradley Johnston and it is in tribute to him that we are all here today. You have all been emailed details of this perplexing problem. I'm sorry that you haven't been given more time to think about it, but you will appreciate the urgency."

There was a murmur of agreement from the group.

"Justine, would you like to tell us your ideas?"

A young, red-haired woman stood up.

"Yes, I am Justine Baker and I work in quantum physics at UCLA. Rachael has asked me here today to try to explain something that has been bothering a lot of people. How can this creature, if indeed it is a creature, be in multiple places at the same time? In the world of 'normal' physics, this is clearly impossible, but in quantum physics, it is unexceptional. In 2012, Doctors Serge Haroche and David Wineland won the Nobel Peace Prize for their work, which confirmed earlier theories stating that electrons can be in two places at the same time. Quantum mechanics predicts the bizarre notion of the 'multiverse' – the existence of multiple parallel universes. It is my personal belief that this creature inhabits one such parallel universe, and has the unique ability to venture into ours to feed. At least, part of it can. Perhaps it lives on a parallel Earth, or perhaps somewhere that the concepts of solid and void are reversed, I don't know. The only thing that we know for certain is that its physics are very different from ours – and that it is not a vegetarian."

A titter arose from the audience.

"The portal that it creates between the two universes is small and very unstable. Somehow, it can reach through and grab things from this side. Living things. To my knowledge, it has never taken an inanimate object – except for a video camera harnessed to its operator. You've seen the images. Now, the team at Oxford have made a computer simulation that predicts this thing's appearances in the next month. I am told that the nearest predictions are fairly accurate, but as time passes, the locations may drift somewhat. The folks in the UK are going to attempt to intercept the creature in a remote region of Wales. The idea may sound a bit wacky, but they plan to catch it like some giant fish, using a bull as bait."

There was more murmuring from the audience.

"There is no precedence for an operation of this kind. It could all go horribly wrong. I think that it is our job here, to offer any gems of wisdom that we can. Has anyone else got any ideas?"

A man with a beard and glasses stood and raised his hand.

"Hi, Howard Landry, Stanford. As an exobiologist, this is about as close to 'field work' as I am likely to get. I'd dearly love to go over there and watch all this going on first hand, but I can't. There is one aspect of all this that has me puzzled and I wonder if anyone else has any theories. From the briefing document I was sent, I see that they had a specimen, a part of a limb, in a lab in England. This specimen, somehow, managed to create a small 'worm hole' and disappear into it. I have known limbs cut from animals to twitch for some time after being separated from the main torso, and also heard of headless chickens being able to run around. I wonder why this happened, and how?"

Rachael answered.

"My friend, Doctor Sarah Frobisher, was the biologist working on this, and this is what she told me. Her team noticed that ultra-violet light had an odd effect. It gave a small sample of jelly, scraped from a microscopic section of the limb, the ability to create a micro-rift and disappear into it. As far as the larger limb specimen is concerned, she believes that the stray UV light from the fluorescent tubes in the lab may have had the same effect. The tiny specimen could only travel back to its own universe temporarily; it didn't have the critical mass required for a permanent exit. As to why, I don't know. It clearly didn't belong in this universe, maybe there is a natural force that we don't know about that attempts to create equilibrium between two parallel universes?"

A tall South African man stood up.

"Joseph Mbote. I am an electrician. Okay, a high-tech electrician, but I do work with voltages that most people would find scary. A thunderstorm can generate in excess of a hundred million volts and at a current of over three hundred kilo-amps. We saw from the video at the music festival, that the creature was able to generate plasma and make multiple copies of itself. It was able to use this enormous power source in our universe to cause, what our colleague Doctor Baker here would call a quantum paradox. You've heard of Schrödinger's cat? I believe that, were it possible, constructing a Faraday Cage around the creature would isolate it from the power that it needs to multiply."

"I don't think that stopping it from multiplying is the immediate problem," said Lu Chen, theoretical physicist. "However, if any more detached limbs were to become available, putting them in a dark, Faraday Cage might stop them from escaping."

Rachael was furiously taking notes on her laptop. When the meeting ran out of steam, she was relieved. She rung her hands to ease the pain in her fingers.

"Can I just thank everybody for coming here today," she said, "and for all your very useful ideas. When I have tidied up my notes and corrected the typos, I will let you all have copies. I need to get copies off to Doctors Calvin and Frobisher in

England. They are the ones on the front line."

Chapter 60 - Snowdonia

Having been warned that there would be a lot of military activity in the area, it occurred to Steve that it would be better to go two days early and get dug-in, rather than have to run the gauntlet.

He knew that he didn't have room in the boot of his small sports car for all the gear he would be taking to Snowdonia, so he went to his local car accessory shop and managed to get a rack that clipped on to his boot lid, giving him somewhere to put his large rucksack. With the hide taking up most of the passenger seat, it was a tight squeeze and a long trip, nearly five hours' drive. He had put a pile of CDs and bars of chocolate into his glove compartment, but now he realised that he was going to have extreme difficulty in opening it.

They would probably have thermographic cameras mounted on helicopters to search the area, so he would take a couple of space blankets to help disguise his heat signature, and keep warm.

He entered the GPS co-ordinates that Marion had given him into his satnav. He cursed when he saw how far from a main road that it was. Probably just as well, he thought, his bright red car would stand out like a beacon. On his map, he identified a small car park off the A4212 used by hikers going to the mountain. It worried him that there might be road blocks that would leave his car as the only one.

From the car park, he would still have a kilometre

to walk across the fields to get to where he wanted. He also needed the advantage of elevation. Luckily, the foothills of Snowdonia were rocky and had plenty of bush cover.

Not wanting to leave his car and expensive camera equipment unattended, Steve ignored the M6 motorway service stations. As he bowled along the motorway at a steady seventy-three, he became aware of a burning smell.

"Bloody hell," he screamed, as grey fumes started to emanate from his heating vents. He thumped the emergency stop button on his dash and swerved over onto the road's hard shoulder. He threw his door open to a blast from the horn from a passing truck that just missed it. After checking that it was safe, he released the bonnet catch and jumped out of the car. When he raised the bonnet, the smoke and burning smell became even more apparent.

"Fan belt," he said to himself. "That's just great. It would go when I'm in a hurry."

He rang the emergency roadside assistance. They took nearly an hour to arrive.

"Hello," said the man who got out of the van. "Sorry I took so long to get here, but I didn't have a fan belt for your model. I had to pick one up. Can I just see your membership card?"

Steve took his card from his wallet and showed it to the man. He wrote the membership number down on a form.

The van driver noticed that Steve's car was

packed to the gunwales.

"You need a bigger car, mate," he said, pointing at the hide squeezed into the passenger seat.

"Yeah," said Steve, "haven't had it long. It was a case of heart over head, I have to admit, but this is not a typical outing."

The van driver was now under the hood with a spanner.

"So, what's with all the camouflage gear?" asked the man.

"Oh, I'm shooting birds in Snowdonia," said Steve.

"Is that legal?" said the man, standing up from his work.

It took Steve a few seconds to realise what that meant.

"Photography, not guns," he grinned.

"Oh," said the van driver, and continued with his job. "I'm thinking of getting a new camera, could you recommend a good one?"

Steve had been asked this question many times before, and came up with the same answer.

"What brand of spanner do you use?"

"No idea," came the reply.

"Does it work?"

"Of course it does," said the man looking up quizzically. "Why do you ask?"

"A camera is like a spanner, it's just a tool. How good it is comes down to the user, not the device itself. Get the best one you can afford and learn how to use it properly."

"Mmm," said the van driver. "Okay, that's your fan belt fixed. Can you just sign this?"

Steve signed the form and waved goodbye to the driver as he drove off.

Steve wound down his windows to get rid of the lingering smell, checked his mirror and pulled out into the road.

He drove all the way to Chester before taking a turning onto a smaller road through Wrexham that would take him towards his goal. Eventually, he found the car park he was looking for, surprisingly full. He managed to just squeeze in between a 4x4 and a stone wall. He had familiarised himself with the species of birds he was supposed to be photographing; Red Kites, Peregrine Falcons, Chough and Merlin, in case anyone asked him. He had gleaned enough knowledge about them to bluff his way, if challenged.

Steve had only partially unpacked his car when it struck him that there was no way he could carry this lot to his vantage point over a kilometre away. He was going to have to make two trips. His two precious cameras couldn't be left behind, either in the car or in the hide. It was remote, but not that remote. He was going to have to keep them with him. He was quite happy to lock the hired telephoto lens in his boot. It was easily worth more than his two cameras together, but it wasn't his and he had paid for comprehensive insurance. He tied the collapsible dome hide onto his back with webbing and slung his camera bag over his shoulder. He could just manage one tripod in his left hand and extended one leg to act as a walking aid on the rough terrain. His smartphone could be used to navigate to the area where he was going to be setting up camp.

The going was rough. Steve stopped for a breather and surveyed the landscape around him. Mount Snowdon was in the middle distance behind him, and in front, small rocky outcrops and coarse grass. There was no sign of any people or animals, just the odd bird crossed the blue sky, calling as it flew. He didn't know what it was. He realised that he wasn't as fit now as he used to be when he played football. The terrain wasn't all that difficult, maybe it was the load?

The exact location he was looking for was on a shallow hillside. There was a small valley, and then another hill opposite covered in gorse, heather and small bushes. Perfect! After a root around, he found an ideal spot between two gorse bushes, flattened the grass with his boots, and slipped the hide out of its bag. It was ridiculously easy to erect, practically springing into position by itself. He pushed a few metal stakes into the earth to hold it steady. Last thing he wanted was for it to go blowing across the hillside with a gust of wind.

He unzipped the side. It was going to be a tight squeeze. There wasn't much room in it. It was a hide, not a camping tent. He knew that he was going to have to compromise. He would have to curl up to sleep. He stowed his tripod inside, backed off a few metres and looked back. The hide was well camouflaged amidst the gorse. He just hoped that he could find it again when he came back and made a mental picture of the surroundings. There was a taller bush nearby with half of its side missing that could be used as a landmark. Now he had to go back to the car for the second load.

As he headed back towards Mount Snowdon, his mind was rehearsing the details for tomorrow. He had enough food and water. The only thing he was not entirely happy about was the visibility of his hide. It did have a pattern that disguised it against the terrain for an observer at ground level, but how would it look to a helicopter in the sky above? He could cut off some gorse branches and spread them across the top, maybe that would help. A yelping from behind him made him turn around. A large black Labrador was bounding towards him.

"Oh no," he thought, "guard dogs, I hadn't thought of that. Camouflage won't hide me from them."

The dog came running up to him and started sniffing and growling.

"Buster," came a voice from over the hill. There was a man in wellington boots and a waterproof jacket striding towards him with a second dog.

"Buster, here."

The dog ran back towards the man and circled

around behind him.

"It's alright, he won't touch you," said the man. "You are some way off the beaten track?"

"I am," said Steve, lifting his cameras in the air. "Birds."

The man walked up beside him and smiled.

"There are plenty of those around here, anything in particular?"

"Red Kites, Peregrines, anything like that," replied Steve.

"There are some about here, but I haven't seen any today. You might need to come a bit earlier, morning's the best time."

"Yes, I know," said Steve. "I'm planning on staying overnight so that I can be up at the crack of dawn."

"Good luck to you," said the man as he wandered off. "It might be a bit damp tomorrow though."

When Steve got back to the car park, the 4x4 that he had parked beside was gone. His car was looking very lonely and vulnerable. Hopefully, if anyone did find it, they would assume that he had gone hiking up the mountain.

For his next load, he took the two rucksacks. The larger one had clothes and his space blankets. The smaller one held food; mostly cans of beans and tuna. He wasn't going to be able to light a fire. He also had some breakfast bars and three large bottles of water. He hoisted the large rucksack onto his back, hooked the smaller one and long lens over his shoulder and locked the car. He hoped that it would be safe in this remote car park. With its soft top, it was very stealable.

He found his hide without too much trouble, although he wouldn't have if it were not for his smartphone and its accurate GPS readout. He put all his gear inside the hide and squeezed in beside it. He was exhausted. This cramped space would be his home for the next few days – unless, of course, he was caught.

That night, Steve had a bad dream. He dreamt that he had unzipped the hide and the rippling distortion was just outside his door with flailing arms reaching out towards him. He tossed and turned as the image replayed over and over again. He awoke in a cold sweat. The space blanket was pulled across his shivering body. He went back to sleep.

Chapter 61 - Camp

"Hello Marion," said Sarah, holding her phone between her shoulder and her ear while she leafed through some sheets of paper.

"I've passed Rachel's contributions on to Charles Millar. He said that they were very useful, but he still hasn't come around to the fishing idea. They are going ahead with it, but he says that he has taken some 'contingency measures', whatever that means."

"I do hope they don't do something stupid," replied Marion.

"Marion," said Sarah. "How do you fancy a little drive to Snowdonia? They say it's lovely at this time of the year."

"You don't mean…?"

"Yes, I do mean. I don't know about you, but I wouldn't miss this for the world," said Sarah.

"But they won't let us within five miles of the place," replied Marion. "It will all be all cordoned off."

"Yes, it will, and further back than that," said Sarah, "but our good friend Charles Millar said that he can swing it for us to be in the command and control truck, as scientific advisers. It will be a couple of miles from the actual site, but they will have a live TV feed from a helicopter. We'll have a veritable grandstand seat."

"In that case, you don't have to ask twice," laughed Marion. "Can you give me a lift?"

"Yes, it's a four-and-a-half-hour drive, so we will have to make an early start."

"Why don't you stay overnight at mine?" suggested Marion. "I have a sofa bed that you can use."

"Good idea," said Sarah.

"I wonder what these contingency plans are?" asked Marion.

"I guess we'll find out the day after tomorrow," said Sarah.

* * * * *

"I would have liked something more heavy duty," said Charles Millar.

"There are plenty of heavier vehicles," said Major Mervyn Donaldson, "but we have to get it over some very rough terrain. The big trucks will only run on proper roads. That narrows our options considerably. This one is the ultimate 4x4. It can go up and down 45 degree inclines and has a powerful winch up-front that can easily pull a tank out of trouble."

Indeed, the Unimog was a large, muscular pickup truck sitting high on its suspension over chunky off-road wheels. The three-pointed star on its front grille betrayed its Mercedes Benz heritage.

"As long as it's well tied down," said Millar.

"It will be," said the army major.

"And the choppers?" asked Millar.

"We have three on standby, two Apache attack ships and a Wildcat for personnel and cameras."

"And what about our bait?" asked Millar.

"Ah, we got an old bull off a local farmer. It hasn't got long to go – Bovine Respiratory Disease Complex. He was glad to have it taken off his hands as he couldn't sell it and would have had to pay for disposal in the not too distant future. We did him a favour."

"Have you briefed the local police?" asked Millar.

"Yes, they will put a five-kilometre exclusion zone around the site from midnight. Nobody will be able to stray in there. We will also scour the area with the thermographic camera on the Wildcat in case of campers."

"Good," said Millar. "I'm going to station our command and control vehicle in this car park, here," he said pointing at an ordinance survey map. "My team will be monitoring everything on the feed from the helicopter."

"I just hope that the computer prediction for time and location is accurate. Don't want to have to drag a sick bull a couple of hundred metres across that ground for no good reason," said Donaldson.

"Quite!"

* * * * *

Steve poked the long lens though the snoot on the side of the hide. He knew approximately where to point it. Unfortunately, the Sun was in the wrong place, he was facing south, so he would be shooting into its glare. He had no idea how this was going to play out. Would he be behind the distortion or off to the side? There was no way to know at this stage.

Steve decided that it was time to eat. When he pulled the ring-pulls to open the tins it reminded him of when he had gone camping years ago on a school trip. Then, they had a campfire to do the cooking and there was hot tea and a singsong. It wasn't much fun here camping by himself. The cold beans and tuna weren't too bad; a hot drink would have been welcome.

When he heard the thrashing of rotor blades in the distance, he rolled himself into a ball inside the hide and covered himself with both space blankets. The helicopter passed directly overhead, circled a few times, and headed back in the direction from which it came. Only a day to go. He opened a bar of chocolate.

A few minutes later, Steve heard voices in the distance. He straightened up and opened the lens-flap at the top of his hide. He couldn't see anyone, but the voices were coming nearer. The gorse bushes on either side of his hide were obstructing his view, so he pulled on his camouflage jacket and khaki beanie hat and crawled out of the hide. He pulled a gorse branch aside and peeked out. Three soldiers, complete with rifles, were plodding though the long grass, obviously sharing some lewd joke. They came to the flat slope where the target was due to materialise the next day and stopped. One of the soldiers had a computer tablet and was swiping across the screen. He couldn't make out what they were saying, but saw the soldier with the tablet pointing at features in the landscape. He pointed toward him. Steve hunkered down. Another soldier walked towards him.

"Here?" called the soldier.

The officer held up a thumb. The soldier marked the ground with his heel. He was only twenty feet away. Steve couldn't guess what was going on 'here'. It was too close for comfort, whatever it was.

After ten minutes, the three soldiers disappeared off to the East. It was only when they were out of earshot that Steve climbed back into his lair gingerly. Suddenly, a thought struck him. A devastating thought. What if 'here' was the location that they expected the thing to appear? What if his phone GPS wasn't all that accurate? The military had access to much more accurate GPS co-ordinates than civilians were permitted. Surely his co-ordinates couldn't be that far out? He remembered his dream with the tentacles reaching out towards him. He shook his head. Never mind the tentacles, what if they opened fire on the creature with bazookas or missiles? He would be blown to pieces. If he moved his hide, it would be to a less good vantage point, he might not get the photos he came for. He might even be spotted.

Steve stood up beside his camouflaged hide and looked all around. Was there another location he could use? He was about to walk out across the hillside when he heard the soldiers again. This time, there were more of them. He squatted against the ground, his head as low as possible. A soldier came up to the location where the heel-mark had been earlier. He stuck a long red and white striped pole into the earth. In the distance, three other soldiers were doing the same. They were marking out the square arena. Its centre was some two-hundred metres away. He gave a sigh of relief.

A helicopter throbbed past overhead. Steve quickly dived into his hide and covered himself with a space blanket again. The chopper seemed to circle for ages. He daren't look out, a thermographic camera would spot him with no trouble. After fifteen minutes of circling, it flew off. As the noise subsided, he could hear the soldiers' voices recede into the distance. Was he alone again? He carefully crawled out of the hide and lifted his head above the bushes. Yes, he seemed to be safe, for now!

Chapter 62 - Baited

Sarah had no idea where she was going, she didn't know North Wales. She had already entered the location that Charles Millar had given her into her satnav and was following the spoken directions. She and Marion had left at half-past five in the morning before the Sun had come up. Now, it was a bright, clear day. It would have been enjoyable, if it wasn't for the sense of foreboding.

They pulled in to a services area for some petrol and a hot drink. On the way in, Sarah noticed an army truck parked well away from all the vehicles. A group of soldiers were leaning against it, drinking from paper coffee cups.

"I wonder if they are going to the same place as we are," said Sarah.

"I very much doubt it," said Marion, "they could be going anywhere. You are just putting one and one together and coming up with three."

"Yes, probably," said Sarah. "I realise that I'm a bit obsessed with all this."

With another stop an hour and a half later, they still made their destination by a quarter to eleven. The long, unmarked command and control truck was already parked across the empty car park. Empty, that was, apart from a small red sports car against a wall. Sarah pointed at it.

"That looks familiar," she said.

"Ah" said Marion. "It looks like Steve is here."

"Steve, the photographer we had a drink with in London? How come he's here?"

"A little bird must have told him what was happening," smiled Marion.

"Oh, Marion. You? That wasn't very smart. What if he's found? You will be implicated, and in turn, so will I. The Official Secrets Act!"

"Don't be such a worrier, Sarah. It's a coincidence, that's all. Just like the soldiers at the service station."

Sarah tried to hide her annoyance.

They got out of the car and Sarah rapped on the door of the truck.

"Who is it?" came a voice from inside.

"Sarah Frobisher and Marion Calvin," said Sarah. The door opened slightly.

"Ah, come in," said Charles Millar. "Sorry, it's not very salubrious, purely functional."

As they climbed the metal steps, another, smaller army vehicle pulled up beside.

Inside the back of the truck, there was a definite military feel – olive drab and scruffy. Three television monitors on the wall showed test patterns. A loudspeaker produced only static. Every now and then a voice broke in, saying something fast and unintelligible. One of the monitors flickered and an image appeared. It was a landscape with Mount Snowdon in the background.

"Ah, the aerial feed is coming in," said Millar, picking up a headset. "Zero One, come in Zero One. We have your signal."

"Roger," came the reply.

The image on the monitor stopped swishing past and steadied. It zoomed in. In centre frame was a bull, standing in the middle of a grassy patch. A long tether ran from a harness around its body to the front of a small army vehicle.

"The line is baited and ready," said Millar. Another officer in the truck was jabbering furiously into a microphone. He turned around.

"Zero One is going to refuel." Millar nodded.

The picture cut off.

"How long have we got?" asked Marion.

"Slightly more than an hour," said Millar, indicating to Sarah and Marion that they should sit down on a seat near the front of the compartment.

* * * * *

Steve needn't have worried about the sun shining in his lens. When the early morning mist had lifted, the sky was grey and overcast, but it wasn't raining. He had watched the soldiers arrive with the Unimog truck towing a large cattle trailer. The poor old bull was pushed, prodded and dragged out of the box by four men, and the trailer detached. Long metal stakes were driven into the soft ground by the same four burly soldiers, working in pairs. Chains were run out, attaching the stakes to the chassis of the truck. The scene was set.

Occasionally, Steve would stick the telephoto lens out through the snoot near the top of the hide and check the focus. When the helicopter with the camera turret slung under its nose arrived, he pulled a space blanket over him like a cloak and hood. Only his eyes were visible.

The bull just stood there patiently chewing grass, as bulls do. Steve thought that had it known what was about to transpire, it might have been a little more agitated.

The cattle box was pushed further down the hill and its wheels were wedged with small rocks. Only the driver was left in the Unimog. Two other soldiers lay on the grass beside it with their rifles ready. All the rest took cover behind the cattle box.

Steve fired off a few shots of the tableau. Had it not been for the din from the helicopters, he would have been worried about some keen-eared soldier hearing the clacks from his shutter. He checked his back up camera. It had a shorter zoom lens, which wasn't really powerful enough to take decent images at this range. He hoped that he wouldn't need it.

* * * * *

The swish, swish, swish in the distance heralded the approach of three helicopters, two gunships and the one with the spherical camera mount on its nose. In the command truck, the three television monitors sprang to life, showing views from each of the helicopters. The officer was shouting orders into his microphone as he watched the three blips on his radar screen converge on the target.

"Zero One, I need you at six o'clock. Zero Two at

three o'clock and Zero Three at nine o'clock. Range, one hundred metres," ordered the officer in the control truck.

"I feel sorry for the bull," said Sarah. "Poor old thing. What a way to go. How long now?"

"Sixteen minutes," said Millar. "Now please sit there and be quiet, ladies. This will all be over in a very short space of time. We only have a thirty second window at best and I don't want to be distracted."

They could hear the helicopters throbbing in the near distance and watched the monitors intently.

As the countdown clock on the monitor ticked silently downwards, Sarah could feel the hairs on the back of her neck bristle. She took Marion's hand and held onto it tightly.

"I'm now beginning to wish I had stayed at home," whispered Sarah. "I'm not used to all this excitement."

Millar gave her an annoyed look. She got the message and shut up.

"Two minutes to go," he said. "Everybody be quiet."

Chapter 63 - Tug of War

The first shimmers were seven seconds late according to the numbers on the screen, and a few metres from where they should have been. It was not a problem. The ripples spread outwards forming a three-metre circle. There was no sign of anything coming out. Steve took a few shots of the distortion, but there was virtually nothing to focus on. A few seconds later, the first two stalks with the sensor organs emerged, sweeping to and fro seeking prey. The bull instinctively sensed the danger and started to bellow. In an instant, the two blobs transfixed themselves onto the terrified bull. Then something very strange happened. The entire distortion floated towards the bull. It could move! The bull turned to face it and pawed the ground in defiance, roaring and snorting. The snake of cable connecting the bull to the truck winch tightened as the driver took up the slack. Steve was now concentrating on the bull. He could see the orange, nylon webbing wrapped tightly around its body. It was only then that he noticed that the bull was wearing two rucksacks, one on either side of its neck. What could those be?

Back in the command and control truck, Sarah and Marion craned their necks to see past the technicians' heads. The helicopter views of the apparition and the feisty bull were visible, but there was no audio. They were totally oblivious to the racket it was now making. Through the small window in the side of the truck, Sarah noticed another helicopter landing; a blue civilian model. As the rotors slowed down, a figure emerged holding tightly onto his trilby hat. It was Ewan Cummings. He climbed over the low stone wall with difficulty, and mounted the steps into the back of the truck. His jaw dropped when he saw Sarah and Marion sitting there.

"What the hell are you doing here?" he spat.

"And good afternoon to you too, Mr Cummings," said Marion, with a forced smile. "We are the official scientific observers."

Cummings didn't know what to say. He certainly hadn't authorised this. His attention was quickly drawn to the screen showing the ripples with two stalks sticking out. He pushed a uniformed technician aside and peered at the screen. The sensor organs were followed by a number of other, black tapered shapes reaching out slowly and encircling the bull's horns and front legs. Longer arms wrapped themselves around the bull's body, causing it to tumble over onto its side and kick furiously. The cable running between the bull and the truck tensioned further.

Steve's vantage point was at a forty-five-degree angle to the plane of the ripples. He held his finger on the shutter release and the camera took frame after frame. The creature's arms were now perfectly taut as they pulled at the stationary bull. Steve could see the Unimog tilt forward on its suspension and hear the vehicle's engine revving and straining, grey smoke belting from its vertical exhaust pipe. As the tug-of-war continued, neither side was giving an inch. Another sound joined the bull's squealing and roaring. It sounded like a whale song. For a few seconds, a horrible hexagonal mouth broke the surface of the ripples. It opened, uttered an unholy screech and vanished again. The chains tethering the Unimog to the ground were stretched out straight. Something had to give. Just then, another distortion appeared in the air. Then another. Soon, there were dozens of them forming a circular shape around the main one. They weren't very large, ranging from a metre in diameter down to twenty-five centimetres. Steve was expecting more arms to emerge from each one, but that didn't happen. Instead, the central pool of ripples spread out to envelop the smaller ones making one huge pool. There was an almighty discharge of electricity, then the bull stiffened and fell silent. In the sky, people pushed buttons. The bull exploded in a blood-red cloud as a hail of shells from the two attack helicopters ignited the fragmentation mines in the rucksacks. There was a series of explosions. Small pieces of the animal shot off in every direction. Among the chunks of red and white meat and bones, severed black arms flailed through the air. The firing stopped. Steve was aware of shards of metal shrapnel zipping past his hide. One ripped a hole in the top, missing his head by a hair's breadth. On the ground where the bull had been, lay a sickening mass of bones and entrails. Above that, black stumps that had once been arms, thrashed helplessly and ineffectively. The one remaining eye stalk was bent over like a bulrush in a flood. The ripples in the air bubbled and the whole thing spun wildly on a vertical axis. As it rotated, the hexagonal mouth came to the surface and screeched. Steve realised that his finger had been on the shutter release for the entire episode. His battery was drained. He threw down the camera with the long lens and picked up his back-up camera. The short zoom lens wasn't up to the job, so he crawled out of the hide and walked deliberately towards the spinning distortion taking shot after shot. He ignored the soldiers' shouts. As he got closer, he could see electricity arching between the remains of the arms, most of them had been decimated by the grenades. The one arm that seemed almost intact was trying desperately to support the battered eye stalk. It spotted Steve. The entire mass floated towards him, stumps flailing. He walked backwards, with his camera still to his eye.

"Look," shouted Sarah. "That's Steve! The fool. He is going right up to the thing." The aerial shot from the helicopter showed how close he really was. As he walked sideways, still shooting, a soldier rugby tackled him and brought him crashing to the ground. The soldier pushed his head flat against the grass and held it there. Just like the spot on an ancient black and white television set, the ripples collapsed into a central point, paused for a second, and faded out.

Two other soldiers came running up with their guns pointed squarely at Steve. He climbed to his feet and raised his arms above his head.

"You bloody idiot," said the sergeant. "What the hell do you think you are playing at? You could have jeopardised our entire mission."

"Unlike you," said Steve diffidently, "I've done this before!"

The sergeant snatched the camera from where it lay at Steve's feet. It was still switched on.

"I'm keeping this," he said.

"Oh, no. That's my livelihood," said Steve. "Take the memory card if you must, but not the camera. Please."

The sergeant motioned to Steve to give him something and handed him the camera. Steve opened the flap on the side of the camera, ejected a memory card and handed it to the sergeant. By this time, another soldier had discovered Steve's hide further up the hill, and beckoned the sergeant over. Steve followed, with a gun still pointed at him. The sergeant retrieved the camera with the long lens from inside the tent.

"This one too," he said, tapping the memory card flap. Steve removed the card and very deliberately, kissed it goodbye.

Having completed their mission, the two Apache Helicopters banked steeply and headed for the horizon. The one with the camera was still sweeping the scene. Soldiers were removing the chains from the Unimog. They pulled some crates from the back of the pick-up and opened them. Inside were shovels and heavy duty black plastic bags. Donning protective suits and breathing apparatus, they waded through the bloody mess on the ground, picking up what was left of the tentacles and shovelling them into the bags.

The picture on the control truck monitor went black as the helicopter left.

Chapter 64 - Biohazard?

Steve slid down from the back of the Unimog and pulled his gear after him. His car was still sitting in the corner of the car park by the wall.

"Steve," shouted Sarah, running over to him.

"Oh, hello," he said as he recognised Marion's friend from the pub. Marion, herself, was right behind her.

"Dr Calvin," he said, with a degree of surprise. "What are you two doing here?"

"Who is this," asked Ewan Cummings, walking over. "Is this some kind of private party or can anyone come?"

Marion explained that it was Steve who took the original photos at Cobham, the ones that made the headline news.

Cummings looked unimpressed.

"He won't be making any headlines this time, "said the sergeant, tapping his buttoned top pocket.

Steve opened the boot of his car and started loading his gear.

"How did you find out about this event anyway?" snapped Cummings.

Steve didn't want to get Marion in trouble.

"I was just photographing birds," said Steve. "It's a good spot for Red Kite."

Cummings grunted.

"I find that just too much of a coincidence. I expect that one of you two is involved," he said to

Sarah and Marion. They shook their heads sheepishly.

"You were lucky that you weren't arrested," snarled Cummings to Steve. "Maybe you will think twice next time."

"Since when was taking photographs of birds in the open countryside a crime?"

Cummings opened his mouth to speak, but just waved Steve away. Steve just smiled. With his equipment all stowed away, he got in and started his car. He winked at Sarah and Marion as he drove off. Marion was giving a discrete 'phone me' signal with her fingers.

"We've managed to pick up what is left of the creature," said the sergeant. It's wrapped in lightproof plastic bags inside those metal crates as you instructed. Sorry we can't do the full Faraday Cage thing; we can't earth the boxes in a moving vehicle. That will have to wait until you get it back to Wiltshire."

"I have something suitable ready and waiting," said Sarah. "As long as we have excluded ultra-violet light, we should be alright."

"We have a clean-up team on its way," said the sergeant. "It's quite a mess down there. If we find any more bits of the thing, we will get them to you Doctor Frobisher."

"Thank you for your help," she said.

Sarah and Marion said goodbye to Charles Millar and the technicians in the control truck.

"And thank you for the tea," said Marion.

Sarah gave her a funny look.

"It was disgusting," she whispered.

"Yes, it was," said Marion, "but they don't know that, why disillusion them!"

On the drive back home, Sarah was so glad that they weren't transporting the creature's leftovers. She had seen, first hand, how they could reanimate and disappear. Did they go back to where they came from and regenerate into new horrors? Was each piece able to reproduce like plant cuttings? It certainly wasn't a plant and she had no knowledge of how it reproduced, if at all.

"Poor Steve," said Marion. "All that trouble for nothing. He could have been killed and they took all his photographs. What rotten luck."

"Shame," said Sarah. "So, what happens next? We don't know if the creature is dead or alive. If it's able to regenerate itself, we will be back where we started."

"We will find out in a couple of days," said Marion. "Remember, its next appearance is due in Glasgow in about fifty-six hours. If it's a no-show, then we can assume that it's been finished off. On the other hand, it might just turn up very pissed off. Please excuse my French."

* * * * *

"That changes everything," said Brian Harding. "They have interfered with the creature's natural cycle of occurrences. By holding onto it in this world for longer than it would normally stay, the whole rhythm could have been altered. It has missed a beat. My model's future predictions may no longer be valid."

"Oh dear," said Marion. "Is there no way that we can fix it?"

"Not without a couple of hundred new data points," said Brian. "Even then, I can't guarantee it."

"So, what will happen now?" asked Marion.

"Remember, I don't know how this works, I only know that it has. It might be that the time intervals stay the same, but that the locations change. Maybe the locations are constant, but at different time intervals. It is more likely that both have changed. Nothing is predictable anymore."

"So, there is no point in going to Glasgow tomorrow?"

"I'm sorry Doctor Calvin, but I can't say one way or the other."

"It's not that I want to go all the way up to Glasgow, it's just that if something does happen there, I would hate to miss it," said Marion. "Oh, I don't know what to do. I'll ring Sarah."

When Marion rang Sarah at the lab, she was outside supervising the unloading of crates from an army truck. Normally, deliveries marked as 'Biohazard' would be unloaded into a high security freezer, but Sarah knew that what was being unloaded was not biological in the usual sense. She directed the soldiers to the storeroom fitted out with the Faraday Cage.

When she returned to her desk, there was a note that Doctor Calvin had rang. She immediately rang her back.

"Are you going to Glasgow?" asked Marion.

"I can't," said Sarah, "I have to get to work on these new specimens. I've had orders from the top. Are you going?"

"No, Brian tells me that the predictions are all rendered null and void. Cummings and Millar are going. I hope that they enjoy the Scottish air."

"What about Steve?" asked Sarah.

"No idea," said Marion. "He's probably still licking his wounds after what happened in Snowdonia. I suppose that I'd better call Rachael and tell her the news. She won't be seeing anything on television."

Chapter 65 - Arizona

It was a place where people stopped off on a long trip from Los Angles to Phoenix or beyond. It had a gas station, a bar, an eatery, a post office and a small motel. The rest was just farm machinery lots and car wrecks. The total population was less than a thousand souls.

The small army convoy didn't bother to stop. It drove five miles past the town and branched off onto a dirt track running through rectangular, agricultural plots. Low hills rose on either side in the distance.

The leading vehicle looked military with its armour-plated sided and barred windows, but it had 'Homeland Security, Police Rescue' stencilled on its side. Daniel Malloy was in the passenger seat.

"Nearly there," he said. "Best to form a wide circle around the target and dig in."

The twelve vehicles drove around the designated spot over rough ground and took their pre-arranged positions. Tarpaulins over three flat trucks were removed to reveal heavy machine guns and a rocket launcher.

"Major, I need you to emphasise to your men that they are not to be trigger happy. What they are about to witness will definitely come as a shock to them, but it is essential that they hold fire until they are given the order."

"They are all hand-picked and well briefed," said Major John Harris. "You can rely on them, believe me."

"Now, the location we have been given is a computer prediction, I don't know how accurate it is," said Malloy. "We will have some air support shortly which will give a better overview. The time I have been given is 1013 hours, which is thirty-nine minutes away."

"What exactly are we dealing with?" asked Harris, "is it some kind of space alien?"

"Alien? Yes, I suppose you could call it that. It is certainly not from this planet, but then, I'm told that it's probably not from any other planet either."

"Huh?" asked Harris. "It must be from somewhere."

"You would think so," said Malloy. "It's just that it's not anywhere that we know about. As far as I know, it materialises out of thin air, looks for a meal and if there is any living thing nearby, it grabs it and disappears."

"I doubt that it will find much of interest here," said Harris. "It's not like there are any cattle or anything else to eat."

"Exactly," agreed Malloy, "it won't hang about for long."

Two large tadpole-shaped aircraft appeared on the horizon, heading straight for them.

"Here come the choppers," said Malloy, lifting the mic on his radio set. "Come in Titan One, this is Zeus actual. Standby. Over."

"Copy that," came the reply. "Reading you five."

"Titan One, you are to observe only. Do not, I

repeat, do not get involved in this mission. Over."

"Copy, Zeus. Wilco. Over."

The two black shapes in the sky came to a standstill and just sat there waiting.

Malloy was pointing a pair of powerful binoculars at a bare patch of ground. All the soldiers lay underneath their trucks except the two pairs operating the heavy machine guns on top.

They waited.

"What can we expect, here?" asked Major Harris. "The worst part is the waiting."

"Yes, I know," said Malloy, "Previous reports have mentioned a distortion in the air, like ripples on a pond, followed by two sensory organs that come out of the ripples to look for prey. If prey is identified, it deploys a multiplicity of arms, or tentacles, that reach out and snare the prey which is pulled back in through the ripples. Then that's it. Gone."

He clapped his hands for emphasis.

"I think I'd rather deal with fundamentalists," said Harris. "At least you know what they are."

As the countdown clock on the vehicle's dashboard approached zero, soldiers cocked their rifles and one lifted a heavy missile launcher up from the ground and aimed it.

The countdown had reached +21 when the air started to ripple. It wasn't in the middle of the circle of trucks but well to one side. Malloy refocused his binoculars. Something emerged. It looked like a black cobra with a large egg-shaped head, except that it had no eyes or mouth, just a faint blue glow. The object seemed to be supported on a second limb wrapped tightly around the area just behind the head. Before Malloy could comprehend what he was looking at, the complete pool of ripples floated straight towards one of the machine gun trucks with the men on board. Stumpy arms lashed out at the belt-fed machine gun team. The two men flattened themselves against the floor of the truck as, in a shower of sparks, the arms tried desperately to grab hold. The machine gun was ripped off its mount and tossed aside leaving the two soldiers completely exposed to their assailant. One soldier managed to get to his sidearm and rolled over onto his back. He emptied an entire clip towards the mass of ragged, stumpy arms, but with little effect.

From below the next truck, a soldier used his elbows to creep out. He could see the danger his gunners were in. He removed a grenade from his belt and pulled the pin. Blue forks of lightning shot towards him and lifted him off the ground. He was held dangling in the air for a fraction of a second, and then whipped into the midst of the cauldron of plasma and bubbling ripples. The two gunners watched aghast. From somewhere beyond the ripples, there was a bright, silent flash. The surface bulged slightly. A group of stumpy black shapes fell onto the ground and the ripples flattened out and vanished.

Three soldiers came running over with machine guns and pulverised what was left on the ground.

"Cease fire, cease fire," yelled Malloy. The machine guns spluttered to a stop. He went running over to the side of the truck and checked the dazed soldiers.

"Martinez, it got him," cried the heavy gunner. "Just whipped him away from where he stood."

"You were ordered not to shoot," screamed Malloy.

They saluted.

He went over to the debris on the ground and touched it with the toe of his boot. The largest piece was a bulbous object, lying there cut to shreds.

"Collect this stuff up and bag it," ordered Malloy, angrily.

From the back of one of the nearby trucks, two soldiers arrived with armfuls of clear polythene bags and shovels. They started to fill them.

When they got back to base, the polythene bags were removed from the truck and taken to a storage room. The scientists would have a field day with this lot. Malloy made a phone call.

"John, we have some body parts from the interception in Arizona, I don't know what to do with them."

Senator John Wilson stroked his chin.

"Dan, we have never been in this situation before, but I think that this is a job for our friends at NASA. Let me make a few calls."

Chapter 66 - NASA

The next day, a team from NASA arrived, packed the polythene bags into metal crates and whisked them off in a transport helicopter. In a few hours, they were being opened on a lab bench at a NASA research centre in San Jose, California. Dr Ben Cantor was reading notes on his computer screen.

"This is unbelievable," he said. "Julia, have you seen this?"

Julia Bertram peered over his shoulder.

"Yes, I was told that the material would be coming here for analysis. What have we got?"

Cantor went over to the lab bench and moved some pieces around with a pair of stainless steel tongs.

"I wish that they hadn't chopped it up so badly. There's not much to go on here."

"What about this?" asked the female, pointing at the shredded remains of a larger piece.

"This is what's left of one of two sensory organs, apparently," said Cantor, lifting it clear of the rest with his tongs and turning it over. "It would be very interesting to find out how this works."

He looked back at the notes on his screen.

"It seems that there is a group at Stanford who have been studying this. There is a phone number for a Rachael Hartmann, who seems to be the main contact."

Rachael was very surprised to hear from a NASA scientist.

"Yes, I suppose that I do know as much about it as anybody," said Rachael. "I would love to see what you have there."

"Any chance you could come over here?" asked Cantor, "I'd love to talk to you before we go any further."

"San Jose, yes, I can be there in an hour," said Rachael. "Can you arrange a pass for me?"

Ben Cantor met Rachael at reception and led her to the research lab. This was a different world from her usual university surroundings.

"What area do you work in?" asked Cantor.

"Anthropology," replied Rachael.

"Ah, now that's something we don't do a lot of at NASA," he replied.

She briefly explained her involvement and relationship to the Late Professor Bradley Johnston. She also told him about the work being done in England, not that she knew very much detail.

"I do know that it is not organic in the conventional sense," she said. "Nor is it mechanical. The people who have examined it closely in England have drawn a blank in that respect."

In the lab, Rachael was introduced to Julia Bertram.

"Rachael Hartmann is in close contact with the team in England who have also got some of this material. It seems that they got it the same way as we did, with explosives."

Rachael looked up at the light fittings.

"I'm glad to see that you don't have fluorescent tubes in here," she said. "Ultra-violet light has a strange effect on this stuff."

"Like what?" asked Julia.

"Like making it disappear," replied Rachael. She recounted the incident in Sarah's lab. "LED spotlights should be okay."

Rachael noticed the tattered sensory organ.

"It originally had two of these, it is now effectively blind. It no longer has any arms either so it won't be able to feed, unless it has some tricks that we don't know about. What we don't know is if it can heal itself, you know, regenerate. It might be a very long time before we find out."

Ben Cantor poked at the organ with his spatula.

"Looks pretty lifeless to me."

He yelled when a violent shock ran up his arm. The blunt end of the object glowed a dull magenta for a few seconds then reverted to its original black.

"Not as dead as you think," smiled Julia. "There must be some residual energy left in it."

"No, it doesn't work like that," said Rachael. "In England, they keep their samples in a Faraday Cage to eliminate any external electromagnetic influences. It seemed to be able to draw energy, at will, out of one of those aerial distortions that act as a portal between its world and ours."

"Harah!" exclaimed Cantor. "I wish that somebody had told me that before I was electrocuted."

"You'll live," said Julia. "We'll just have to be a bit more careful when we start to dissect it."

"Ah, you can swear in Hebrew," said Rachael. "I haven't heard that word for some time, since my schooldays, in fact."

Ben looked at her for what seemed like a long time, and then smiled.

"We didn't go to the same school by any chance?" he asked, with a frown.

"The David Stein Jewish High School?" said Rachael.

"I thought I recognised you in reception. My, you have changed," said Ben. "I remember now, you had braces on your teeth."

"Yes, I did. For years," she groaned.

"Hey, we'll have to meet up and talk about old times," said Ben.

"Yes, I would like that," replied Rachael.

Chapter 67 - Bernie

"Ah, Sarah," said Geoff Hamilton, "no doubt you've seen the dictum from Frank Fahey?"

"Yes, it's obvious that he is being leaned upon by Cummings. I have three crates of samples in the storeroom, all wrapped up tightly in lightproof bags and protected from external electromagnetic influences in a Faraday Cage."

"You didn't learn that stuff in your biology classes," smiled Geoff.

"No, I've had a little help from a friend at Stanford."

"Shall we go and have a look then?" asked Geoff.

Sarah tapped the keypad on the secure storeroom door. The lights came on automatically.

"Here we are," said Sarah, undoing the lock on a metal crate. Inside, was a black plastic bag sealed tightly with a nylon fastener. Inside was what looked like a chopped up black rubber hose, still covered in blood.

"Oh, that stinks, it looks like jellied eels," said Geoff, holding his nose. "I think that we need to get those samples washed off."

"Urgh, I'll get one of the technicians to do that," she said, turning her head away and closing the crate lid. She went off to find somebody to do the dirty work. A few minutes later, a woman in a white biohazard suit and air filter arrived and Sarah gave her instructions to wash the blood off the samples. She left hurriedly.

Back in the lab, Sarah closed the door tightly and took a perfume atomiser out of her top drawer. She gave her lab coat a liberal spray. Geoff said he was going for a shower and left the room.

Bernie, the lab technician was having great trouble cleaning the bull's blood off the samples. The two tungsten spotlights in the Faraday Cage were making it very difficult to see what she was doing. She opened the door and looked around to see that nobody was watching and took the large stainless steel tray of black, tapered shapes out into the storeroom. She switched on all the fluorescent lights, put the tray into a large sink and turned on the tap to give the samples a good hosing down. She went off to the cleaners' storeroom and rummaged about for a sponge or a brush to make the process a bit quicker.

Back in the sink, a black shape twitched and sparked. Then another. Bernie returned with a scrubbing brush and went over to the sink. She lifted a section of the black tubing and started to scrub. She held it under the tap as she worked the bristles along its length. The blood was coming off and running down the plughole. She set down the cleaned piece and picked up another. It coiled around her arm. She screamed. Bernie tried to unwrap the object from her arm, but another grabbed her. She tried to shake them off. They were stuck fast. One by one, the sections of the creature's arms slithered and entwined themselves around Bernie's white protective suit.

They found a way inside. Nobody heard the terrified screams as the technician's suit turned from pristine white to bright crimson. A distortion appeared in the air and the suit, with the woman inside, disappeared into the ripples. It vanished.

Over her nausea, Sarah decided to go back to the storerooms to see how Bernie was making progress. The storeroom door was open, and so was the Faraday Cage inside. Sarah called out.

"Hello. Bernie. Where are you?"

No answer came.

"Bernie, you should keep the doors closed."

Still no reply.

Sarah found the room with the sink. There was blood all over the wet floor. When she saw the water running into the empty tray, she suddenly realised what had happened. Her legs folded under her and she grabbed the sink to steady herself.

"Oh my God," she screamed. Managing to summon a little strength, she hit the alarm button beside the door.

"You can't blame yourself, Sarah," said Geoff, handing her a strong cup of tea. "Here, drink this. It will steady your nerves."

"I shouldn't have left her there alone," wept Sarah. "I just had to get that horrible smell out of my nostrils."

"It wasn't your fault, you told her to keep everything in the cage. You didn't know that she would take it upon herself to drag it all out into the open. She made a small mistake and paid for it with her life."

Sarah put her arms on the table and laid down her head.

"The best thing you can do, Sarah, is to go home, have a stiff drink and go to bed. If you don't feel like coming in tomorrow, that's alright by me. In fact, take a couple of days off, I insist."

Sarah slurred her way through a conversation with Marion that evening. She'd had four large gins, without much tonic, and was half asleep.

"So, you think that all those samples went the same way as the first one?" asked Marion.

"Yes" said Sarah. "I'm … I'm pretty certain that that's what happened."

"God knows where they've gone," said Marion. "There is no evidence that they can re-constitute themselves. I think it is just a reflex, an instinctive reaction. According to Brian's original projections, something should happen in the middle of Glasgow tomorrow at nine minutes past five in the afternoon. They aren't taking any chances; all the roads will be closed off and the people evacuated. There will only be a few soldiers – and Cummings and Millar. I shouldn't say this, but I wouldn't be too concerned if it got them!"

"Did you speak to Steve?" asked Sarah, having difficulty forming her words through the alcohol.

"I tried to ring him, but only got an answering

machine. I don't suppose that he will ring back tonight."

"I have to go," said Sarah, and ended the call abruptly.

* * * * *

Meanwhile, Steve was at a noisy club in Central London with Andi. They were locked in an upright embrace as multi-coloured lights flashed around them. Andi had told her parents that she was having a sleepover at Jill's house. It was the third time this week. They pretended to believe her.

Chapter 68 - Slots

When Marion got fed up with waiting, she rang
Steve at half past ten in the morning. He was still in
bed. Andi was moving around in the kitchen making
breakfast, wearing only his shirt.

"Hello Doctor Calvin," he yawned.

"Ah, so you haven't gone to Glasgow then,
Steve?" she asked.

"Oh no, I wouldn't get near the place. I was well
and truly rumbled in Wales. No point in pushing my
luck."

"I don't think that Cummings bought your story
about the bird watching," said Marion.

"No, he didn't look too convinced," said Steve.
"Had he been a detective, I might have been arrested
and locked up for questioning, but I think that he
had other things on his mind at the time. It could still
happen though! Maybe I should leave the country?"
he joked.

"It doesn't matter so much about me, but Sarah
was very worried that she would be carted off to
the Tower of London, or wherever they put traitors
these days," said Marion. "Oh, I do hope that there is
nobody listening in to our conversation."

"I'm sure that they have better things to do now,"
said Steve. "Those fragmentation grenades cut the
thing to pieces, I doubt if there is very much left."

"I feel so sorry for you having all your photos
taken like that," said Marion. "It must have been

quite a blow to lose them after all your efforts."

Steve sniggered.

Marion wondered what was so amusing.

"If that soldier had known anything about professional cameras, he would have realised that they have dual card slots. On mine, one card is reserved for unprocessed RAW files, the other for compressed JPEGs. Every shot I take is saved to both cards. I gave him the cards from both cameras with the JPEGs. The RAW files are now with my photo agent in London. He's holding them back until we see what happens in Glasgow. Then … then I'm going to be really rich!"

"Oh, I'm delighted for you, Steve. If some of those photos were to accidentally fall into my inbox, I would be a very happy bunny."

"The photo agency will only buy a few shots, the ones that they consider best. They will have the syndicate rights for those photos, but the rest remain my copyright, so, sure, you can have any of those for 'academic research'."

"Thank you, Steve, I am very grateful. What are your plans now?"

"Not sure," replied Steve." I have never been one for making long-term plans. Who knows what's just around the corner? As long as it doesn't have tentacles, I'll be quite happy."

Chapter 69 - Glasgow

A deathly hush hung over Glasgow's George Square in the warm afternoon light. No noisy traffic passed by, no bustling people. A statue of Sir Walter Scott looked down from his twenty-four-metre-high column onto small groups of soldiers hunkered behind sand bags, brandishing grenade launchers and flame throwers. The flame throwers had been Charles Millar's idea. In a built-up environment like this, they were much more controllable than fragmentation grenades. Grenade shrapnel could take out windows all around the square, never mind the damage it could do to valuable statues and monuments. If the worst happened, they would have to be sacrificed.

Just beside the cenotaph, the command and control vehicle waited, Ewan Cummings and Charles Millar firmly ensconced inside. Pictures from the two hovering helicopters filled the television monitors, and spotlights criss-crossed the shadowed square.

Millar barked orders into his radio headset microphone.

"All personnel keep firmly out of sight. Do not fire until I give the orders."

Cummings paced the length of the long vehicle. He was agitated.

A remote hillside in Snowdonia is bad enough, but duelling with this monster in the middle of a crowded city is even worse, despite what those above me think."

"I think that you are more worried about your career than the people of Glasgow," said Millar.

"Bloody impudence," shouted Cummings. He wasn't used to being taken to task, especially by someone he considered subordinate, but then that included just about everybody.

"Just make sure that any damage is kept to an absolute minimum," he snarled.

"We have no idea what is going to happen," said Millar. "The thing was clearly injured by the grenades at Snowdonia. I don't think it will have much fight left in it."

"How do you know that it can't heal itself?" argued Cummings. "I do know that lizards can grow new tails when they lose one. Cut a worm in half and you get two worms."

"That's an old wives' tale," answered Millar. "Cut a worm in half and you get two dead worms!"

"Whatever," said Cummings, brushing off the comment. "But if that thing has managed to heal itself, it will be very angry. Who knows what it is capable of?"

"No, we don't, but we are about to find out," said Millar. He pressed the transmit button on his radio mic.

"One minute to zero hour. Hold your fire."

At precisely 17.09, and as predicted in Brian Harding's original model, a very small ripple disturbed the air. It was so subtle in fact, that nobody actually noticed it. The countdown reversed.

"I was warned that the deadline might wander," said Millar. "The boffins think that the last incident might have thrown the predictions off. They said that both the time and location could be different."

"You mean that we might be waiting in the wrong place?" asked Cummings, "that it might be snatching people in Dundee as we speak?"

"Could be Dundee, could be Melbourne, I don't know," replied Millar.

Cummings grabbed what little hair was left on the sides of his head and roared.

Seventy minutes later, Cummings, Millar and the whole kit and caboodle packed up and went home. George Square stuttered back to life.

Chapter 70 - Futures

"And how do you feel this morning?" asked Marion.

"It's not morning anymore," said Sarah, looking at the clock on her wall. "Yes, a lot better after a long lie-in."

"When are you going back to work?"

"I'm not," said Sarah. "I've been thinking about it. I just rang Geoff and told him that I was taking a year's sabbatical. He was a very annoyed at first, but eventually came around to my way of thinking. He said that when I wanted to come back he would still have a job for me, but I don't think I'll be going back. Biology is supposed to be a placid occupation, peering through microscopes and writing up notes. What I've gone through in the past few weeks is not at all what I signed up for."

"So, what will you do?" quizzed Marion.

"I have some money put by and I will rent out my house. After hearing about all the wonderful adventures that you and Brad had on the far side of the globe, I've decided that I might become a travel writer. I don't know if I'll be any good at it, but I'm going to have a go."

"That sounds wonderful, Sarah. I wish you every success."

"And what about you, Marion? Are you going to continue with your university work until the grim reaper knocks at your door?"

"No, I've always promised myself a little place in

Greece," said Marion. "Nothing fancy, just a humble flat with a sea view, I don't need much. It was always something to look forward to, a reason to keep on slogging. I mean, I don't have a lot of incentive to stay in England. The only family I have left is my brother, Roger, he's a dermatologist in Harley Street and we only really contact each other once a year. We were never all that close. I've never had much of a social life outside the university, so I don't have a huge circle of friends either. When I met Bradley Johnston, he changed my whole perspective on life, but after all this rigmarole, I no longer have the will or energy for the upheaval of moving myself and all my stuff to Greece. Greece was only a pipe dream, I should have realised that. I was lying to myself."

"So, what will you do?" asked Sarah.

"Well, this place belongs to the university, I only rent it. As soon as I retire, I will have to move out. I've always been careful with my money, so I've managed to save a nice little nest-egg. It's not enough to buy that proverbial cottage with roses around the door, but I'll get something. I will lose myself in a little herb and vegetable garden; canvas gloves, a little dibber and trug basket. Then, I'd like to write a book. I'm sure that someone will find my life story interesting, especially the last few years. Nobody has ever told a story like that. I was thinking of calling it 'Exopod', what do you think of that?"

"Go for it, Marion. That's a sure winner," said Sarah.

"Yes, that will keep me happy for the rest of my days. Rachael promised to pop over any time she is in England, but now she tells me that she has found a young man, a scientist at NASA no less, and they are pretty serious. I don't know."

"Well, I will certainly come and see you when I get back," said Sarah, "we can compare notes."

"Yes, Sarah, that would be lovely," said Marion.

They said goodbye.

* * * * *

Steve Markham had always told himself that he didn't do relationships. He had always considered girls to be disposable arm candy. Now, he was a little older, a little wealthier and he did like Andi. She was fun to have around.

"Andi, are your parents not suspicious about this 'sleep over' thing at Jill's? They might be thinking that you two are having a girlie affair."

She giggled.

"When I said that I was staying at Jill's last week, Dad gave me a very obvious wink. They know fine well that I'm not staying at Jill's. They even rang up and checked. They aren't stupid. They have put one and one together and come up with two. Us two. I have neither confirmed nor denied it, but Dad said that the next time I see you I should tell you that you owe him a new bird watching hide."

"Well, yes," said Steve, "I suppose I do."

"Steve, I have my half term break coming up next

week. How about we go away somewhere for a few days?"

"Huh? What will Paul and Lizzie say?"

"I hinted that it might be a possibility," said Andi, coming over and sitting on his lap.

"And what did they say to that?"

"Oh, Mum just held up a finger and said 'be careful'."

Steve gave her a meaningful squeeze.

"Why not, the royalty payments will still come in even if I'm not here. Where were you thinking?"

"Oh, somewhere away from it all. How about North Wales?"

It looked like she'd hit Steve over the head with a brick, judging by his expression.

"No way," yelled Steve. "If you want to go to North Wales, it will be by yourself."

Andi grinned and did that thing with her eyelids.

"Not even for me?"

"No, anywhere but North Wales or Cobham. Anywhere else."

"Cornwall?" she prompted.

"Yes, Cornwall is fine. I have no bad memories of Cornwall," said Steve.

"When I was younger, my parents used to go to a little place near St. Just. I have very happy memories of strolling along the clifftops and climbing the headland at Cape Cornwall. I could do some panoramic landscapes for my project," suggested Andi.

"As long as we don't get their famous ninety-miles-per-hour fog," said Steve. "Or bulls!"

He rocked Andi on his lap, pulled her over and kissed her lightly under the ear.

Chapter 71 - End

A pod of dusky dolphins gambolled playfully in the South Pacific Ocean some one hundred miles southwest of Hawaii. As they skipped across the water, they didn't notice what was happening a few metres above them.

The air bubbled and took on a texture mirroring that of the swelling seas beneath. The distortion rippled outwards from the centre, as if a rock had been thrown into a village duck pond by some bored youth.

A mass of twisted and broken limbs broke through the surface of the ripples. They twitched feebly and ineffectually in the direction of the dolphins. In the middle of the convulsing clump, a hideous hexagonal mouth appeared. It opened and closed, opened and closed, its six triangular flaps curved back against the extremity of its lips. It gave an ear-splitting shriek that only the dolphins could hear. The intervals between the opening and closing of the mouth became longer and longer until finally, it came to a frozen stop. It was as if it was wheezing its last breath.

A bulbous hump that encircled the mouth burst into view. The air rippled outwards much further than before and the plane of the pool in the sky tilted downwards. A massive circular disk manifested itself from the tormented air. It fell forward and downwards towards the sea, like a massive, flat, black blancmange being poured slowly from a dish. It jerked to a halt. The air shook all around it. Between the suspended disk and the rippling air above, filaments of pure blue energy strained and sparked. The rippling waves in the air flashed with lightning that tore at the very fabric of space and time. One by one, the dancing electric filaments changed from bright blue to dull grey and snapped. The salt water erupted in a cloud of steam as the creature smashed into the waves. It bubbled and boiled effervescently as the creature sank into the depths.

In the sky, the rift healed over and evaporated.

* * * * *

Sarah sat at the poolside table drinking an early morning coffee. She wished she had paid just a little extra for her hotel. This one was clean and comfortable, but it was just too big. It hadn't occurred to her when she booked, that half the population of the United States of America would be vacationing there with her. Still, it was only for a few days, she wasn't going to be staying any place for very long.

"Newspaper, Miss?" asked the waiter, holding out a tray of papers towards her. She took one off the top, even though she didn't have any great interest in local Honolulu news. As she sipped her coffee, she flicked through the pages – mostly advertisements for other hotels and night spots. She wouldn't be needing any of those. She noticed something a few pages in…

'First manned expedition to deep sea volcano reveals mysterious life.'

She wasn't a marine biologist, but she read on, 'mysterious life' always interested her. A three-man submarine had descended to explore the environs of a thirteen thousand-foot volcano on the Pacific Ocean floor. Undersea volcanoes, even those that are dormant, transfer rich nutrients into the surrounding water and are a haven for a vast multitude of creatures. Sarah marvelled at the colour photos of the previously unknown species of animals, coral and sponges. Suddenly, she stopped. Even though all the photographs showed bizarre, alien creatures, one looked strangely familiar. It wasn't any recognisable octopus or squid. It had a large, flat, circular body, almost like an upside down jellyfish, with arms or tentacles protruding from the centre. Two of the arms terminated in bulbous blobs. She gasped as she read the caption.

'Unknown species of cephalopod. Just one juvenile from a large family found around the Cook seamount.'

The End

About the Author

It all started with Dan Dare in the mid '50s. In the Eagle Comic and on Radio Luxembourg, a young Joe Gillespie learned of 'spaceships' and 'Saturn' – and was hooked.

Born in Belfast in 1945, he won a place at The Royal College of Art and graduated with a Master's Degree in Visual Communication.

He worked in the advertising industry in London before setting up his own company, Pixel Productions, developing interactive multimedia for Apple, Microsoft and other leading technological companies.

An ardent classic sci-fi reader, he used his writing skills developed from advertising copy-writing and penned numerous short stories and longer projects that unfortunately ran out of steam due to pressure of work.

Now retired to sunny Dorset, he lives a less hectic life involving bird watching, astronomy and catching-up on ideas to change the universe for the better.

For more information, visit
http://joegillespieauthor.com

Also by Joe Gillespie…
Hayden's Realm

Hayden's Realm (Chapter 1)

Max Hayden was a smug, self-centred bastard.

As he left the tall office building, he had smugness written all over his face. He was good, and he knew it.

He strolled out to his car, opened the door, tossed his briefcase into the back seat and climbed in.

Taking a smartphone from his inside pocket, he swiped across and brought-up his contact list. Near to the top, his finger stopped at 'Katie Cowell'. He was about to press 'Call' but stopped. He smirked and put the phone away.

Pulling out into the main road, he leaned across slightly and pushed the 'Play' button on the in-car entertainment system. He wound Bruce Springsteen's 'Back in the USA' up as loud as he could bear and bowled along the motorway.

Max turned his key in the lock of the solid wooden front door.

His shirt was unbuttoned at the top and his tie half undone. He set down his briefcase just inside and put his suit jacket on top.

A young woman was absorbed in grating carrot into a bowl of salad. He crept up behind her and put both arms around her waist, swung her around and pecked the nape of her neck.

Katie acted a little surprised, although she had heard him come in. She turned and smiled.

"Well, how did it go?" she asked excitedly, nodding her head in encouragement.

Max put on a poker face and looked her straight in the eye.

"You are only…"

He breathed on his right finger tips and stroked his collar lightly.

"…Looking at the new Technical Director of McGregor Aerospace!"

She smiled and nodded deliberately.

"Oh…" she said.

He picked her off the ground again in a tight hug. They jumped up and down in a joyful dance.

"I just knew you would get it," she whooped.

He stuck out his tongue at her.

"So did I!"

He took the salad bowl from the kitchen worktop, opened the refrigerator door and stowed it inside.

"Tonight, we are celebrating," he said.

Katie gave him another big hug and kissed him again.

"Where would you like to go?"

"Giovanni's?" she asked, pausing slightly with a question on her voice. "Can…we afford it?"

"Whatever," he said. He lifted his briefcase from the hallway, unlocked the catches and removed his laptop. He took out a manila folder, reconsidered and promptly put the folder and computer back in again. The briefcase was locked and pushed back under the hall table out of sight.

"They put me through three interviews but I had

this sneaking suspicion that they'd given me the job already. It was just a matter of getting the head honcho on board," he continued.

"If we are going to Giovanni's, you might want to ditch the jeans and sweater."

Katie liked to dress casually - jeans, white trainers, sloppy jumpers. Her short blonde hair bobbed around her ears. She also liked to wear lipstick. Max hated it.

She knuckled him on the shoulder.

"I'll go scrub-up," she mocked, heading out into the hallway and up the stairs.

Max fetched the briefcase, unlocked it and took out the manilla folder. His eyes glazed over as he flicked through the turgid contracts.

His mind wandered.

Max was neither tall nor thin. His scalp was shaved short, a perfect complement to the designer stubble on his face.

He had joined the Royal Navy as a graduate with a good degree from Cambridge at the age of twenty-five. That was eleven years ago. He had stayed in the Navy for five years and was licensed to fly both fixed-wing aircraft and helicopters. Most of his work was in avionics and control systems. When he left the Navy, he went to work for Advanced Aviation and had become a star player in his field. Now he had been headhunted by a major competitor and was about to move on.

Katie was ten years his junior. They had met in a pub where he often had lunch or drinks after work and hit it off right away. Within six months, they were living together.

In her teens, she had planned on becoming a fashion model. She certainly had the looks: tall, long legs, beautiful face. An unfortunate set of circumstances involving bulimia, anorexia and hospital put paid to that.

It was totally by accident that she fell into the antiques business. Her friend Judy asked her to help out at a fair one day. She really enjoyed it and was soon dabbling on her own, making a few quid here and there. It was more of a hobby than an occupation but she bought an old Mini Countryman so that she could lug stuff around.

Katie liked Max because…well, she never really worked that one out.

He loved her just because she was Katie.

Max put a measure of Arabica beans into his hand-cranked coffee grinder. He was a coffee snob, although he preferred the word 'connoisseur'. He tipped the aromatic grounds into a filter cone lined with unbleached filter paper. The boiled water was allowed to cool for a minute before he poured it over the coffee grounds. Fresh black filter coffee. He couldn't think of anything better.

Nearly half an hour later, Katie came back downstairs. Max was finishing his coffee in the kitchen.

"Will I do?" she asked.

Max gave a low wolf-whistle.

"Where did that come from?" he asked, nodding at the slinky red satin dress.

"Oh, just a little something I put away for a special occasion," she teased. "Isn't this a special occasion?"

"It certainly is," replied Max.

He put his suit jacket back on and straightened his shirt cuffs.

As they left, he double-locked the front door and opened the door of the black Audi A5 in the driveway.

"Are you sure that you'll be able to drive home?"

"I don't intend overdoing it," Max said, looking down at his watch. "I need to get into work tomorrow early and type-up my resignation letter."

"Don't you have to work out three months?" asked Katie.

"Theoretically," replied Max, "but when they hear that I'm joining McGregor's, I'll get the bum's rush. I'll be asked to clear my desk right away."

"So, what are you going to do for three months?"

"I have a few loose ends to tidy up and quite a lot of research to do, but McGregor's have asked me to go in a couple of weeks to meet the management so that when I do start in October, I can hit the ground running."

Katie pulled down the vanity mirror and checked her make-up.

They turned into the restaurant car park and found a vacant space between a yellow Porsche and a red Ferrari. The other cars around them were just as grand.

"Mmm," said, Max tapping his Audi steering wheel, "I feel a tad underdressed in this!"

Katie chuckled.

Max removed his jacket and slung it over his shoulder casually. In a place like this, he didn't want to look like he worked for a living.

Giovanni's was right on the shore with a stunning view over the bay. The decor typified Italian chic – an odd mixture of traditional and ultra-modern that just somehow worked.

"Do you have a reservation?" asked the smart waiter as they stood in the foyer.

"Er, no," stuttered Max, "is that a problem?"

The waiter looked at them for a moment.

"Two?" he asked.

Max glanced around to see if anybody else had followed them in.

"Yes, two." He added "idiot" silently.

The waiter took menus from a rack and beckoned them to follow.

The restaurant was barely a third full. They were ushered to a table for two by a large panoramic window. The waiter pulled the seat out for Katie and pushed it back in under her. He handed them each a menu folder and tidied-up the cutlery and glasses on the table fussily.

"Would you like to see the wine list?" he asked.

Max took the thick bound drinks menu and pointed to the most expensive bottle of bubbly.

The waiter bowed and walked away.

He returned a few minutes later holding up a bottle of champagne to Max. He nodded. The waiter removed the cork with a twist and poured some into Max's flute and waited. Max waved has hand in dismissal and pointed to Katie's glass.

"So, what does the new job involve," asked Katie. "Is it much different from what you were doing before?"

Max lifted his glass and stared at it thoughtfully.

"They didn't say very much other than that it will be a 'little different' from what I'm used to. I don't know exactly what they have in mind for me but the 'remuneration package', as they call it, is double what I'm on at the minute. Then there's the Beemer that goes with the job."

Katie pulled a tight smile.

"I'll know more about it in a couple of weeks – but I won't be able to tell you anything," he smirked dryly. "Not only do I have to sign a watertight non-disclosure contract, there is the Official Secrets Acts too!"

"Ah," said Katie nodding knowingly, "military stuff?"

"That's par for the course in this business," explained Max. "In aerospace, it's just like that."

They passed on starters and ordered their main meals. Katie went for the pan-fried mackerel, Max the grilled fillet of beef. Max didn't want to embarrass himself attempting to pronounce the long Italian names.

Throughout the meal, Katie plied Max with

question after question, most of which he couldn't or wouldn't answer. She gave up.

"How was yours?" asked Max, as she put her knife and fork on the virtually empty plate.

"Absolutely wonderful." The waiter was already hovering with a dessert menu.

"I'll just have the amaretto syllabub," Max indicated and looked across at Katie.

She patted her tummy and shook her head.

"No, full up!"

"Would you care for some coffee?" asked the waiter.

"Could we have two espressos on the veranda?" Max replied.

The waiter nodded graciously and left.

The veranda bathed in the warm glow of a July evening. Seagulls wheeled in the sky as waves lapped softly on the sandy beach, where a few oystercatchers pecked purposefully amongst the seaweed.

"This is so lovely," sighed Katie. "A perfect end to a perfect day."

Max put his arm around her and kissed her cheek. He presented her with a white rectangular box, opening it to display the contents. Her eyes widened.

"Maxie, it's lovely!" she exclaimed, taking the Victorian pendant necklace and holding it up to the light.

"Amethyst, my birthstone!"

Max smiled.

"For the luckiest girl in the world."

She fumbled with the clasp and put it round her neck.

"Thank you, oh thank you," she said.

Katie looked around to see that no-one was watching and went to sit on Max's lap. She put her arms around his neck and they kissed deeply.

On the horizon, out over the bay, sails bellowed lazily in the sea breeze.

"Oh, I'd love to have a boat," sighed Max, "maybe I'll be able to buy one now. Just imagine, lying back under the stars and drifting off to Nineveh."

Katie closed her eyes and took Max's hand.

She gazed out over the bay at the pale orange band of sky that spanned the horizon. Cotton wool clouds caught the last sun rays and were edged in the same soft, fiery glow. She would remember this night.

Max and Katie cuddled on the veranda but straightened-up abruptly when the waiter arrived with the two coffees, each with an amaretto biscuit on the saucer.

"Can I have the bill?" asked Max. The waiter nodded and walked off.

Max started drinking his coffee. Katie leaned back in her chair and drunk in the atmosphere. She could have coffee anytime.

"Oh look, Max. Can you see that cloud shaped like a polar bear?" asked Katie.

Max looked.

"I can't see any polar bear."

"There's its head and there are its front paws."

Katie pointed.

"Pareidolia," said Max.

"You what?" asked Katie.

"Pareidolia. It's the psychological phenomenon whereby the human brain tries to make sense out of random shapes."

"Oh, you and your big words," scowled Katie.

"Some people can use them and some can't," said Max, giving Katie a gentle shove.

"Anyway, that's definitely not a polar bear, looks more like a squirrel to me," said Max.

Katie tightened her lips and continued to draw the outline in the sky with her finger.

"Aw, it's changed shape," she moaned.

She looked for more shapes in the clouds.

"Max, what's that?" she asked, pointing to a cloud in the distance.

"What now?"

"Look, there. There are three dots sitting just above that cloud." She moved her fingers in a circular motion.

"I can't see anything," said Max, shaking his head.

Then he sprang to his feet, putting his hand across his forehead to cut out the glare.

"Odd," he said, "I have no idea. Can't be birds, too far up and they're not moving. Not planes either, planes can't stop in mid-air. Too high for helicopters as well. I don't know," he shrugged.

"Are they UFOs, perhaps?" smiled Katie.

"Well," he laughed, "they are flying objects and I can't identify them so, therefore they are, by definition, UFOs. That doesn't mean that they are alien flying saucers or anything like that. There will be some perfectly ordinary reason for them being there. Weather balloons, atmospheric distortion…"

He shook his head. "There were reports from China recently of cities apparently floating in the clouds. Just a freak weather condition it turned out. Hell, I don't know, could be anything. In my business, you see a lot of things in the sky that you don't understand. You have to learn to live with it or it will drive you mad."

The three objects began to move off, first in formation and then shifting into line one behind another. For a moment, they were obscured by a fleecy cloud and should have re-emerged from the other side. Only one came out. It accelerated at an impossible rate straight upwards. The other two had just vanished.

Max and Katie stared at one another for an instant, mouths agape.

Max shook his head as if he had awakened from a bad dream.

"Odd!"

He took Katie by the hand and led her back into the restaurant. He paid the bill and left a tip on the plate

Back in the car, Max started the engine and turned the radio on. He pushed the pre-set for the news station. After a few minutes of banal jingles, the newsreader spoke.

"Reports have been coming from all along the coast about strange objects in the sky this evening. Let's go over to our reporter Milly Barnes…"

"Yes, I have here with me, some people who have just witnessed bizarre and unexplained happenings in the sky. Tom, tell me what you saw."

A man with a thick country accent spoke into the microphone.

"I was just coming down the lane on my tractor when I saw these three…don't know what you call 'em…just sitting up there. They didn't have no lights or anything, they were just grey. Then, all of a sudden, they shoot-off like bullets from a gun. Odd thing is, two of the three just disappeared into thin air. Strangest thing I have ever seen in my whole life, it was."

"And Tracy, can you tell me what you saw?"

"I was coming home from work and there was a lovely sunset. Three flying saucers came out from behind a cloud – but I don't believe in those things," she giggled. "I don't know what they were. One was a sort of triangular shape and the other two were – oh, maybe they all were. They were a bit hazy, not distinct, like."

"And what happened to them?"

"Dunno. One minute they were there and the next minute they're gone," said Tracy.

"Thank you both. And with that, I'll hand you back to Carole in the studio,"

"So we weren't seeing things," coughed Katie, groping for a handkerchief in her pocket.

"T'would seem not," said Max, as they sped off home.

The four-armed alien monster reared up and gave a ferocious snarl. Sticky goo drooled from its extended mandibles and its bony arms flailed wildly towards the figure on the ground beneath it. The scantily-clad female screamed and put her arm across her face. The leviathan's red eyes were aflame with rage as it lifted the girl off the ground and glared. It raised its head to the sky and gave a triumphant roar.

"Oh Maxie, what's that rubbish you're watching?" asked Katie, sitting down beside him on the sofa.

Max didn't answer but pressed the volume up button on the remote.

"Do you want a drink?" she asked.

"On the rocks," he answered. His eyes didn't leave the screen.

Katie returned from the kitchen with two glasses. One held Soave, one had just ice cubes. She set the glass of ice beside him on the coffee table.

"Ta."

To the swooshing of plasma cannon fire, Max lifted the glass to his lips and recoiled. Just ice? He took two cubes from the glass and pulled back the neck of Katie's soft woollen jumper. She squirmed and shouted.

"Max! Don't you dare. Maxie!"

She clamped her two hands against the back of her neck to block the ice cubes from sliding down inside the back of her jumper. Max moved them round to the front and dropped them in.

"Ahhh!" she screamed as the cold ice slid down into her cleavage. She lifted the front of her jumper and shook the ice cubes out onto the floor. Before Max could get them, Katie picked them up and tried to get them inside Max's shirt. He was too strong for her and just held her wrists while the ice melted in her hands. He wrestled her down onto the floor rug. They fought some more. Max swept Katie up in his arms and lifted her off the ground. He raised his head to the sky and gave a triumphant roar. She put her arms around his neck and kissed him wildly.

"Take that, space cadet," she smiled.

Max managed to pick up the remote control and flicked the television off.

"Now look what you've done," he said accusingly.

"What?" she asked.

"Made me miss a classic," smirked Max as he carried her towards the stairs.

* * * * *

"Who the hell is this guy, Landers?" asked CIA Director Michael Thornton.

Schakowsky, sitting opposite replied, "He's a maverick. A pain in the ass that heads-up a group out at Groom Lake and has ambitions far beyond his station."

"What does he want from us?" asked Thornton.

"He's been requesting intel on encrypted radio

signals localised to a small airfield in the East Coast England."

Thornton rocked back and forth on his chair.

"He contacted GCHQ in England," said Schakowsky, "and they told him to piss-off."

Thornton grimaced. "I imagine they did. Under what authority is he making these requests?"

"He told the Brits he was CIA. He's not. He has only the most tenuous connections with us but he is a master of bluff. He doesn't come right out and say it, he suggests it and lets the other party reach the wrong conclusion."

"And, what do we know about these signals?" asked Thornton.

"We know that they are military-grade encrypted. If we had to decrypt them, given enough time and resources, we probably could. We just don't have any good reason to do that."

"What do we know about the airfield?"

"Private. Belongs to McGregor Aerospace. They run a couple of Lear Jets from there with avionics test rigs. Mostly Brit MOD stuff. All above board. So, there's a perfectly good reason for military grade encrypted signals coming from there. It's not really any of our concern."

"So, why am I even being bothered with this?" asked Thornton.

"I'm just worried about Landers, Michael. He has history. When somebody like that becomes a liability, they are usually promoted out of harm's way. He was, but it didn't work. He's ended-up in a no-man's land between CIA and military but it's one where he gets to call the shots."

"I don't understand," said Thornton. "He must answer to someone?"

"That's it," replied Schakowsky, "he is a law unto himself and seems to get off with it."

"But, he must have some areas of interest," argued Thornton, "somebody's paying him."

"There are budgets allocated to research work that even we don't know about. People in government with pet projects. They find the money and no questions are asked."

"Pet projects," repeated Thornton, "such as?"

"Groom Lake, Area 51. Do I have to draw pictures?" asked Schakowsky.

"Somebody is spending good money on that nonsense? Flying fucking saucers? Are they believing their own mythology?" asked Thornton.

"One man's mythology is another man's culture, is another man's way of life. Who am I to say?" shrugged Schakowsky.

"Look, let me make this clear," said Thornton." I'm not wasting CIA resources on this bunch of clowns and their pet projects. If Landers asks for any more intel from us, just tell him to go shove it. He gets zilch. Okay?"

"And if his backers start making waves?"

"Refer them to me," barked Thornton, tapping his chest.

Hayden's Realm by Joe Gillespie
Available now from Amazon and good book
shops everywhere.

www.ingramcontent.com/pod-product-compliance
Lightning Source LLC
Chambersburg PA
CBHW071159250626
47159CB00001B/139